ADVANCE PRAISE FO

M000103354

"Gregory Shepherd's *Sea of Fire*, a super-charged thriller about big trouble in North Korea that could result in a nuclear war—hits the bulls-eye on multiple levels: the writing is swift and sometimes even brutal, the situation is right out of a *New York Times* headline, his deep knowledge of the Korean language, customs, and politics is authentic, and the believable characters he builds brick-by-brick pulls you by the collar into their troubled world. His is a new, important, and entertaining voice on the thriller scene. Hat's off for a fine read!"

—David Hagberg, author of the Kirk McGarvey series
(https://www.goodreads.com/series/57660-kirk-mcgarvey)

"Gregory Shepherd's *Sea of Fire* is a magnificent novel, a real page-turner to the end. The plot is a great mixture of the protagonist's struggle with his demons, love interest, east and west, nasty villains, and conflicted heroes that keeps the reader engaged and guessing up to the last minute."

—Michael Breen, author of *The Koreans*
and *Kim Jong-il: North Korea's Dear Leader*

"Hold on for a wild ride! If you like fast-paced spy thrillers filled with high-powered suspense, you'll love *Sea of Fire*."

—John Wehrheim, author of
Bhutan: Hidden Lands of Happiness

"Gregory Shepherd's *Sea of Fire* is a timely and marvelous novel. Taking place after the death of North Korean dictator Kim Jong-il, it is timely as the world waits to see what his successor will do with his father's legacy. It is a marvel in the meticulous research required to give the novel the details that bring the story and characters to life. Shepherd's writing is also brilliant, setting mood and emotion with a deft and sure hand. He never shies away from giving us the truth of the danger and cruelty at the hands of North Korea's sadistic henchmen. And yet, Shepherd also gives us a sweet romance that matches the intensity of the thriller's main storyline. You will find that you will not want to put this novel down as the main characters, covert agent Tyler Kang and his friend-turned-enemy Patrick Featherstone, must save each other, if not the world."

—Todd Shimoda, author of *The Fourth Treasure*

SEA OF FIRE

Gregory Shepherd

PERMUTED
PRESS

A PERMUTED PRESS BOOK

ISBN: 978-1-68261-952-0
ISBN (eBook): 978-1-68261-970-4

Sea of Fire
A Thriller
© 2020 Gregory Shepherd
All Rights Reserved

Cover Design: Linda Shimoda, shimodaworks.com
Book Design: Carol Sullivan, carolsullivandesign.com

PERMUTED
PRESS

Permuted Press, LLC
New York • Nashville
permutedpress.com

Published in the United States of America

For the people of North Korea who suffer under an unimaginably cruel and repressive regime. May the "Rising Tide" of the book come to pass in the not-too-distant future.

C H A P T E R 1

KOREAN PENINSULA
February 15

"Raise your hand if you would like to die today."

The tour guide on the bus to the DMZ now had the complete attention of his passengers. The silence on the bus was broken only by the low rumble of the engine that powered the heater on this bone-chilling morning.

"Thank you, ladies and gentlemen. First of all, I want to make it absolutely clear to all of you that your visit to the Joint Security Area at Panmunjom will entail entry into a hostile area as well as the possibility of injury or death as a direct result of enemy action."

He went on to say that the Joint Security Area is a neutral but divided area guarded by United Nations Command military personnel on the south side, and Korean People's Army on the north. He ended his presentation with, "Technically, we are still at war with North Korea, especially now that the peace talks have ended in failure. We're literally back to square one. I must emphasize that we cannot guarantee your safety and will not be held accountable in the event of a hostile enemy act." The tourists were then required to sign and date a document attesting to their full assumption of risk before being allowed to leave the bus.

Unlike the other tourists, who were uniformly Caucasian, one passenger had the high cheekbones and tight, perfect skin of the soldiers who glared menacingly at each other from their respective sides of the border. Despite the near-freezing conditions, the man's movements off the bus and toward the border area were fluid and unhurried. He was alone.

An hour later an announcement came over a loudspeaker for everyone to return to the bus that would ferry them back to Seoul. As the tour guide was shooing shivering oldsters back onto the bus, the man tucked a file folder more securely down into his jeans and removed from his jacket a metal object no larger than a soda can. Pulling on a tab that ran down its top, he tossed it in the direction of the fence that separated the two countries. A deafening explosion and bright flash from the object, an M84 flashbang grenade, caused everyone in the area to duck and turn away from the blast.

At the sound of the explosion, soldiers of the Quick Reaction Platoon from Camp Bonifas not far from the tourist site came barreling down the trail leading in the direction of the parking lot. As they rushed past him, the man feigned a look of shock and yelled "Oh my God!" over and over as the others did. However, as soon as the last soldier had come up the trail, the man ran in the opposite direction and scaled the barbed wire fence of the DMZ.

Once on the other side, he deftly made his way through the snow-patched minefield, pausing cautiously here and darting forward there. After proceeding about a quarter mile, he heard loud voices shouting at him in Korean, a language he spoke like a native, and then he felt a bullet whizz by his ear. He hit the frozen mud to avoid being hit and immediately felt a sharp, stabbing pain in his hand. He lay where he was and waited for the shouting men to come closer. A moment later, four North Korean soldiers rounded a bend and quickly surrounded him with rifles aimed at his head. One of them kicked him roughly in the back and ordered him to get up.

The man didn't move. He didn't dare. As the squad leader brought his leg back for another kick, he looked into the eyes of the man on the ground. Then he looked at the man's hand. The squad leader's eyes went wide as he realized why the man was immobile. He had fallen on one of the DMZ's millions of high-powered land mines. If he moved an inch, there would be little of any of them left.

After a munitions expert had disarmed the mine, the leader of the squad walked up and shouted something in the man's face.

The man on the ground shook his head. "English?" he said.

"Who are you? What do you want?" the leader then demanded in broken

English. Ever since several American GI's had defected decades earlier, platoon leaders were required to have at least a rudimentary command of English.

"My name is Tyler Kang. I am a CIA officer. I want to defect to the Democratic People's Republic of Korea."

PYONGYANG
The next day

"What is your *real* name?"

"I told you! Tyler Kang!"

Slam!

"What is your nationality?"

"American."

Slam! His left elbow erupted in pain.

"Why have you come here?"

"Look, I've answered all these questions at least five times!"

Slam! His shins this time.

"Answer again. Why have you come here?"

"I wish to defect to the Democratic People's Republic of Korea."

Slam! His wrists.

"Liar! You are a spy! Do you speak Korean?"

"Only a few words."

Slam! Slam!

"Dammit, I've given you the most sensitive missile secrets the Americans have!"

Slam! Slam! Slam!

By the end of the interrogation in an unheated army barracks, Kang's face was black, blue and swollen. A mixture of blood and snot flowed from his nose, and each new blow of the truncheon ignited a searing agony that engulfed his entire body. Two days later, the beating stopped. In walked his minder, Mr. Hyun, who had been with him ever since he was taken captive.

"I am very sorry, Mr. Kang, but we needed to make sure you really are who you say you are."

Kang squinted mutely at him through the scrim of blood and sweat that coated his eyes.

An hour or so later, after he had cleaned up as best as he could using a basin filled with freezing water, Kang gingerly spooned the thick soup that had been brought to him in the barracks where he was being held, guarded around the clock. It was his first food since jumping the border at the DMZ. Both of his hands were deeply bruised and covered in weeping wounds, and it was close to impossible for him to maintain a grip on the eating utensils.

"Are they finished with me?" he slurred through broken lips to Mr. Hyun as he slurped the lukewarm soup. He had managed to convince Mr. Hyun and the others that he had only picked up a bit of the language from his parents. In actuality, he was more fluent than some of the sadistic thugs who had tortured him.

"The interrogation?" Hyun replied. "Yes. We are convinced that you are who you say you are. But we have questions regarding the validity of the documents that you brought."

"I will only talk about those with the Supreme Commander, Kim Jong-un, himself."

Mr. Hyun laughed derisively. "I'm afraid that is quite impossible," he said, lighting a foul-smelling cigarette.

"Then go fuck yourselves."

Hyun's face reddened. "Would you like us to resume the interrogation, Mr. Kang?"

Kang scowled. "No. But I'm only giving up what I know to someone very high in the regime. And I *would*, at some time, like the opportunity to meet the Supreme Commander. My fondest dream was to meet his father, but since he is no longer with us, I would like to offer my respects to his son."

Hyun stared at him with suspicion in his eyes. "Perhaps that can be arranged for some time in the future. Not now, however. As for the information you have, I have told someone very high up in the regime about you, and he would like to question you personally."

"Who is he?"

"You will know soon enough."

Less than an hour later, Tyler Kang was driven to a gray, six-story building in downtown Pyongyang. There were no signs on the building indicating what it was, but it was heavily guarded by uniformed soldiers. Inside the upper echelons of the Korean Workers' Party, it was known as Bureau 39.

Once inside the building, Hyun flashed his ID, and the guards parted to let him and Kang pass. As Hyun and Kang ascended in an elevator, Kang thought he might be hallucinating from the beating he had received. For, penetrating the death-rattle of the elevator motor came a sound like that of a circus calliope. Kang shook his head, but the sound only increased in volume the higher they ascended. When the elevator doors opened, the sound reverberated eerily throughout the empty hallway. Hyun took Kang by the arm and moved him in the direction of a corner office.

As they walked inside, Kang saw an impeccably dressed older man sitting in front of a window playing the accordion. Kang would soon learn that this was Comrade Moon, an utterly ruthless man who years earlier had shot his first wife to death at one of Kim Jong-il's drinking parties in order to demonstrate his loyalty to the Dear Leader. As a reward for this and other demonstrations of fidelity, he was given the directorship of Bureau 39, the shadowy section of the DPRK government that deals in all manner of illegal activities, including counterfeiting, drug smuggling, arms sales to terrorists, and sale of goods made in the slave labor camps.

At the sound of the door closing, Comrade Moon stopped put down his accordion and turned in the direction of Kang and Hyun.

Mr. Hyun directed Kang to sit in a large office chair facing an enormous teak desk.

"Your name is Tyler Kang," Comrade Moon stated in English, reading from a file Hyun had given to him. The documents that Kang had brought with him over the DMZ lay open on the desk.

"Yes."

"And what is this information you have that is so important?"

Ten minutes later Kang finished summarizing the details of South Korea's clandestine nuclear program, and how any attack by the North would be met with apocalyptic retribution. South Korea had been prohibited from possessing nuclear weapons under the terms of the Nuclear Non-Proliferation Treaty, but the United States had recently given its approval of a secret program owing to the fact that the American president was withdrawing the bulk of U.S. troops from the South.

Moon said nothing the entire time Kang spoke. He then gestured for Hyun to take Kang and leave. When they had gone, he made a series of overseas phone calls on his cell phone. Half an hour later he pressed a button on his desk. In walked his right-hand man, Pung Min-ho, whose tiny cobra eyes bugged out of an impossibly large head.

"Yes, Comrade?"

"The southern puppets have nuclear weapons. Pack a bag, you're going to Tokyo. Bring two million in cash."

Moon got up and stretched his legs. "This is just the opportunity I needed. You're not to say a word about the South Korean nuclear program. We don't want to tip our hand. As far as they're concerned, we know nothing about it, and I want to keep it that way. And not a word about their defector yet, either. Let's have the Americans wonder what happened to him for a while. Always keep the enemy off balance, Pung. It's one thing I've learned in life."

"Yes, Comrade Moon."

CHAPTER 2

AMEYOKO PACHINKO PALACE
Ueno district of Tokyo
February 18

An hour before opening time, Goro Takara, the proprietor of Ameyoko Pachinko Palace, made the rounds of his hundred or so machines, making sure none of the *chimpira* mafia punks who lounged there all day had jammed the coin slots with gum after a losing streak. Between the gum in the slots and the riceballs hurled in disgust at the plexiglass screens by those same customers, Takara's work started long before opening. Suddenly there was a knock on the front door.

Who the hell is that? Some fucking punk wanting to come in early? He strode quickly to the front door ready to send the offender on his way with a torrent of well-chosen profanity, but stopped short when he saw who it was. With trembling hands he undid the lock and opened the door. His stomach tightened as the thickset North Korean known to him as Mr. Pung hurried through the door carrying a soft-shelled suitcase. Pung trailed a cloud of cigarette smoke that mixed with the parlor's ambient odor of overpowering cologne and cheap perfume.

What does the bastard want this time? he thought as he bowed with feigned cordiality and brushed back the comb-over on the top of his balding head.

"Hello again, Mr. Pung, so nice to see you!" he beamed obsequiously at the man he secretly hated. Pung grunted through a scowl as he came closer. Takara felt an involuntary tremble as Pung got closer.

"Hide this," Pung said breathlessly, handing the suitcase to Takara. "I just paid two million dollars for it."

Takara was luckier than his competitors whose pachinko parlors had been shuttered in recent years as a result of Japan's economic woes. But his luck was largely due to Pung who was the main enforcer of the Chosun-kai, a powerful organization with ties to North Korea that had seen Takara through the worst of Japan's economic bubble...at a steep price. For Pung had turned his pachinko parlor into a transshipment point for most of the narcotics coming into the Tokyo area from Comrade Moon's Bureau 39.

But today Takara could tell from the look in Pung's eyes that the North Korean was transporting something far more dangerous than the usual drugs Takara was forced to warehouse in his basement. As Pung departed, he warned Takara that the suitcase would detonate if anyone tried to tamper with it.

All that night after closing time, Takara sat on the floor of his basement with his knees to his chest, frantically rocking back and forth.

What am I going to do? What am I going to do?

Before Pung had even shown up that day, Takara had been worrying himself sick over his daughter Yumi. She was still despondent over her breakup a year earlier with her fiance, a foreigner named Patrick Featherstone. Finally that night, Takara plunged into a dark depression. His mind conjured faces of dead children and their grieving parents, and he knew that he was at least a partial reason for their misery. For years he had been able to ignore any consideration of the victims of his vicious trade, but now, thinking of the suffering his daughter was going through over a mere broken heart, for the first time he felt a stabbing remorse for all the lives he had helped to destroy. And now this suitcase with what surely contained enough explosive power to snuff out many more lives.

What am I going to do? What am I going to do?

As Takara stared fixedly at the suitcase, he suddenly got up from his spot on the cold basement floor.

No, he said firmly to himself. *No more. From now on, I live for myself. For myself and for my Yumi.*

As he picked up the suitcase, he knew there was only one thing to do to make things right.

BUREAU 39
Pyongyang
The following day

Comrade Moon was beside himself with anger.

"But how could he just disappear?" he screamed at Pung. "And with the package, no less?"

Pung had just informed him that Goro Takara, owner of Tokyo's Ameyoko Pachinko Parlor, was nowhere to be found. More important, the suitcase that Pung had brought, or "the package" as Moon had taken to calling it, had disappeared as well.

Pung shuffled on his feet. "I'm sorry, Comrade, I have no idea where he went. He's always been my most reliable man in Japan."

Moon paced the floor of his office. "Don't you understand how serious this is? I thought you said he could be trusted! The other members of Commission will be furious. Do you know what that means?"

Pung kept his head lowered. The Commission that Moon referred to was a group of fabulously wealthy and ruthless men from around the world who were constantly on the lookout for new opportunities to slake their avarice. Violence always followed when their wishes were thwarted. They had met recently to discuss a pressing matter: their interests in North Korea were being threatened by the actions of its young leader, Kim Jong-un, toward the United States. And when the profits from a particular country are threatened by politics, the Commission member from that country is expected to step up and do something about it. Comrade Moon was that member. He had promised his fellow Commission members that he had a plan, and the contents of the missing suitcase were pivotal to the execution of that plan. As he continued pacing, his mind went back to the last meeting of the Commission when he had made his case:

Gentlemen, he had said, *in addition to Kim Jong-un's acts of belligerence, another danger to our enterprise comes from General O Jun-suh of the Korean People's Army. I am quite certain that he has designs on the premiership himself through a military coup. If he were ever to come to power, there is little doubt in my mind that he would establish himself as dictator and take over Bureau 39. He is, in my opinion, even more dangerous to our interests than Kim Jong-un. My plan is to have Kim Jong-un assassinated and simultaneously annihilate General O and his entire corps of the army. At that point, I will declare myself the new leader of North Korea...*

The members of the Commission had stared skeptically at Moon when he finished. They had assumed that he would simply steer Kim Jong-un away from his aggression against America. But the plan Moon had just proposed was grandiose in the extreme. That notwithstanding, at the end of the meeting the members of the Commission voted grudgingly to approve Moon's plan. If he failed to come through within a reasonable amount of time, he would be expelled from the Commission. And the last time a Commission member had been expelled, he was never seen again.

Moon shuddered as he contemplated his own fate, now that the suitcase had gone missing. He turned angrily to Pung.

"I want you to do whatever is necessary to find Takara. Find a way to flush him out. Does he have any family? Kidnap them, kill them, I don't give a shit. I need that package," he said through a clenched jaw. "A lot more than I need you," he added balefully. Pung hurried out the door.

CHAPTER 3

THE WHITE HOUSE
February 23

President Evan Dillard rubbed his temples and exhaled a deep, yawning sigh. He hadn't slept well the night before due to the situation on the Korean peninsula. Not even the tantalizing scent of freshly baked muffins and gourmet coffee that wafted through the White House Situation Room held much appeal to a sleepless man, and he accepted only a small glass of orange juice from the butler. He looked around the room. His heart sank. There she was, his Secretary of State, Bernadette Hilton, glaring at him accusingly from across the long conference table. She had been his opponent in the last presidential primary election, and was promised the post of Secretary in exchange for conceding. They hated each other, especially after the president's unilateral decision on the Korean situation the previous week.

For her part, Hilton recalled the meeting of the Joint Security Council at which the president had announced that he was going to redeploy the American troops stationed in South Korea to the Middle East, and allow South Korea to arm itself with nuclear weapons instead of relying on American troops. His reasoning was that the situation on the peninsula had degenerated to the point where troops on the ground would't make much of a difference if the North attacked. Something far stronger would be needed, at least as a deterrent.

He hadn't even consulted with Hilton first, and she was absolutely livid when he announced it to the Joint Security Council. Now, however, there was a major glitch: the withdrawal of American troops had begun in earnest, but South Korea was experiencing one problem after another with its missile delivery system. And the United States couldn't just send them the missiles, either, since the South was crawling with North Korean spies who would immediately report to Pyongyang any such large-scale movement. The nukes themselves were small enough to hide from prying eyes, but now they were like bullets without a gun.

We don't have enough troop strength to deal with both the Levant Liberation Committee and North Korea, the president had said the week before. An involuntary smirk came to Bernadette Hilton's lips as she recalled the president's approval of a plan to send a mock defector, Tyler Kang, over the DMZ to warn the North Koreans about the South Korean nuclear program. Now the South had no means of delivering the warheads. On top of that, Kang, purportedly one America's most reliable undercover agents, had not only gone dark, he had also taken top secret documents with him, presumably to hand over to the North Koreans. From all appearances, he had really defected. Hilton stared at the president and thought to herself, *It was your decision alone, asshole. Now deal with it.*

The President looked at his watch, anxiety etched into his weary features. "Where's Larry Conover?" he barked hoarsely, referring to his Director of National Intelligence.

An aide was on his cell phone trying to raise Conover. "I'm sorry, Mr. President, he's not picking up for some reason," he said in a panicky voice. Suddenly, the door flew open and Conover raced in. With his black, plastered-down hair, deep voice, and unblinking eyes, he resembled an undertaker to many, but, like a master chess player, no one was better at formulating plans that were one move ahead of everyone else's. Except maybe this time. He was the one who recommended to the president that Tyler Kang be sent over as a mock-defector.

"Very sorry," he gasped, out of breath. "I had an early meeting that ran over."

The President glared at him. Lousy excuse. "What's the status on the defector?" he said without any attempt to hide his irritation.

"Actually, that's what my earlier meeting was about. We're trying our damnedest to get some word, anything, on what's going on over there. We really don't know what happened to him."

"And what about those missing documents on our missile program? Did he take them with him?"

"We're not completely sure, sir, but it would appear so."

"This is *not* how it was supposed to go down," the President growled, now in an even darker mood. "He wasn't actually *supposed* to defect." He tapped his desk, lost in thought. "It's too late to pull back on our redeployment of the troops from South Korea to Syria. That new Levant Liberation Committee retook Idlib last night, and I need boots on the ground before those fuckers go after Aleppo and restart the whole ISIS thing. Annihilating them once and for all takes precedence over everything at this point, even North Korea."

"But what if Kim Jong-un makes good on his father's promise to invade the South if we withdraw?" asked Bernadette Hilton tauntingly. "We all know the South Koreans won't be ready with their nuclear deterrent for weeks, if not months."

The President looked off into the distance and exhaled in frustration. Turning back to Conover, he said brusquely, "You let me know the minute you hear anything from that Tyler Kang. And it better be good news."

"Yes, Mr. President."

CHAPTER 4

KAMAKURA, JAPAN
February 25

In a spartan cabin at the top of one of the low mountains that ring the seacoast town of Kamakura, sixty miles from Tokyo, a man in his early 40s lay staring at the ceiling just before dawn. A wisp of pine-resin incense curled hypnotically out of a metal urn on the shelf next to him. He had awoken as always to the memory of a dead child on the mountains of Serbia.

His black Irish features were a legacy of his father's ancestry, as well as a goodly portion of his mother's, although the mother, who had grown up in Hawaii, was also one-eighth Japanese, a combination of bloodlines which gave the man's skin an almost olive complexion. With deep-set, jade-green eyes and gray-flecked black hair, he could have easily passed as a local in Turin or Mantua— and never gone lacking for female companionship.

But solitude was Patrick Featherstone's only companion these days, ever since he had announced unceremoniously to his former fiancée, Yumi Takara, that he had chosen a quest for spiritual enlightenment over marriage. She had taken the breakup badly. He had moved on.

After rising, he sat in meditation for half an hour and then started in on his various *kata*, beginning with ink-brush painting, continuing outside with martial arts, a three-mile run, and concluding with target practice in the mountains using a silenced Colt .45 1911A semi-automatic pistol that had belonged to his father. The oversized walnut grip was his father's own design. It held a hidden extra round accessible by breaking off the inside panel. Through these various *kata*, and especially through his meditation practice, he was free of the image of the young boy dead on a mountain in Serbia.

When he finished his shooting *kata*, Patrick thought of the day ahead. A few days earlier he had been contacted by the CIA, an agency he had once done work for. He had been an operative in JSOC, the Joint Special Operations Command, as part of an elite commando unit that had been posted in Serbia during the time the countries of the former Soviet axis began to disintegrate. Now the intelligence world wanted Patrick Featherstone back, if only for a little while. Later in the day they would visit him personally to make their case.

But why would they want me back? Me of all people? he thought. *Especially after last time...*

The last time Patrick had worked with the Agency, in 1995, he had been part of a botched sniper mission in Serbia that had left the young boy dead. He was court-martialed, found culpable, and discharged. His life was ruined.

Upon returning to Kamakura from Serbia, Patrick spent most of his time in his cabin drinking alone. Like most heavy drinkers, he did so to forget, but, of course, that only made the image of the dead boy on a mountain in Serbia more nauseatingly horrific when he awoke.

One night on a binge, he was about to fall headlong into a drainage ditch when a hand reached out and grabbed his arm, saving him from what would surely have been major injuries, perhaps even death. Patrick looked dumbly at the man who had caught him.

"You are very drunk. You could have died," the man said, although since it was a cloudy night, Patrick couldn't make out his facial features. The man led him to a temple down the narrow road in front of which sat an urn that held the smoldering stubs of dozens of incense sticks.

"There was a funeral here a little while ago," the man said. "He was a young man, maybe your age. He had a wife and two small children. He died of cancer. He didn't drink. How is it that such a man died? How is it that you didn't?"

The man seemed to be directing these questions to himself, rather than to Patrick, as if he were contemplating the fairness of life. Patrick said nothing but continued to allow himself to be led by the man who had saved him from himself. Once inside the temple, it became apparent that the man, whose head was shaved, was a Buddhist priest, and that this was his temple. He was elderly, but had an inner light and vitality about him that belied his age.

"You will stay here tonight," he said to Patrick in a voice that brooked no dissent as he led him to a small room with a futon on the tatami floor.

"Who are you?" Patrick managed to ask in a ruined voice.

"I am Yasuhara. Some people call me 'Roshi', but they are my students. You are not my student, so call me Yasuhara. Now go to sleep," the priest said. Patrick fell onto the futon and passed out.

The next morning Yasuhara Roshi was gone when Patrick awoke, so that evening Patrick returned to thank the priest for literally saving his life. He saw for the first time the name of the temple: Eiwa-ji, the Temple of Eternal Peace. Over the coming weeks Patrick found himself coming back to the temple, both for the fatherly guidance of Yasuhara Roshi and also the daily meditation which he took up avidly when he discovered that it helped him forget the young boy dead on a mountain of Serbia.

At one of Yasuhara Roshi's lectures, Patrick heard the word satori, enlightenment, and learned of the possibility of a life-changing experience that could wipe away all of one's doubts and fears. Maybe even the nightly image of the dead boy. Redoubling his efforts in zazen, Zen meditation, he found that his troubled soul was gradually settling, although Yasuhara Roshi assured him that enlightenment was still quite a ways off. As with everything he did, Patrick threw himself single-mindedly into his Zen practice, vowing not to stop or be sidetracked until he had reached enlightenment.

And then Yumi showed up.

Yumi Takara, an artist in her mid-twenties, had taken up zazen to improve her concentration as a practitioner of traditional Japanese calligraphy and ink-brush painting. One day Patrick entered the kitchen where Yumi sat chatting with Yasuhara Roshi. When she saw Patrick, she stopped and stared. Patrick stared back at her with his lips parted. The rest of the world fell away. The very air around her took on an incandescent glow. Her thick, lustrous hair was full of lights that burned holes in his heart. In no time they had fallen in love.

As the months progressed, they made tentative plans for marriage. In time, though, something in Patrick's heart longed to resume his single-minded pursuit of enlightenment, perhaps to the point of becoming a monk and devoting himself to it exclusively. But monks didn't marry in Yasuhara Roshi's lineage. On the last day of a visit to Sado Island off the central west coast of Japan, he let Yumi know that he had had a change of heart. She should find someone else. She called him a self-centered bastard for leading her on. He agreed with her but didn't change his mind.

Now, a year later, he was sure he had made the right decision. He would not consider marriage or even a close relationship until he had plumbed the depths of this enlightenment which became the end-all and be-all of his life. The memory of Yumi faded from his mind. He was serene in his solitary life of meditation. And as long as he meditated, he was free of the image of the dead boy.

But now the CIA wanted him back. He would hear them out, but he had at last found a measure of peace of mind after so many years of anguish over the boy. He had even given up Yumi for his quest for enlightenment. He was not about to give up that quest and re-enter the world that had taken that peace from him to begin with. Still, his curiosity got the best of him, and he wondered what on earth the Agency wanted from him this time. He looked at his watch. He would find out soon enough. They were arriving at noon.

CHAPTER 5

SADO ISLAND, JAPAN
February 25

Located an hour's ferry ride from the west coast of Japan, Sado Island offers the perfect wedding venue for young people looking for something more adventurous than the usual banquet in a Tokyo skyscraper. That was the plan, anyway, for Patrick Featherstone and Yumi Takara who traveled to the island from the Tokyo area a year earlier. Yumi, the daughter of Goro Takara, the missing pachinko parlor owner, was particularly drawn to the breathtaking scenery of Myotoiwa Beach, which features two large rocks nestled close together in the water. Dubbed the "Husband and Wife" in local lore, she felt the rocks added an auspicious element to their trip. But at the end of their stay on the island, Patrick told her he had come to realize they had no future together. He was bound and determined to become a Buddhist monk. Now, a year later, Yumi walked alone as sunset approached. Measured in time, a year is not very long. Measured in heartache, it is an eternity.

Dressed in jeans, T-shirt and hooded sweatshirt, Yumi walked barefoot at the waterline, sloshing listlessly through the cold foam. The sea-rounded stones tossed up by the waves made a clattering sound like dice in a cup. Two of her friends sat on a hillock watching her with concern, hugging themselves to stay warm. They were there to lend moral support but they felt utterly helpless in the face of her despair.

Why have I come back here? she wondered, especially when she caught sight of the Husband and Wife rocks in the near distance. But an overwhelming force had drawn her back, against the urging of her friends and father, and against her own better judgment. Back to the place where her future ended.

Back to the place where she had last seen Patrick Featherstone.

Has it really been twelve months since I last saw him, and on this very beach? She thought of his face, but was alarmed that his features seemed to have receded from her memory. She tried to conjure up his jade-green eyes, sometimes dancing with delight, at other times flashing with anger, and still other times lost in their own world. That was the trick, she thought. *Think of his eyes, and the rest of his face will come along, too.* Not this time, though.

A sigh of profound sadness that started in her gut came rushing out of her lips for the ten thousandth time, like the waves that swelled, crested, and dashed themselves upon the shore. It had not gotten any easier, not even a little. The boundless futurity of youth was fading fast behind her, and she contemplated a life lived alone. Unlike Patrick, though, she would not be doing so voluntarily. *Damn him,* she cursed under her breath, as she had also done ten thousand times over the past year.

But although a solitary life seemed to be her destiny, on this morning she was not alone at all. Had she not been so absorbed in her contemplation of long years ahead filled with silent meals and lonely walks on the beach, she might have noticed a man lurking in a dense growth of bushes at the sand line just above her friends' hillock.

The waves crested higher along the shoreline, and when a giant one broke loudly on the beach, the man sprang from his hiding place. As Yumi absently watched a motorboat on the horizon bobbing just behind the Husband and Wife, she heard a sharp, whooshing sound, like air being discharged through a small opening. She turned in shock to see her friends drop to the ground with scarlet tulips blossoming from their foreheads.

The man ran to Yumi and in one motion had her in a headlock and forced a wet sponge over her nose and mouth. Almost immediately she felt a dizzying sensation, as if she had drunk too much sake. When her body had gone completely limp, the man tied her hands and stuffed a gag into her mouth. He then signaled to the operator of the small motorboat Yumi had been watching. The boat pulled up to the beach, and Yumi was carried aboard.

When she awoke, her head throbbed with each beat of her heart. Straining to focus her eyes, she realized that she was in a larger vessel on the open sea. The boat's motor vibrated with a low, incessant hum she could feel in her guts, and the heavy salt-tang in the air mixed with noxious diesel fumes nauseated her even further.

"Feeling better?" said a gruff voice from behind her in Korean. From her father's association with North Koreans in his pachinko business, Yumi spoke and read the language with considerable fluency.

"Where am I? Where are you taking me?" Yumi said in Korean in a voice made husky and deep-pitched from dehydration.

"Here," the man said, flinging a blanket at her head. "It's going to get a lot colder tonight, and we have a long way to go."

"But why am I here?"

"You're here because your father stole something from someone very important."

The man's voice was familiar. Finally it dawned on her where she had heard it before. It was a man whom her father worked for, a man whose beady eyes staring coldly out of a scowling face never failed to make her tremble with fear. Mr. Pung. She lay back in the boat and moaned, too miserable from seasickness to ask anything more. Compounding her misery was the fact that she was being kidnaped over something her father had done. She loved him dearly, but part of her now cursed him for the chances he was always taking, chances for which she was now paying the price.

PYONGYANG

Following the long boat ride came a long car ride to Pyongyang, at the end of which Pung opened the back door of the car and motioned with a jerk of his head for Yumi to get out. With enormous effort, she pushed and pulled herself out of the car, at which point Pung grasped her by the elbow and pulled her into the building. They rode the elevator upwards in silence.

At the top floor, the door of the elevator opened and Pung roughly guided her toward an office down the corridor. Everything was silent except for an eerie musical sound which echoed in the silence. Pung opened the office door and pushed Yumi into a chair. A tall man dressed in a perfectly-fitted suit stood with a cigarette dangling from his mouth while playing an accordion and watching another man fiddling with a computer. When Yumi's chair creaked as she sat down, the man with the accordion stopped playing and turned.

He looked Yumi over with heavy-lidded eyes, unstrapped the accordion, and took a seat in a tall leather office chair that accentuated his air of authority. Lighting another cigarette from the one he had just finished, he raised his head to blow the smoke into the air almost daintily and again fixed Yumi with a steady gaze that was more curious than hostile, at least initially.

"Inspector Choy, come back and finish your work later," he said to the person who had been working on his computer. His eyes never left Yumi as he spoke.

"Yes, Comrade Moon," Inspector Choy said as he left. He glanced back at Yumi as he shut the door behind him.

"Your father has something that belongs to me," Moon began.

"I know nothing about any of this," Yumi replied with exasperation in her voice. "All I know is that I was taken from Japan against my will." The authoritative contralto she had heard coming from her throat earlier had been replaced by a pinched, almost desperate squeak.

Moon snorted in derision. "See if Senghori will improve her memory," he said to Pung.

"Right away, Comrade Moon," replied Pung, and he left to arrange Yumi's transfer to the country's most notorious prison camp.

Comrade Moon was in a bind. The Commission was already nipping at his heels for a status report on his plan to turn North Korea into the Commission's own fiefdom. The suitcase Yumi's father had stolen was vital to that plan. If Senghori Prison didn't squeeze the information out of Yumi about her father's whereabouts, nothing would. And that would really be a problem.

EN ROUTE TO SENGHORI PRISON

After two hours of driving in the direction of the Demilitarized Zone, Pung

27

pulled off the highway and began a steep descent down into a valley on a pocked dirt road. A half hour later, they came to a halt just inside a gate that had been opened for their arrival. Pung ordered Yumi out and said a few words to the sentry who nodded and went back into his little shack to use the telephone. Soon an ancient Russian-made jeep from inside the compound pulled up, and a uniformed man got out of the back before it had come to a full stop. Pung handed the man the papers for Yumi's incarceration.

"From here on in, this is your most important prisoner," Pung said. "Her father has stolen something very valuable from Comrade Moon." With that, he got into the truck and was on his way back to Pyongyang.

The man from the jeep looked at the papers he had been given and then at Yumi.

"You are here for *kuryujang*," he said, using the official word for "questioning". Then he quickly ran through his usual spiel to incoming prisoners: "You must adore Kim Il-sung, Kim Jong-il, and Kim Jong-un with all your heart," he said. "And you have to give up being human if you want to last very long in this place," he added. With that he motioned for a young guard to take the new prisoner for processing and assignment to a miserable little hut she would share with eight other prisoners. The guard grabbed Yumi's arm and, even though she did nothing to resist, he applied as much pressure and torque as possible. She cried out in pain.

"Shut up, bitch, this is the easy part," he hissed.

The next morning Yumi was roughly awakened at 5 a.m. along with the other prisoners. This day was unusual, though. A voice came over the camp's loudspeaker system.

"Today there will be two executions. All prisoners must attend or there will be more than two executions."

The man who spoke had a sallow, oily complexion and a galaxy of acne scars on his face. He was the superintendant of the prison, known to the prisoners as the Rat Catcher. The nickname derived from the fact that he deprived them of practically their only source of protein and did God knows what with the rodents he trapped. Once the prisoners were all assembled on the execution grounds, the Rat Catcher called out through a bullhorn.

"Bring the prisoners!" he shouted, and immediately four troll-like figures dressed in rags skittered up to a tree dragging a woman who looked to be 60 but was 37, and a girl who looked to be 8 but was 13. They had tried to escape two days earlier.

The Rat Catcher strutted forward and addressed the condemned in a stentorian voice. "On account of your perfidy in betraying the country that nurtured you, you are condemned to die."

Then turning to the assembled prisoners he continued, "You are witnessing how miserable fools end up. Traitors who betray their nation and its people will meet the same fate!"

In most other countries, the prisoner would then be allowed some last words, but here they had stones stuffed in their mouths in order to prevent them from shouting any words of defiance. A noose hung from a tree limb. An order issued during Kim Jong-il's reign that was still in effect had stipulated that prisoners be shot in the head because their brains were full of "wrong thoughts," but they could only spare one bullet for the day.

Yumi watched in horrified fascination as they lifted the woman onto a chair, fitted the noose tightly around her neck, and the head guard knocked her legs out from under her with a hickory club he carried. Her body twitched and writhed spasmodically for a few seconds and then went slack.

"Bring the next traitor forward." This time the Rat Catcher was almost casual in the way he rushed through the words of condemnation. "On account of your perfidy in betraying the country that nurtured you, you are condemned to die." There was no emotion of any kind in his voice, not hatred, certainly not pity. His only thought was that he would now be allowed to attend a vocational college in nearby Kaesong the following year, his reward for having met his quota of executions.

The young girl was shoved forward, a little matchstick of a figure covered in bloody rags. Her arms had only the barest layer of skin covering sparrow bones, without any intervening muscle tissue. Her eyes were long beyond fear. They had the wide-open but blank expression of a doll that had been discarded in a dump. Because of her age she would not be hung. The head guard, nicknamed Bastard Cho by the prisoners, walked up behind her and fired his pistol once into the back of the young girl's head. She went down without her body making the slightest sound as it hit the earth. Yumi's body trembled as if from a terrible fever. She felt completely alone in the universe.

CHAPTER 6

ON THE SHUTO EXPRESSWAY FROM TOKYO
February 25

The two "cultural attaches" from the American Embassy in Tokyo drove in silence toward the town of Kamakura, forty miles down the coast from Tokyo. The driver, Norm Hooper, was actually the CIA Station Chief in Japan, a stockily built man in his early 50s, about 5'8", with dandruff-dusted black hair shorn down to an early-astronaut style crewcut. The other man, Harmon Phibbs, was a year or two younger, tall and pinch-faced with papery skin and white-blond hair that hung slack down his forehead like tiny fiber-optic cables. He sipped coffee while Hooper drove.

"So who's this guy we're visiting, anyway?" Phibbs asked.

"Patrick Featherstone's his name," Hooper said. "American. Kind of a recluse, but Jack Fitzroy in Technical managed to track him down."

"You mean he lives in this country willingly? How'd he wind up here?"

"He was born here. His parents were missionaries. Ran an orphanage in Kamakura. Actually, his old man was one of ours during the Korean War."

"How did the son get involved in our line of work?" Phibbs asked as he took in the scenery.

"It started when he was in college in Tokyo. An art major, of all things. His Korean painting teacher, a guy named Professor Park, was a good friend of his father's during the Korean War and one of our recruiters. Patrick learned Korean from the guy who also taught him this secret martial art called *kakuremu*, which means 'hidden warrior.' Now that's some heavy shit, let me tell you. You can kill a guy with just a finger thrust to the temple or throat. Anyway, after art college Featherstone joined our life. They recruited him into the Joint Special Operations Command."

"You serious? JSOC?" Phibbs said.

"Right. 'Sharp edge of the knife', 'snake eaters', take your pick of clichés. He was part of a special sniper unit in Serbia with that guy Tyler Kang who was only supposed to make believe he was defecting to North Korea a while back. Featherstone got fucked up in the head."

"Shot?"

"Nah, fucked up psychologically. Some young kid got killed on their last mission. Featherstone thought Kang should take some of the heat for it, but it was all on Featherstone. He came back here after the Serbia fuckup, pulled himself out of a whiskey bottle and went looking for enlightenment. Zen Buddhism, the whole bit."

"And what are we supposed to say to him when we get there? 'We need you back to find your old sniper buddy who's defected to North Korea'?"

"The first thing we're going to do is find out if Kang ever gave any indication of disloyalty when they knew each other. Back in Serbia."

"I get the feeling they didn't exactly part on good terms."

"Oh, you got that right. They used to be like brothers. Still are, in a sense, if you count Cain and Abel. Featherstone got court martialed and Kang testified against him."

"How do you know all this stuff, Hoop?"

"I was there. Hey look, there's the turnoff for Kamakura."

Patrick's noontime meditation was interrupted by a neighbor's dog frantically yapping down the road leading to his cabin. The dog was his early warning system. He rose from his round *zafu* meditation cushion, stood to his full six feet and walked out onto his porch. Two Caucasian men appeared on foot from around the bend in the road leading to his cabin. They had been forced to leave their Lincoln Navigator down the steep mountain. Haggard and exhausted, they looked as though they had just trekked across the Gobi Desert.

"Featherstone?" gasped the first of them to make it to the cabin.

"I am. You are?"

"Harmon Phibbs," he huffed and sat down in a heap on Patrick's porch steps.

His straggling companion smiled wanly at Patrick as he trudged closer, his chest heaving but his eyes not leaving Patrick's. Patrick said nothing. The man's face was familiar, if older, but the feelings it engendered were something quite a bit less than affection. Finally he spoke.

"Hello, Hooper," he said, purposely using the man's last name in order to drive home the point that there was no love lost between them, not even for old time's sake. Especially not for old time's sake.

"Hello...Patrick." The man's words were labored from the hike up the steep hill. He spoke in a low, almost apologetic tone, as if they were friends who had had some words and now would sort things out. He waited for any hint of a smile or cordiality on Patrick's face. He would have had to wait for a very long time.

"Mind if we come in? It's kind of chilly up here on Mount Everest."

Patrick nodded in the direction of his front door.

As they entered his cabin, Patrick winced. "Shoes outside, please," Patrick admonished Phibbs with barely concealed contempt. Phibbs snorted ever-so-slightly as he removed his shoes. *Gone native,* he thought to himself.

Seeing no chairs in the main room of the cabin, Hooper and Phibbs lowered themselves uncomfortably onto cushions on the tatami floor.

"Well, what is it you want from me?" Patrick asked, cutting off any possibility of introductory chitchat.

Hooper chewed the inside of his cheek for a moment, as if trying to find the exact words to explain his presence. He hadn't expected to get to the purpose of his visit so abruptly. Finally, he inhaled and exhaled quickly, blowing out his cheeks before speaking.

"It's about Tyler Kang."

Patrick was silent for a long moment. "I haven't seen him in a very long time," he said finally.

"He ran over the DMZ to North Korea," Phibbs said.

"He always liked to travel."

"Actually, we sent him there," Hooper said, pausing to gauge Patrick's reaction before continuing. "He was supposed to tell the North Koreans he was defecting, but it was a cover for something else."

"A confusion op."

"In a sense. But not to feed them disinformation. We needed to get a message to them without broadcasting it all over the world."

"So you had him mock-defect. What was his cover? He missed home-cooked kimchee?"

"The cover was that he had grown disgusted by the work he had been forced to do for the Agency," Hooper said. "The North Koreans think everything the U.S. does is controlled by the CIA, so it seemed a natural 'in'."

"And they're too sophisticated to believe anyone who says they're defecting in order to live in a socialist paradise," Phibbs added. "Not even they believe in that anymore."

Patrick laughed. "So he tells them he's disgusted by the work he's done for the Agency. That's brilliant! A perfect cover! How could anyone doubt a story like that?"

Hooper's face flushed. "We've made our share of mistakes, sure, but on balance, I'd say the world's done pretty well by us."

"You mean like going into sovereign countries and assassinating the bad guys? A certain Serbian named Ranko Djanic comes to mind. And if innocent people get killed, well, that's just 'collateral damage', isn't it. Do you guys still use that term?"

"We live in the real world, Mr. Featherstone," Phibbs said. "We don't try to make believe that if you feed the hungry and give shelter to the poor that there won't be some scumbag out there ready to blow us all to shit anyway."

"And that gives you the right to take out the scumbags before they can do any more harm, is that it? And in the name of 'regional stability'? Like the black op in Serbia where a five-year-old kid got killed?

Hooper raised his hand. "Look, I'll be honest with you, we..."

"Don't break any habits on my account."

Hooper lowered his eyes and inhaled deeply, struggling to maintain his composure. Phibbs glared at Patrick.

"You mentioned regional stability a moment ago," Hooper said finally after exhaling. "Now, I'll grant you, that thing in Serbia was a major fuckup. But the last thing anyone wants now is a North Korea that's any less stable, especially now with Kim Jong-un's aggression against us and South Korea. For one thing, their nuke program has the brass in Washington as skittery as a kitten on meth. They think the ICBM tests and threats against Guam might be a lead-up to an attack on the South. Testing the shark-infested waters, if you will, to see what our response will be. It may even have something to do with a power struggle for control of the regime, since Jong-un's hold on power is more than a little iffy. Either way, it could get ugly, but it would be uglier if we tried anything…precipitous. That's where Tyler came in."

Hooper had Patrick's attention. A power struggle on the Korean peninsula. Where his father had fought in the last conflict. But Patrick had long since given up trying to fill his father's shoes. The last time he had tried that, innocent blood was spilled in Serbia. Still, the topic held a natural interest for him.

"What about the summit talks? Kim Jong-un and the president face-to-face," he asked.

"A total bust. As if anyone's surprised. They pulled the same bait-and-switch bullshit they did in '85, '94, '95, '96…shall I go on?"

"I get the point. Alright, so why have you come to me with all this?"

"Tyler's gone dark."

"And what, he's being held in a dungeon somewhere? What if he's been doubled? Drank the Kool-Aid? Did you even *have* a contingency plan for that? It wouldn't be the first time. Maybe he's become a proud member of the Democratic People's Republic of Korea. 'Hero of the People'. Ever thought of that? He always did have a knack for selling people out."

The men from the Agency said nothing. Phibbs nervously tapped his fingers on the low table. Patrick just looked at the two of them, his lips set.

"Okay, so I get drummed out of JSOC and now they want me back in so that I can go to North Korea and rescue Tyler Kang, is that it?"

"If he's innocent. Some sensitive missile technology documents have gone missing, and the fear is that he took them with him. If he did, it's pretty clear that your scenario would be right, that he really has defected. And if that's the case, then we need him neutralized."

Patrick's eyes widened in disbelief, and he laughed from deep in his belly. Then his face became serious again.

"Gotta love the passive voice. *'Need him neutralized'*. Are you perchance referring to me as the *neutralizer?* Look, Hooper, I wouldn't piss on Tyler Kang if he was on fire. But I wouldn't light the fire, either. Besides, he had a tendency to crush the toes he stepped on, I'm sure there's a long line of others who would jump at the chance to take him out."

"But you still blame him. And you *did* say you would kill him, after the court martial, I mean."

Patrick sighed wearily. "Do you really think I'm that gullible? That you can use what happened all those years ago to get me to go into a country we're still technically at war with and grease the guy?"

"If necessary. You always wanted to get back at him. Tell me I'm wrong."

"You're wrong."

"I don't believe you."

"Don't, then. I left that world far behind a long time ago," Patrick lied. He carried it inside all the time. He sat silently and looked out the window.

"I'm sorry you've come all this way for nothing," he said finally. "This isn't my fight. I'm not going back to that life ever again."

"Look, do me a favor," Hooper said. "Don't give an answer right away. Think about it for a few days and see if you feel the same way. Here's my card." Hooper placed it on the low table when Patrick made no move to take it. Then the two Agency men rose stiffly from their seats on the floor and exited the cabin.

That night
...*Tyler's gone dark*
...*we need him neutralized*
...*you still blame him*
...*you did say you would kill him*

...you always wanted to get back at him

With Hooper's words echoing in his ears, Patrick was suddenly back in Serbia years earlier. His spirits plunged as the image of the five-year-old child being shot replayed over and over in his mind. Finally, with his head throbbing with remorse and depression, he could stand it no longer and took down an unopened bottle of Jack Daniels that he kept on a top shelf as a passive *kata* in self-control.

In the morning he awoke with a mortal hangover and flew bleary-eyed and shaking on business to Macau, the Switzerland of Asia when it comes to secret bank accounts. He had to gulp down two glasses of sake before he got on the plane just to settle his nerves. As the plane leveled off at its cruising altitude, he accepted a third glass from the flight attendant and anxiously wondered if he was slipping back into his post-Serbia pattern.

His father had been lost at sea years earlier when his fishing boat went down in a gale off Kamakura, and his mother had left him a decent sum of money when she died. A banker he knew on Macau had turned it into a sizeable portfolio that would support him comfortably, if not lavishly, for the rest of his life. Patrick had moved the money to Macau to avoid Japan's inheritance tax while his mother was still alive, and the Lucky Star Bank, though legal, operated in a netherworld of sub rosa financial dealings, which was why Patrick chose it. It was able to fly under the radar of government oversight and was as secure as a bank this side of Zurich could be.

After taking care of business, Patrick relaxed for the rest of the day on the veranda of his room at the Grand Lapa Resort, absorbing the last rays of the sun and sipping wine, cautiously relieved that he didn't as yet have a craving for anything harder.

As he reclined on the lounge chair, his thoughts turned again to Hooper and Phibbs's visit. Tyler had mock-defected to North Korea and gone dark. Patrick contemplated the puzzle of Tyler's disappearance until he nodded off.

Later that night the sound of the telephone trilling insinuated itself into the edges of his sleep. Forcing himself awake, he checked the time, cleared his throat, and picked up the receiver.

"Hello," he croaked, his brain pulsating with disjointed dreams.

Silence on the other end of the line. Just as Patrick was about to hang up, an angry voice spat out the words, "Yumi Takara has been abducted to North Korea." The speaker had a heavy Korean accent. Then the line went dead.

Despite the late hour, Patrick dialed the last number he had for Yumi Takara, the woman he had almost married.

"Moshi moshi," a frantic female voice answered almost immediately.

Patrick identified himself.

The voice on the other end of the line was borderline hysterical, but Patrick was sure it belonged to Mrs. Yoshii, the Takara's housekeeper. "Takara-san is missing," she managed to say between garbled sobs. "And so is Yumi-san. I went to the pachinko parlor, but no one was there. And I just got a call from the police on Sado Island that Yumi's friends were found dead on a beach! I am so afraid that something terrible has happened to Yumi and her father!"

"Did either of them ever say anything about North Korea?" Patrick asked.

There was a pause on the other end of the line. Finally the housekeeper spoke. "I know there was a man named Mr. Pung that Yumi's father associated with at the pachinko parlor. I think he was from North Korea. I don't know what they did together, but I think it was probably illegal. I could tell that Takara-san hated him."

"Thank you for letting me know, Yoshii-san, I'll look into this."

After hanging up, Patrick contemplated the odds of two of the people he had been closest to in life now being in North Korea, the most closed country on earth. Had it just been Tyler, he would have washed his hands of the whole thing. But with Yumi in the picture, the equation had changed, especially if she really had been abducted. They had been as close as two human beings could be at one time, even though he had instigated their breakup. He couldn't just sit by and do nothing, especially in light of the information coming out about the horrendous conditions in the prison camps over there. Patrick shuddered to imagine what conditions she might be in at that very moment. He picked up the phone and made another call. This one was to Norm Hooper, CIA Station Chief in Tokyo.

CHAPTER 7

TOKYO
February 26

The next morning, Patrick rode his Harley Road King directly from the airport to the American Embassy in the Akasaka section of Tokyo. On the ride over, his thoughts went back to Tyler Kang with Hooper's words from the other day filling his ears:

...you still blame him

...you did say you would kill him

He remembered when he first met Tyler. Together they had been brothers in arms in a secret commando unit known as Team Red based at Fort Bragg in North Carolina. Now he regarded him as a mortal enemy...

Eighteen years earlier

"Ah, here he is," Patrick's commanding officer said. *"Patrick, I'd like you to meet Tyler Kang. He's over from Army. Spent part of his boyhood in South Korea, but his parents are American, so he's a dual, like you, and..."*

"Were," Tyler interjected.

The C.O. gave a puzzled look. "Pardon?"

"My parents were American. They're both dead. Plane crash in 1988."

"...Oh, sorry," the C.O. said, embarrassed at the gaffe. He cleared his throat and continued.

"Tyler, this is your sniper partner, Patrick Featherstone. Dual citizen, U.S. and Japan. Three languages, just like you. He's one of our best, so you have your work cut out for you. We're expecting great things from you two."

Patrick chuckled at the compliment as he shook the hand of the newcomer who took the opportunity to squeeze Patrick's hand in a vise-like grip while smiling playfully.

"How's it going, Sempai", he said casually, addressing Patrick with the Japanese word for someone who is senior in a relationship. They were almost exactly the same age, but Patrick had entered JSOC first. The way Tyler said it had the mocking overtone of "What's shaking, old timer?" Tyler had learned his Japanese from his Korean aunt and uncle who had grown up during the Japanese occupation of Korea. He grinned as he combed his hair back with his fingers. A second later it fell right back across his forehead.

"At your service, Kohai," Patrick replied with a needling smile of his own, using a Japanese word with the connotation of "underling". And so, from their very first meeting Patrick Featherstone and Tyler Kang were both colleagues and rivals.

Patrick's grip on the handlebars tightened involuntarily. The speedometer on his Harley read 90. He had to force himself to slow down as he continued to remember...

During their tour of duty in Serbia, their commanding officer sent for them one afternoon. A man in civilian clothing was seated on a folding chair. The CO explained that they had a special mission. They had been chosen over three other sniper teams.

"This one's black," the CO said. "Off the books, never-happened kind of thing. This is Norm Hooper. He'll give you the specifics of the mission."

Hooper introduced himself only a bit more fully. He was from the Special Operations Group of the CIA's Special Activities Division.

"We have a very thin timeline, gentlemen, so let's get to it." Hooper nodded to the CO who unfurled a topo map of the area. "This is the town of Pale, about ten klicks from here. Right in between here and Pale there's this castle." Hooper used a long pointer with a black rubber tip to indicate a king's crown on the map.

"There's a guy living here called Ranko Djanic, a local warlord. Brings in *heroin from the Bekaa Valley in Lebanon, sells it, and uses it to buy arms. He's looking to profit from destabilizing the whole Balkan area. Sells to both sides, profits from both."*

Hooper paused and looked at Patrick and Tyler. "He has to go. You guys get to punch his ticket."

"One question," Tyler said. "Why is it black? Why not go with regular rules of engagement?"

Hooper replied without hesitation. "Because we want to send a clear message to anyone else who might be entertaining the same idea: we can operate outside the law like they do. And they just might be next on our honey-do list."

Patrick then remembered their preparation for the mission as though it were yesterday. Patrick would be the shooter and he would use an M16 rifle and speedy 5.56mm NATO rounds because of the wind. The speedometer of his motorcycle began inching up again as he thought of Hooper's instructions that day...

"You're going to hook the rifle up when you get there to one of our latest toys, a computerized scope. It'll give you an instant read on all the things you'll need to know in terms of windage, sightline, etc. It even corrects for parallax. 15X magnification. I think you're gonna like it."

"How's it work?" Tyler asked skeptically.

"It's a new technology that combines fiber optics and tritium gas in the sights. We're still trying to miniaturize it, but it's been 100% effective in its current iteration. When you get to this position," Hooper indicated a rise on the topo map above the castle, "you'll see the computer unit in place. Plug it in and you're good to go. Totally user-friendly."

Once they were in position, Patrick attached the scope to the rifle and Tyler plugged the cable into the computer. Just as Patrick was marveling at its imaging capability, the sight picture suddenly went grainy and indistinct.

He shook his head in disgust. Even after all these years, Patrick recalled what happened next with total clarity…

"This thing is fucked," Patrick muttered. Tyler said nothing, his eyes fixed on the castle. Just then, a large limousine pulled into the central entrance to the castle.

"Target approaching," Tyler whispered. He peered intently through his own 20X scope. "Acquire and hold target."

Patrick went back to his sight picture, though its clarity was now greatly diminished. As Ranko Djanic's limousine entered through the main gate, Patrick chambered a round into the M16. The back door of the limousine was opened by a soldier who jumped out of the front passenger's seat as soon as the vehicle came to a halt. Ranko Djanic exited. Tyler put his hand on Patrick's shoulder, a signal that the final phase had begun.

Patrick snuggled the stock into his shoulder and dug his feet into the ground for stability. He closed his right eye and willed his muscles to ignore the surge of adrenaline that blossomed in his abdomen. He slowly exhaled and could feel his heart rate decreasing incrementally. His finger curled more tightly around the trigger, about a pound of pressure. Waiting. Vacant of thought. Target acquired at the intersection of the cross of the reticle. Suddenly, the sun broke through the clouds. Patrick squinted from the unexpected light in the scope.

"Stand by, stand by. Three, two, one. Execute, execute," Tyler said under his breath…

As Patrick got closer to the American Embassy in Tokyo, he forced himself to push out of his mind what happened next all those years ago. A few minutes later he stood at the entrance gate before two young Marines in dress blues and Corfam shoes who greeted him with an air of menacing courtesy.

"Sir, may I help you," said one of them, not so much a question as a challenge.

"I'm here to see Mr. Hooper," replied Patrick in a measured voice, assuring the Marines through his demeanor that he was not intimidated.

After a brief phone call, another Marine appeared to escort Patrick to Hooper's office. As they walked wordlessly through the labyrinth of cubicles, Patrick noted the security measures that had been taken to prevent eavesdropping of any kind. Foot-thick rubber bricks lined the walls of the room to prevent vibrations from being detected by anyone outside the building. A thicket of antennae bristled from a number of areas around the room in a constant search for radio or microwave transmissions. A spectrum analyzer that checked for anomalies in acoustic waveforms completed the array of electronic surveillance.

"This is Mr. Hooper's office," the Marine said, indicating a door at the far end of the cavernous room. He waited until Patrick had entered the office before turning and heading back in the direction he had come from.

As Patrick entered, Hooper looked up from a memo he was dictating to a secretary. He said something to her and walked quickly over to Patrick.

"Come on in the back," he said in a voice that had a tone of subdued urgency about it.

Once inside a smaller room at the far end of the work area, Hooper closed the door.

"We can speak freely here," he said, indicating the room with his head.

Patrick nodded.

"First of all, I want to thank you again for coming. We're all glad to have you back on the team," he said.

"Not to be rude, but I don't really consider myself part of any team," Patrick replied. "Just to get that established from the beginning."

"Well. Anyway. We've had a few new developments since our conversation in Kamakura," Hooper said. Patrick wondered if he might be alluding to Yumi's apparent abduction.

"Things have gotten a little jumpy in Pyongyang lately."

"Jumpy in what way?" Patrick asked. It did not appear that Hooper had been referring to Yumi.

"I don't know how much you know in-depth about the current situation in North Korea..."

"Just the scary headlines, really," Patrick replied. Actually, he had spent half the previous night on the internet poring over everything he could find about the situation in North Korea. But he wanted to draw out Hooper to see what kind of spin he would put on the facts of the case.

Phibbs walked in as Hooper was about to continue. "Come on in, Harmon, I was just giving Patrick the lowdown on Kim-land." Then to Patrick, "Harmon just got back from gambling on Macau." He turned to Phibbs: "No wonder you're broke all the time."

Phibbs grinned. "Finally won this time." He turned to Patrick. "Welcome back to the wilderness of mirrors. Care for a donut?" He held up a multicolored paper bag. "Got them in Macau. Real Portuguese malasadas."

Patrick shook his head no. "I was just there myself. I hope you won more than I did."

Phibbs just grinned and bit into a malasada.

Hooper took up from where he had left off before Phibbs had arrived. "Patrick, before we start, you'll need to know the background on what's happening. As you no doubt remember, the oath of secrecy you took when you joined JSOC was for life. I need you to agree in writing that what you see and hear in the conduct of this mission will remain in the strictest confidence."

Hooper already had a document out on his desk. He held out a pen for Patrick to take. Patrick read the document carefully, surprised at how lacking it was in the usual fine print.

"You realize that I'm just saying I won't tell anybody anything. I haven't agreed to go yet."

"I understand," said Hooper. Patrick signed the document. Hooper continued. "Now let's get to the heart of things: the President has ordered a drawdown of our forces in South Korea for redeployment to the Middle East. Syria, to be exact. The last time we redeployed was back in 1950. North Korea invaded within a month. The reason we sent Tyler over was to let the North Koreans know, without issuing a press release, that the South is now equipped with a nuclear arsenal capable of taking out their whole pissant country if they try to repeat history. Now we have several problems. For one thing the South

Korean missile delivery system is defective. For another, since Tyler's gone dark, we don't know if he got through to the upper level of the North Korean regime. And on top of that, he brought over Top Secret info on our own missile delivery system. So now we have to find out what happened to him and take appropriate action. And as if all that's not enough, this morning we find out there's yet another wrinkle: last night we got some inside dope that at least one coup plot is in the works. We need to know how likely it is to actually happen, and who's behind it."

Patrick said nothing at first but looked off into the distance as he always did when deep in thought. "So now there's a lot more involved than just finding Tyler."

Hooper and Phibbs nodded in unison.

"So who are the players? And how likely is a coup? I thought Kim Jong-un was the 'Supreme Commander' over there."

Phibbs began. "There's a humongous power vacuum opening up. For one thing, Kim Jong-un has developed a nasty habit of executing his top guys in the Politburo. Plus, the military brass hates his guts, because he knows jack about military leadership but thinks he's the new Sun-tzu. The army thinks that if they ever have to go to war with this psychopathic frat-boy in charge, they're all dead. They want their own guy in, a total nutcase in his own right named General O who's threatened to turn South Korea into a 'sea of fire'. As if that's not enough, there's a guy named Comrade Moon who's General O's main rival. He's one of Kim's relatives by marriage, and he might be the real power behind the scenes. If there's a coup, it'll be one of these two behind it."

Hooper's turn. "All of this stuff makes President Dillard a very nervous camper. Shit can happen if there's a coup. Shit like nukes going off. The North now has ICBMs capable of hitting D.C. What we need is regional stability, but that doesn't look likely to happen anytime soon. That pretty much sums up the situation."

"The whole kit-and-kabuki," quipped Phibbs with a self-satisfied smile as he licked sugar off his fingers.

Patrick sat with his arms crossed on his chest as they spoke and leaned slightly back in his chair. When they finished, he waited a few silent moments before he spoke.

"You have to realize that *if* I go, it will be NOC" — non-official cover— "I don't work for you, you don't know me, I'm on my own. The proverbial 'army of one'. Clear?"

Hooper had been expecting this. His eyes moved from side to side, a sign to Patrick, whose read of faces was nearly flawless, that Hooper was assessing all options before speaking. Finally, he blew out his cheeks and spoke.

"If you're NOC and anything happens to you over there, we can't do anything about it. And there aren't any civilized rules over there, Patrick. If they catch you, you *will* go to the gulag…or worse."

"I'll take my chances."

Hooper sighed. "Alright," he said after a long moment. "But remember: anything too far off the rez could be enough to start World War III. You'll need to have a risk-of-capture briefing before you go. I also need for you to meet with Fitz."

"Fitz?"

"Jack Fitzroy, our tradecraft specialist. Best there is. Come back tomorrow and we'll take care of the remaining details."

During Patrick's ride down to Kamakura, his mind went back once again to Hooper's words of a few days before: *You* did *say you would kill him, after the court martial…*

And with that a torrent of memories was unleashed, memories he had tried for so long to forget…

At the exact moment that Tyler called for the shot, a five-year-old boy ran out from behind a tree where he had been hiding in a game with his friends and raced obliviously in Ranko Djanic's direction, laughing giddily as his friends tried to catch him. Patrick's and Tyler's focus was through telescopic lenses that narrowed their field of vision to Djanic's upper body and head. Patrick squeezed the trigger through its final ounce of pressure, and a tremendous echo resounded through the mountain pass. But instead of hitting Djanic, the young child who had run into the sight picture was practically blown in two. His body lifted briefly into the air and then fell inertly to the ground.

"Jesus!" Patrick yelled in disbelief, adrenaline igniting his viscera. "Why didn't you tell me the kid was there?"

"I swear to God I didn't see him!" Tyler screamed back.

"And now he's dead, you fucking idiot!"

"I told you didn't see him, dammit!"

The keening wail of the boy's mother could be heard even from a half mile away as Patrick and Tyler trudged back separately to their command center. Neither said a word from the shock of what had just happened.

A mandatory After-Action Review ensued, and Patrick, being the shooter, was court-martialed. Tyler, on the advice of his JAG lawyer, testified that the shooter has final responsibility for making sure the target area is clear of civilians, and that Patrick had taken the shot anyway. He also testified that he didn't know that the high-tech scope had malfunctioned.

"I told you that right before the limousine pulled in!" Patrick shouted out in court.

"Your exact words were, 'This thing is fucked,'" Tyler retorted. "I thought you meant the mission, not the scope."

Patrick just glared at Tyler, hatred in his eyes.

None of what had happened could be allowed to reach the public, of course, since it would have implicated the United States in an attempted political assassination. Everyone associated with the case was sworn to secrecy. Patrick was found not guilty, forced to accept an honorable discharge, and advised to try and put the incident behind him. Instead, he moved back to Kamakura in a booze-fueled tailspin. Tyler, for his part, took two years off to earn a Master's degree in aerospace engineering, after which he returned to active duty with JSOC. The two former friends never spoke to each other again, their last words coming during a brief encounter after the court martial in the hallway when Patrick hissed under his breath, "You set me up. I wish I'd aimed at you."

CHAPTER 8

TOKYO
American Embassy
February 27

Patrick returned to the Embassy the following day. Hooper greeted him and had him sign a risk-of-capture form which stated that if anything happened to him, the United States would disavow any knowledge of who he was or what he was doing. Hooper then escorted him down a narrow winding staircase that led into the bowels of the embassy where most of the top-secret technical work took place. The staircase was like something out of a European hotel of the 1920s, but it served the dual purpose of impeding progress up or down in the event of a security breach in either direction.

Down in the basement, a knot of technicians in white coats peered intently at computer screens or tinkered with various gadgets set out on long tables. A constant loud whirring came from further back in the basement, and no one looked up as Hooper and Patrick made their way across the rubber-coated floor toward a tall, thin, bearded man in his 60s who gazed in rapt absorption at the ceiling tiles seemingly lost in thought. He caught sight of Hooper and Patrick and waved his hand at a technician in the back. The loud whirring suddenly stopped, and Patrick felt his ears both clear out and echo in the silence.

"Hello, Norm," Fitzroy called out to Hooper, a smile crinkling his eyes.

"Hey, Fitz," Hooper replied.

"Make yourselves at home. I'll be over in just a bit. The passports are on the table."

As they waited, Hooper filled Patrick in about the man. A career CIA veteran approaching retirement, Jack Fitzroy headed the Asia branch of the

Office of Technical Services which specializes in the nuts and bolts of covert ops. Hooper handed Patrick the passports Fitzroy had mentioned. "You'll be going over as a Canadian national. These are exact duplicates of each other. Keep one in a safe place at all times."

Patrick took the passport and flipped through the opening identity portion and then through the phony entry and exit stamps from all over the world.

"I know nothing about Canada," he protested.

Hooper shrugged dismissively. "Who does?"

"But what if someone asks me about Canadian football or something?"

"Christ, I don't know, just tell them you're too embarrassed to talk about it. Oh, here's Fitz. Patrick, this is Jack Fitzroy. Fitz is the one who located you for us. Fitz, I'd like you to meet Our Man in Pyongyang, Patrick Featherstone. He's a 'Canadian art dealer'. What do you think?"

Fitzroy scratched his graying beard absently, giving Patrick an appraising look. "I suppose you look the part. How are your languages?"

"English, Japanese, Korean, all native fluency."

"Good. But you might want to keep the Korean part under wraps. You don't want them to have any inkling you're Agency. Oh, and be sure to bring lots of duty-free booze and cigarettes. It's the coin of the realm in North Korea."

"Okay, will do. And by the way, I'm not really Agency."

"Anything new in the spycraft world, Fitz?" Hooper asked, changing the subject before Patrick got going on his latest pet peeve.

"As a matter of fact, yes. Let me show you something."

Fitzroy led them to an open area that smelled of fresh paint and cordite. He disappeared behind a partition and emerged a minute later with a 9-millimeter Glock which he handed to Patrick.

"Shoot me," he said.

Patrick looked at the gun. Big deal. Blanks. But just to be sure he racked the slide. A live round was in the chamber.

"No way I'm going to even point this off the floor, let alone shoot someone."

"Norm, you do the honors, then." Hooper took the gun, aimed it at Fitzroy's torso and fired. The slug flattened and dropped to the floor.

"Damn, I forgot how much wallop those Glock 9s pack," Fitzroy said coughing from the impact. He then opened his lab coat to reveal a thin Kevlar vest.

Patrick's eyes contracted. "Alright, I give up. That's too thin a layer of Kevlar to stop a 9 mil."

"It's our latest stuff. The lab coat is Kevlar, of course, but what stopped the bullet is something called STF— Shear Thickening Fluid— made of silica and liquid polyethylene glycol. It transforms on impact from liquid to solid in .0013 seconds. Faster than a bullet. Pretty amazing, no?"

Patrick nodded in awe. "Show him the suit, Fitz," Hooper said.

"Oh yeah, that's another beaut. This way, gents." Fitz disappeared behind the partition and reappeared wearing an ordinary-looking suit jacket. He stood in front of a multi-colored wall pattern and dimmed the lights. The jacket immediately changed into the same color and pattern.

"Behold, the chameleon suit," Fitzroy said beaming with pride. "Unfortunately, you can't take it with you. Too much chance they'll back-engineer it."

"Back-engineer it? In North Korea?" Patrick said. "From what I've been reading, they have trouble making door knobs that work."

"Oh, when they put their minds to something, they can do all sorts of things. You've no doubt heard about the counterfeit $100 bills they make, the Super Ks? Completely undetectable. Very clever people they've got. Diabolically so." He reached back toward the table and handed Patrick a small bottle of STF. "You can take this in case things get rough over there. Just apply it evenly."

"On Kevlar? I'm not sure they'd understand why an art dealer needs body armor."

"You can put it on regular clothing too. Not as much protection, but a lot more than a layer of cotton."

"Sorry to rush things along, Fitz, but Patrick's flight to Pyongyang leaves early in the morning from Beijing. He'll need to go home and pack and make the Beijing connection at 7 tonight." Turning to Patrick, he said, "And your new name is 'Patrick McGrail'. It was my grand uncle's name, believe it or not, so I'm hoping it's lucky for you, too."

"What was so lucky about your grand uncle?"

"He hit the jackpot in Vegas just before he was shipped off to Vietnam. Then he won a posthumous Silver Star after the Tet Offensive and went out a hero."

"Lucky dog," Patrick muttered.

Just then, a voice from the far end of the long work room called out. "Hey, come take a look at this!"

The three of them walked quickly over to where a group had congregated in front of a TV monitor. The logo on the screen was for CNN International.

"We interrupt this program to bring you an urgent bulletin. A little over five minutes ago, North Korea's state media announced an unprecedented live transmission from Pyongyang. We go now to that transmission..."

A man sat before a bank of microphones reading from a sheet of paper.

"My name is Tyler Kang. I am an American CIA agent. I have defected to the Democratic People's Republic of Korea, the land of my ancestors. I am defecting out of devotion to the Supreme Commander, Kim Jong-un, and as revenge against the people who have harmed me and the people I love."

And with that the transmission ended.

PART TWO

CHAPTER 9

THE KORYO HOTEL
Pyongyang, North Korea
February 28

One by one, the long-term foreign residents of the Koryo Hotel entered the hotel's Basement Bar for a little something to make a Thursday evening in Pyongyang a bit more bearable. The twin-towered Koryo, 46 stories tall, was Pyongyang's finest, such a showcase of North Korean hospitality, quipped the foreign residents, that they anticipate your every desire by bugging your room. Most of the men used their rooms for sleeping only and spent most of their waking hours either working or drinking in the run-down bar. The ratty upholstery of the chairs reeked of cigarette smoke and stale beer, and the beer itself was watered down and warm, but this was their clubhouse, their sole refuge in a town where there was precious little else to do.

The art of conversation had died out long ago among the drinkers, and in its place was a tedious litany of cringe-inducing jokes, mutual putdowns and sodden philosophizing. The witticisms and barbs came hard and fast, as if any drop in the repartee might invite in the black dog of depression they all suffered from. Those who had been in Pyongyang for more than a few months rarely even bothered to leave the hotel anymore except to go to their jobs around the corner at the Foreign Outreach Institute. What was the point of going out, anyway, if the only thing to see was a dreary landscape of decaying concrete, monuments to dictators, and streets full of hungry people? The only exception they made was to walk down the block to watch the young gymnasts practicing for the upcoming Mass Games. Their main interest, though, was in the gymnasts' coach, who was a stunner. But for the most part they just stayed in the bar, sipping away their time in North Korea and hoping their livers held out until they made it home.

The last of their circle to enter that evening held the record for the longest time any of them had spent in Pyongyang: almost two years with frequent trips abroad in order to maintain his sanity. Owing to his experience in all things North Korean, the language excepted, Liverpool-born Mack McKenzie was looked up to by the others. Their nickname for him was the "Mayor of Pyongyang."

"Got a good one for you today, gents," he said, green eyes twinkling above a luxuriant chestnut beard.

The conversation around the bar and neighboring pool table came to an abrupt halt as it always did when Mack came in. He spoke as he walked to the bar, unraveling the scarf from around his throat and savoring the air of expectation he had created. The group of men leaned in toward him.

"Kim Jong-un is out inspecting a collective farm and comes across a bunch of cute little pigs. He decides he wants his picture taken with them. That evening, a North Korean newspaper editor had to write a caption for the picture to go in the morning paper. He thinks, 'Hmm, how about *The Supreme Commander Kim Jong-un among pigs*. No, that wouldn't do. I know: *The pigs are with Comrade Kim Jong-un*. No, that doesn't work either.' Finally, he had a burst of inspiration. The next morning's paper ran with the picture on the front page. Underneath it the caption read, *Supreme Commander Kim Jong-un, third from the left.*"

The roar of laughter from the men in the clique went far beyond the humor of the joke, as if they were able to find a group catharsis from the ennui all of them felt from living in North Korea.

The moment he entered his bare-bones room in the Koryo Hotel after checking in that evening, Patrick knew he would be spending as little time as possible within its cheerless confines. After unpacking, he did an about-face and rode the elevator back down to explore the building. Off of the lobby a ceaselessly chattering throng of Chinese tourists packed a microscopic coffee shop, while the adjoining bookshop that sold only books about Kim Il-sung and his son echoed with a silence born of indifference rather than reverence. Patrick descended a stairway and saw a cluster of foreigners loitering around drinking and talking over one another in the Basement Bar.

"Good evening," he said as he walked in.

"Evening," the men at the bar mumbled, suddenly subdued. They had developed the North Korean allergy to strangers. But Mack strode over with an extended hand.

"Name's Mackenzie. These idiots call me the 'Mayor of Pyongyang', but feel free to call me 'Mack'," he said, smile lines radiating from his eyes. Patrick smiled back.

"Pleasure to meet you, Mr. Mayor. I'm Patrick McGrail."

Mack's head inched back appraisingly as he ran a hand through his beard. "I'm a good judge of people, and I would guess you're an educated man, Mr. McGrail."

"I was an art major."

"Then the pleasure's mine. It'll be nice to have an intelligent conversation for a change. Let me buy you a watered-down beer."

"North Korean art!" Mack exclaimed after they had introduced themselves more fully. "Best of luck with that. My guess is that they'll try to get you to stay here as long as they can and string you along for your hard currency. Then when they've taken you for all you've got, they'll say, 'Sorry, we don't want to export any of our art after all, thank you very much.' Hate to be so cynical, but it's the way things run here. The first commandment of doing business in North Korea? Don't."

"Maybe I'll get lucky," Patrick said with a smile.

"Yeah, well. The denizens of this dive are all trying to get lucky, too." Mack turned to face the open area in front of the bar.

As if to prove Mack's point, one of the drinkers said in a loud voice, "I think I'm in love again," as he gazed at the television screen. A group of nubile ballet dancers were performing in the previous year's Mass Games.

"No, you're merely in heat again," called out another. "Besides, they're all virgins, every last one of them. Just like you."

"I bet you at least one or two have done it," the first man muttered without taking his eyes off the TV screen. "They're teenagers, for God's sakes, they *can't* all be virgins. And those gymnasts down the street? I'm sure some of the older ones are getting it on."

Mack took a sip of beer and set down his glass with an air of authority.

"The two of you are hornier than any of them will ever be. As for doing the horizontal watusi, if any of them so much as picked their noses wrong, they'd be out of the Glorious Triumvirate Celebration in no time, bring shame on the family, the whole bit. I'm not saying they'd be sent to the camps, but you can bet that that fetching coach of theirs would find herself in a shit-hole like Chongjin if any of her kids got out of line. And we certainly don't want that to happen, do we, gents?"

The coach Mack referred to was an alluring young woman in her early 30s who patiently taught her charges all of the intricate moves of their routines without raising her voice, as some of the other coaches did, but with positive encouragement as her main motivation tool instead. Her squad practiced on a cul-de-sac three blocks from the Koryo Hotel. Patrick turned to Mack.

"Sorry, what is it that you all do again?" he asked.

"Most of us are language contractors at the Foreign Outreach Institute. Basically we clean up the grammar for the propaganda crap they send abroad. Rough going usually, trying to figure out what the hell they're talking about. The stuff they give me is mostly Korean sentences with English words in various degrees of butchery. Half the time I just make something up. Not a lot of brain power involved, but it pays well, and that's all that matters. Beyond that, one of the things I demanded in my contract was that I be allowed to travel out of the country for at least one weekend a month. My only extravagance in this god-awful place. But it makes life a bit more bearable. Three months to go in my contract, and then 'sayonara' or whatever the hell they say here."

"Where do you go?" Patrick asked, signaling the barmaid for another round which was promptly delivered along with a plate of red hot kimchee.

"Oh, Hong Kong and Tokyo, usually. Sometimes Macau to gamble and raise some respectable hell. No way could I stay full time in this prison of a country." Mack raised his bottle in thanks and took a long pull.

Patrick smiled. He tried to make his next comment sound nonchalant. "I've heard the North Koreans actually kidnap people from abroad and bring them here."

"You heard right," Mack replied, setting his glass down and smacking his lips. Foam had gathered on his beard. "As if they don't have enough homegrown prisoners. They're pretty brazen about it, too, just grabbing people off the streets. They mostly take Japanese so they can pick up the latest slang and customs for their agents to mimic when they go over there to spy. And then there's the idiots who actually defect to this place. They had another American jump the DMZ not all that long ago."

"I heard about that." Patrick said, trying to sound casual and disinterested. He took a sip of his beer. "Where do they keep all these people?"

"I don't know about the ones they kidnap, but there's a special guest house for defectors not far from the hotel. John Robert Drosnik's been in the country since the 1960s. He lives at the guest house with a son he had with a much younger Romanian woman. The son is a gymnast who sometimes practices with the young kids down the street. That guy who jumped the DMZ not long ago is probably there as well."

Mack speared a piece of kimchee with a chopstick before continuing. "Once in a while the Drosniks come over for a drink. I'm surprised the Norks—that's what we call the North Koreans-- let them out, but I guess they figure they're not going to try and go back to the U.S. this late in the game. I'll point them out if they ever drop by."

"Thanks," Patrick said and let the subject drop so as not to appear too interested.

After a bit of casual bar conversation, he excused himself for the evening. *Tyler Kang, right in the neighborhood,* he thought as he returned to his room. Then he wondered what he would do if and when he saw him.

We need him neutralized, Hooper had said.

CHAPTER 10

PYONGYANG
March 4

Landscaped with carefully tended trees and colorful flower beds interspersed along the main thoroughfares, Pyongyang, the "capital of willows", is as green and quiet as seems possible for a city of 3 million. An hour's fast drive from the border with South Korea, it sits astride the confluence of the Taedong River and its muddy tributary, the Potong. In the exact heart of the capital lies the 75,000-square-meter Kim Il-sung Square, directly across from which, on the other side of the Taedong River, rises the 150-meter-high Tower of *Juche*, or "self-reliance", a gray cement monument to the philosophical foundation of the Great Leader's go-it-alone form of socialism.

Inspector Choy Jung-hee of the Ministry of People's Security, aka, the police force, glanced up briefly at the tower as he drove one of the Ministry's ancient Nissan Sentras, the front end of which rattled the whole way. It didn't help matters any that virtually every road he drove on, some the size of the Champs Elysees, was riddled with potholes, some the size of Nissan Sentras. And to think for this he had left the comfort of his couch and his videos of "The Godfather" trilogy that he loved so much. As a police officer, he was allowed to watch foreign videos, as long as he did so on the sly. He took his mind off the bone-jarring ride by practicing lines of dialogue. "What have I ever done to make you treat me so disrespectfully?" was a favorite.

A while later, his thoughts turned to his employment situation. At least the computer work he was now doing part-time for Comrade Moon at Bureau 39 held out the possibility of salvation from the tedium of a police beat. A full-time post at the Bureau would be perfect, he thought, especially on a freezing cold day like this. He imagined himself sitting in his own opulently appointed office, sipping tea while researching the pros and cons of the latest computer software. "My *songbun* is plenty good enough," he said aloud to himself as he drove, thinking of his political reliability pedigree, an overarching consideration for anyone's career chances. Choy's *songbun* derived from his father who had been killed in the Korean War taking a grenade for his commanding officer. But in these days of increased belt-tightening, there was only so far one could ride a *songbun*, even in Bureau 39.

In the years following his graduation from Pyongyang's elite Film Institute, he was recruited into the Ministry of People's Security. He had furthered his technical expertise and mastered new software programs as they became available so that he in turn could teach others in the Ministry. Comrade Moon, the head of Bureau 39, had hired and fired a succession of technical assistants, none of whom had the requisite breadth of knowledge in emerging technologies that the position required. And Moon didn't want anyone in the cyberwarfare unit of the General Reconnaissance Bureau to know what he was up to in Bureau 39. As a result, he was woefully ignorant of the latest advances in IT. So Choy's supervisor, seeking to curry favor with Moon, recommended Choy for the opening, and Choy was offered an arrangement whereby he would work half-time at People's Security and half-time for Comrade Moon. As part of his People's Security duties, he was ordered to take actual patrol shifts throughout Pyongyang owing to the recent proliferation of anti-regime graffiti in the capital.

"Choy, you're the computer expert," Comrade Moon said one day as he practiced the left-hand chord buttons of his accordion while resting his right hand. Inspector Choy was busy installing a new spreadsheet program.

Moon continued, "With this internet thing, everyone's computer is linked up with everyone else's, right?" He continued playing the reedy chords which Choy found intensely irritating, but he made no protest. He inwardly rolled his eyes at Moon's ignorance of even the basic nature of the internet.

"Well, in theory, Comrade Moon, but you'd need. . ."

"So how about *in theory* if someone wanted to get into someone else's computer and find out what's on it. Is that possible?"

Choy stifled a guffaw. "Yes, Comrade. It's called 'hacking' in English."

"Hacking. What a strange language. So how would I go about *hacking* the computers of an organization called Human Rights Watch?"

Choy paused to think.

"Well, one way would be to send them e-mails that contain attachments they might be interested in. All it would take would be someone in their office clicking on the attachment, and that can open up a virus that allows the hackers access to all the data on the computer system. Plus, something called a keylogger could be installed that records their keystrokes."

"Really? Did you think of this yourself?"

"No, actually our General Reconnaissance Bureau has been doing it for years."

"To me?" Moon asked, paranoid alarm in his voice.

"No, not to this Bureau, Comrade. In order to hack into a computer system, you have to *have* an actual computer system. This office's setup is much too primitive to..."

Moon's eyebrows raised.

Choy began again. "Our computer system is ingeniously devised to repel any insidious attempt at hacking by the imperialist enemy. As well as any attempt by dissidents in this country to communicate with foreigners. Or anyone else."

Moon frowned. "Alright. So my system is primitive. How would you go about making it....unprimitive?"

Choy blew out his cheeks. "Well, I suppose the best place to start is with a series of servers. Those are big computers that handle all the incoming and outgoing data."

"Good. Start on it right away."

"But Comrade Moon, we couldn't possibly do it with our phone system that can't even..."

Moon shot him a look.

"...that can even prevent ideologically unsound influences from coming into the office."

"Well, what do we use then? To make it possible, I mean. And I don't mean anything involving the General Reconnaissance Bureau", Moon said.

"If we had a proper phone network, we would then need all sorts of hardware and software. Maybe some of our diplomats from abroad could bring it in by diplomatic pouch."

"And what would you know about diplomatic pouches? Are you a diplomat?"

"No, Comrade. It's something I saw in a film that was directed by the Dear Leader. I'm sure you know the one."

"Of course," Moon replied, shifting his weight slightly. "What I have in mind, Choy, is finding a way to track down the traitors in this country on my own without help from the other Bureaus. I'm thinking of that group called Rising Tide, and especially their leader, Nahm Myung-dae." Moon held in his hand a seditious flyer one of his other officers had brought back from Kim Il-sung University. It had been posted on one of the buildings in the middle of the night and read "Nahm Myung-dae and Rising Tide Will Bring Democracy to Our Nation". "I'm thinking that if anybody knows about that guy, it would be some foreign do-gooder organization. Once we hack into Human Rights Watch, we can find information on Rising Tide and Nahm Myung-dae, right?"

"Well, in theory..."

"I wish you would stop using that word. I want reality, dammit, not theory."

"Sorry, Comrade. What I meant was that *if* this office had the equipment available for an internet connection, and *if* our phone network was allowed to go beyond the impregnable walls of this office, then it might be possible to hack into their computers and find information on Rising Tide. Unless, of course, we went through the General Reconnaissance Bureau."

"I thought I'd made it clear that I don't want to go through them."

"Well, Comrade, if I may be blunt, we're again getting a few steps beyond what our Bureau's current technology allows. How about this: we get a diplomat or two from this Bureau to bring in the hardware— that's the actual solid components of a computer system— and then we figure out how to proceed with hacking into Human Rights Watch without them finding out."

"If I get you what you need, can you set this system up?"

"Of course, Comrade."

"'Of course'? You have too much self-love, Choy. You'll never develop your *juche* consciousness that way. But anyway, stick with me, you'll go far. I'll contact our man at the United Nations. I bet you anything they have the best computer stuff in New York. I was posted there once."

"Actually, Tokyo goes New York one better."

"And how would you know that?"

"That other film directed by the Dear Leader himself mentioned someth..."

"Alright, alright. I'll have our man in Tokyo pick up what you need. Make a list of the best stuff money can buy. Only the best for my 'primitive' computer system." Moon suddenly looked alarmed. "But that will take weeks, what do we do in the meantime?"

Choy thought for a moment. "Well, we could hijack a Chinese ISP—that's an internet service provider— and make it look like they're doing the hacking. That way, we can get the information, and the Chinese get blamed. We could only do it once, though. After that, they'd just shut it down."

"But I thought you said my phone system is too primitive for hacking."

"Not the regular phone system. I was thinking we could use the Ministry of Defense's system."

Moon's eyes went distant. "Ministry of Defense. That's General O's system, correct?"

"Correct, Comrade."

"Get started on it, but not a word to the General Reconnaissance Bureau. And tell the idiots in Defense that it's so top secret that they can't even tell General O. If you run into any problems from them, just say the Supreme Commander authorized it as a matter of the greatest national security. Any leakers will be fed to the dogs like Jang Song-thaek."

"Yes, Comrade."

"And while you're at it, see if you can get anything on the Americans and their puppets in the South. If all these computers are linked up somehow, that shouldn't be too hard for a genius like you." Moon bit hard into the word 'genius'.

Choy lowered his eyes. "I'll do what I can, Comrade."

WASHINGTON

(AP)

The Associated Press has learned that the powerful attack that overwhelmed computers at U.S. and South Korean government agencies for seven hours yesterday was even broader than initially realized, also targeting the White House, the Pentagon and the New York Stock Exchange, according to the Department of Homeland Security.

Other targets of the attack included the Department of Homeland Security itself, as well as the State Department, the NASDAQ stock market and The Washington Post, according to an early analysis of the malicious software used in the attacks. It was not immediately clear who might be responsible or what their motives were. But South Korean intelligence officials believe the attacks were carried out by North Korea using hijacked Chinese internet service providers...

The next day

"You've done well, Choy. Maybe you really are a genius."

Choy blushed.

In the coming days as the hardware Choy had requested was brought in by diplomatic pouch, he began setting up the beginnings of a highly advanced network in Comrade Moon's office, but he dragged his feet on its progress for fear that Moon would replace him with someone from his inner circle once it was finished. The last thing he wanted was to go back to being a beat cop in the middle of winter. When Moon asked him two weeks later how he was getting on, his body language became self-deprecating and modest.

"It will take me more time, Comrade Moon. Maybe months."

Moon's shoulders slumped. "Months? You mean we can't start hacking on our own till then?"

"I'm afraid not, Comrade. The high-speed cable has to be installed, and then there's the LAN connection and FTP capabilities, not to mention the HTTP proxy connections and image dithering...

Moon held up his hand. "Alright, alright. Just keep working on it," he sighed as he turned and walked away.

C H A P T E R   1 1

SENGHORI PRISON
March 6

In her time at Senghori Prison, Yumi's psychological condition began to improve somewhat despite the abominable living conditions of the hut. She had made friends with several of the other prisoners, and being around them in the hut had a therapeutic effect. She no longer had the feeling that she was completely alone in the universe, abandoned and forgotten. She was assigned to a work unit that was housed in a small room completely filled with sewing machines. Her light detail, only fourteen hours a day, consisted of assembling top-of-the-line children's dresses made of the finest silk and lace, and then carefully packing them in boxes bound for Macau where they would be distributed to the corporations controlled by the Commission.

What she didn't realize, however, was that Comrade Moon was lulling her into a false state of security and safety. He hoped that when her questioning resumed, she would be more motivated to tell the truth about her father's whereabouts in order to continue the lenient treatment she was receiving. If she did, she would rejoin the general population and the friends she was making while the information was confirmed. If she didn't, the torture would begin again in earnest.

A week after her period of lenient treatment had begun, Yumi was again questioned about the whereabouts of her father. As always, she denied any knowledge of where he was. She was then dragged to a building the size and dimensions of a gymnasium where guards threw a blanket over her head and began to beat and kick her mercilessly. She was then pushed into a furnace with thick smoke and sparks flying all around her. She fell to the ground. They pulled her out of the furnace and threw cold water on her face and beat her some more. After all that, she still hadn't revealed her father's whereabouts. They were convinced she was holding out on them. So they took turns raping her.

"She must be delirious from the pain." The other prisoners in her hut sat on the dirt floor looking down with concern at Yumi who lay under a thin blanket mumbling incoherently. After about twenty minutes, Yumi's breathing slowed to almost nothing, and they feared she might be dying. But then her chest rose and fell regularly again. The dreams that had been torturing her had finally left her in peace. She slept soundly.

Another hour passed, and Yumi opened her eyes. Several gnome-like shapes milled about the hut. The stench of unwashed bodies and open latrines was overpowering, as was the pain all over and through her body.

"Take this," a voice said. Yumi looked up from where she lay on the bare earth of the hut to see a hand proffered in her direction holding a small bowl of corn gruel. "You need to eat something."

Yumi forced herself to sit upright and saw a woman who appeared to be in her early 40s holding a spoon in front of her. After she had swallowed a few mouthfuls, she felt restored somewhat, as much from the kindness of these wretched people as from the meager food the woman had shared with her. She lay back to rest from the exertion of eating and allowed ragged images of the past several weeks to float in and out of her consciousness: Mr. Pung lifting her out of the boat. The man in the office with the accordion. And what was that about something her father had stolen? Because of that *she* had been kidnapped and tortured to within an inch of her life? How could her father have allowed this to happen to her? Finally, like a flame blazing through a pall of thick smoke, the memory of the gang rape of a few hours earlier consumed her, and she began to suffocate from panic. She tried mightily to draw air into her lungs, but it was as though a tremendous force was squeezing the life out of her.

The woman who had fed her pressed her lips to Yumi's and forced air down into her lungs. Gradually, Yumi's own breathing rhythm re-established herself and she was able to take air in on her own.

"We will take care of you here," the woman said as she continued to hold Yumi close.

"Thank you," Yumi rasped. She fell asleep with Patrick's face filling her field of vision.

A few days after Yumi's torture session, Moon met with Mr. Pung.

"Were they able to get anything from the girl about her father and the package?" he asked his underling.

"Sorry, Comrade Moon, nothing. And I really don't think the girl knows anything. They've tried being lenient on her for awhile and then turning the screws. This last time was brutal beyond what they usual do. She still didn't budge."

"But she *must* know something, even if it's just an idea where he might have gone into hiding," Moon said, more than a hint of desperation in his voice.

"I really don't think we're going to get any more out of her. Do you want to try your backup plan?"

Moon thought for a moment and sighed in frustrated resignation. "Yes, it's probably come to that. Her ex-boyfriend is here now, right, the one working for the CIA?"

"Yes, Comrade, I called him anonymously when he was in Macau."

"Alright. Let's steer him to the girl and see if that leads anywhere. Maybe she's holding back something from us but will give it to him. We've got to find the package before long. I'm running out of time with the Commission."

"Yes, Comrade."

"Choy, how would you like to work for me full-time?" Moon said to Inspector Choy later in the day.

A thrill went up Choy's spine. "I would be most honored, Comrade Moon!" he blurted out. His heart leapt in his chest. *At last I'll be putting the life of a beat cop behind me, he thought. And for a full-time job at Bureau 39 to boot!*

"Good," Moon said. "A man with your computer skills is wasting his talents in police work. I'll let your boss know."

"Thank you so much, Comrade. When would you like me to start?"

"Right away. I want your work on my computer system to be your top priority.

"Yes, Comrade."

"And one other thing. Now that you'll be working for State Security, I want you to get a taste of clandestine operations."

"You mean spying?"

"That's right. There's a new American CIA agent in town. I want you to *schmooze* him."

"I beg your pardon, Comrade?"

"'*Schmooze*'. It's a word I learned when I was posted at the UN."

"Is it English?"

"French…I think. Part of the diplomatic language. It means to flatter someone, make him think you're on his side, find out what makes him tick. Gain his trust by telling him things he doesn't expect to hear— and then stick a shiv in his back."

Choy looked down at the floor.

"What's the matter?" Moon asked.

"I'm sorry, Comrade. It's just that I just have no idea what a foreigner doesn't expect to hear."

"Hmm." It was Moon's turn to look pensive. Suddenly, he brightened. "Tell him about your hobbies, your favorite foods, that kind of thing. Hell, if it comes down to it, tell him you want to defect."

Choy's eyes widened in shock. "Comrade Moon, I would never defect from the fatherland!"

Moon's head cut to one side in exasperation. "Choy, it's an act. You studied acting at film school, right? Alright then. He's here looking for his former lover, that girl that we took whose father stole…something from me. You have to gain his confidence and let him find the girl. Whatever you do, don't give him any reason to suspect you."

"But why not just have someone tell him where she is?"

"Because he's a professional, and he'd smell a trap. He has to think he's finding her for himself and gallantly coming to her rescue."

"I see."

"I want you to keep going to your police job for the duration of this mission. It will make it easier for you to 'accidentally' run into him. Pung will give you the details on how to make initial contact."

Choy glanced over at Pung. The look in his eyes sent an icicle of fear into his gut. "As you wish, Comrade."

Moon left the room. Pung half-walked, half-trotted with the stiff-legged gait of a pitbull over to Choy's computer desk. He hovered menacingly over Choy and growled out the information on the new CIA agent in town.

"He's staying at the Koryo Hotel. An 'art dealer'. Calls himself 'Patrick McGrail'. But his real name is Patrick Featherstone."

CHAPTER 12

PYONGYANG
Army Headquarters of General O Jun-suh
March 10

General O Jun-suh sat at his simple black-lacquered teak desk in his Pyongyang headquarters, waiting for Comrade Moon's arrival. With a close-cropped head atop a tall, powerful body, the 59-year-old army commander appeared to have two distinct visages depending on which side of his face one looked at. The left side had been permanently disfigured from temple to jaw in an attempt some years earlier at defusing a bomb that had been set for Kim Jong-il. While the right side of his face was handsome in a severe sort of way, the left side would remain as though cauterized for the rest of his life.

He held in his hands an ancient ink-brush drawing that depicted his hero, Ulji Mundok, a seventh-century Korean military leader who defeated an invading Chinese army a million strong by luring them into the Chungchon River flood plain and then opening the floodgates. Only 3,000 Chinese returned home. Korea, or Koguryo as the kingdom was then known, prospered thereafter. O held the drawing closer to his face as if to commune with Ulji across the centuries. Ulji Mundok was said to be a quiet, thoughtful man, not given in the least to bombast or swagger, but rather keeping his own counsel until the moment to strike had come. General O modeled himself on that trait as well, especially in these precarious times. And especially when dealing with the ever-treacherous Comrade Moon.

Ever since 1998 when a dozen of his fellow generals had been executed for plotting a coup against Kim Jong-il, General O had been as guarded in what he said and did as was possible for the commander of the 100,000-man First

Army Corps. He would be especially wary with the man he was about to meet, a man whom he hated. He would make the Sphinx look like the village gossip.

Fifteen minutes later General O and Comrade Moon eyed each other warily across O's desk. The hostility of their relationship had never reached the level of unscabbered swords, but both kept hands firmly on hilts. Moon recalled that despite O's outwardly impassive mien, he had presided over the execution of the army generals who were plotting against Kim Jong-il. On another occasion, at a mass rally held in honor of Kim Jong-il on his birthday. General O had suddenly exclaimed to the Dear Leader, "Comrade, someday we will turn the South into a sea of fire!" Moon also knew that O's fervor for following others had waned over the years, and now that Kim Jong-il was long dead, he suspected that O was plotting to overthrow the regime and install himself as leader. Moon began the discussion on an obsequious note.

"General, I want to thank you sincerely for having me here today," Moon began. "As usual, you are working while the rest of the country is enjoying this glorious weather. I must admit to laziness myself on days like this. But I said to myself on the way over, 'If anyone in the country is hard at work today, it will be the great General O!'"

O fought the urge to stick a finger down his throat. Instead, he retaliated with oozing flattery of his own.

"You are far too modest, Comrade Moon. I know that you bear the greatest burden of all of us in advising the Supreme Commander, Comrade Kim Jong-un. But if anyone is capable of it, it is you."

Moon forced his face to hold its smile, but he felt a surge of adrenaline in his gut. The general's tone had been just barely on the safe side of mocking.

"You are kind indeed, General. And you are indeed correct. It is not easy being in the presence of one so great as the Supreme Commander on a daily basis."

General O smiled wanly but said nothing. He knew Comrade Moon's false sincerity better than anyone. And it was common knowledge among the upper echelon that Moon had only contempt for the chubby son of Kim Jong-il.

"General, if you will permit me to be so bold: I have come directly from meeting with the Supreme Commander. He gave me this."

Moon proffered a piece of heavy stationery. O took it and began to read.

"General O: It has come to light that the Americans are planning a sneak attack on the fatherland from across the Demilitarized Zone on or about the day of the Glorious Triumvirate Celebration. You are hereby directed to take your entire 1st Army Corps to the DMZ as a show of strength..." The directive continued in more detail.

O looked up at Moon. "Would it be possible for me to meet with the Supreme Commander to discuss this?"

"I'm very sorry, General," Moon said with a downturned mouth. "He is extremely busy with the preparations for Celebration. But he emphasized how much he trusts you with this directive."

O read the directive yet again. "Alright," he said finally but without enthusiasm. "The Glorious Triumvirate Celebration is not until May 1. It will take that much time to mobilize my divisions."

Moon's face brightened. "You are a great inspiration to your men, General, that is something everyone in the country knows. But I must tell you, you are also a great inspiration to me."

General O just fixed him with a stony stare. Moon held out his hand to shake, a Western practice O detested, but he forced himself to shake it anyway.

After Moon had left, O sat back in his chair and once again took the portrait of Ulji Mundok in his hands. He peered into the wise general's eyes, as if seeking counsel from across the centuries. He could swear he heard Ulji saying, "You'll need allies against that bastard."

CHAPTER 13

WHITE HOUSE SITUATION ROOM
March 11

North Korea once again dominated the agenda of the National Security Council. American forces in South Korea were down to half of what they had been prior to the President's order for their redeployment to the Middle East. Troop strength was on track to dwindle even further until a mere two thousand remained in less than two weeks. But the discussion on this day began not with troop strength or redeployment, but with Tyler Kang's apparent defection across the DMZ. Ominously, the President was already seated at the table in the Situation Room, and as the other Council members filed into the room they took note of the smoldering scowl on his face. No one said a word.

"Larry. What the hell is happening?" President Dillard said finally after everyone had taken a seat. The tension in the room was palpable.

Director of National Intelligence Larry Conover lowered and shook his head.

"I have no idea, Mr. President."

The president flung a document on the table between them. "Your memo here said that Tyler Kang was absolutely the best person for the job. I've highlighted your words in brown…for obvious reasons."

"Sir, he never gave any indication of being otherwise."

"And now he's gone over with a shitload of top secret documents." The President glared at Conover. The others around the table found sudden fascination in their cuticles.

"We sent someone over there to look for him," Conover said in a voice that lacked conviction.

"Oh, great. And would that be the *second* best person for the job?"

"Sir, it was either that or do nothing."

"Who's the new guy?" the President growled as he lit a cigarette.

"Tyler Kang's former sniper partner in Serbia. His name is Patrick Featherstone."

A smoky sigh of frustration escaped the president's lips. "Christ," he muttered. "So if and when this guy finds Kang, I trust he'll know what to do."

"That's an affirmative, Mr. President."

"Let me know the minute you hear anything more."

Conover nodded with downcast eyes.

The President turned to the entire assembly. "We have to move on to the issue of the possible coup over there. Any word on how firmly in charge the son is these days?"

He directed the question to Secretary of State Bernadette Hilton as a way of smoothing feathers that were still ruffled from having been left out of the decision to withdraw American troops from Korea.

"He's in charge on paper, sir, the 'Supreme Commander' and all that. They're planning something called the Glorious Triumvirate Celebration for May Day. It's the son's way of reminding people of his lineage. But his hold on power appears to be even more tenuous. He's executed so many members of the Politburo that it's just a matter of time before they come after him to save their collective skins."

"And the other two, the possible coup-leaders— a nutcase general and an accordion player. That's what's left, right?" the President asked.

Hilton nodded.

"Jesus," the President muttered. "It's like playing Russian roulette with a double-barreled shotgun."

"Actually, we've gotten some back channel reports from China that Moon—that's the accordion player— is a man who can be reasoned with. Certainly a lot more so than General O."

"Be careful what you wish for," said Secretary of Defense Arthur Gottlieb, former ambassador to Japan and old Asia hand. "There's a Korean proverb:

'The dog you trust the most will bite you.'"

"I understand that, Art," the President replied testily. "But we need to make a choice here, and soon. Damascus is surrounded by the Levant Liberation Committee, and I can't afford to keep those troops in South Korea for more than a few weeks, tops. I agree with Bernadette that Moon seems the better of the two possibles. I'm just afraid that if the young Kim kid is assassinated, the whole place is going to erupt into mass chaos. God knows we can't afford a conventional military response there, not with Syria blowing its lid. And the South Koreans still don't have their missile system ready if they're attacked."

The President paused in mid-thought. He turned to General Richard Mather, Chairman of the Joint Chiefs of Staff. "General, what are our military options if they got it in their heads to attack South Korea before the South's nuclear response is operational?"

"Well, Mr. President, half of our troops have already been redeployed from the peninsula to the Mideast, so a ground response would seem unrealistic, but that's from my perspective sitting here 10,000 miles away from the DMZ. Which is why I asked General Carl Merkin, our commander in South Korea, to fly in for today's meeting. With your permission?"

The President shrugged his assent, and the door to the Situation Room was opened. A wiry, compact man with imposing upper-body carriage stood in the doorway. The President turned in his direction.

"Join the party, General."

"Thank you, Mr. President." General Merkin walked in with self-assurance and took a seat. General Mather repeated the President's question regarding a military response in the event of a North Korean attack before the South's nuclear arsenal was operational.

"Well, before answering that question," Merkin began, "I'd like to begin by giving everyone here an idea as to what they have to attack with. It might lend a multi-dimensional perspective on any response on our part."

The President waved his hand for him to continue.

"First of all, North Korea has the capability to attack with conventional arms alone, no nuclear, chemical, or biological warheads needed. They have

74

about 500 medium-range artillery tubes and two hundred multiple-rocket launchers. Without moving a single artillery piece, the North could deliver up to 500,000 rounds an hour against our combined forces for several hours, and that would be just the first phase of an all-out attack. Following that would be a ground force invasion."

"And our response to all that would be?"

"Before my troops began to be pulled out of the peninsula, we had something in place called War Plan 5027. Simply stated, it consisted of a 'defeat in detail'."

"Explain."

"A defeat in detail involves using our conventional weapons and ground forces to abolish North Korea as a functioning state and reorganizing the country under our control. In other words, when we're finished with them, they would not be able to mount any military activity of any kind. To put it in the simplest terms, we kill them all and take over."

"General, you weren't here when I said that anything like a military occupation would be out of the question," said the President.

"Sir, I am just giving an answer to your question. As I stated, before my forces began to be pulled from South Korea, there was War Plan 5027. Now, however, my remaining forces could be destroyed in less than a minute if the North attacked."

"And what do you propose we do about that?"

"A preemptive response might be a viable option if it looked as though they were on the verge of an attack."

"How big a preemptive response?"

"Big enough to thwart any future threat. I refer the Council back to War Plan 5027: wiping North Korea off the map, but in this case with nuclear weapons instead of conventional ones. The South Koreans aren't ready for a response of their own yet. And since we're now lacking an effective ground deterrent, an American tactical nuclear option is the only one left to us, in my opinion."

The President's face darkened. "So their General O wants to destroy South

Korea, and you want to nuke the North first."

"I'm talking about my men, sir."

"You're talking about World War III, General. Look, I understand your concern, but I want it to be absolutely clear that a preemptive nuclear move on our part is not in the cards unless I give a direct order. It's not that it's off the table completely, it's just that I'm calling the shots on that one. Understood?"

"Yes sir."

"Good."

"Question, sir."

"Go ahead."

"If my troops are attacked in the meantime, who will be responsible for their deaths?"

"Your question is insubordinate, General."

"Begging the Commander-in-Chief's pardon, sir."

"You may go, General."

"Thank you, sir."

General Merkin walked out and closed the door behind him.

And fuck you too, sir. No way in hell do I let my men get massacred.

Two hours later, the meeting drew to a close. The President asked Vice-President Lymon and his National Security Advisor, Jonathan Barnes, to stay behind. The President poured each of them a shot of Jack Daniel's.

"You know what's really ironic about the world today?" the President asked once the three of them were settled and sipping their drinks. Lymon and Barnes waited for the President to answer, letting the question hover in the air.

"The ironic thing about the world today is that the wealthiest countries... Sweden, New Zealand, Canada, you name it...are all but defenseless, while these bankrupt shitholes like North Korea, Pakistan and Iran have us all dancing on a string with their nuclear arsenals. They may be small arsenals, but they're a hell of a lot bigger than, say, the *Norwegian* nuclear arsenal." The President shook his head ruefully and stubbed out his cigarette.

The Vice-President spoke up.

"Do you know what the other ironic thing is? After the Kim family is gone, the North Koreans will be ruled by the same people who enslaved them, only this time they'll call themselves 'reformers'. Then they'll loot the treasury, sell off state assets to themselves for a song and become billionaires, just like in Russia."

No one spoke a word, partially from exhaustion and partially from a sense of depression that, with all of their good intentions, the world would just go on grinding so many people down, not the least of whom were the 25 million people of North Korea.Finally, the President spoke.

"Alright. Who's it going to be if the 'Supreme Commander' is struck by tragic bolt of lightning: Moon or General O?"

"Moon," said Lymon.

"Moon," said Barnes.

"Moonanimous," said the President as he downed his drink in one gulp and poured them all another.

CHAPTER 14

PYONGYANG
Basement Bar
Koryo Hotel
March 12

Patrick treated Mack, the "Mayor of Pyongyang", to lunch before the latter headed back to his job at the Foreign Outreach Institute. Patrick had told Mack he would be spending the rest of the day trying to arrange some business meetings with government officials who might be able to connect him to some traditional North Korean ink-brush painters. The rest of the bar was completely deserted except for Miss Ok, the barkeep.

As Patrick wiped his mouth with a napkin, he happened to look up. Two Caucasian men who weren't part of the regular crowd entered the bar and immediately went off in search of a table in the back of the bar. The overweight older man had a full head of steel-gray hair and a starburst of broken capillaries across his nose and cheeks. The young man was in his mid-twenties, handsome with a lithe build and straight blond hair that fell across his forehead.

Mack looked in their direction. "That's the American defector I told you about, the old guy. The young one is his son."

"What were their names again?"

"John Robert Drosnik and his son, Andrew. The old guy defected decades ago, and the son is a gymnast who practices occasionally down the street. They sometimes still use the old man as the typical evil American capitalist in their propaganda movies, but he's getting a bit old for it." Mack looked at his watch.

"Shit, time to get back to the think-tank for a few hours of language butchery," he said as he got up. "Maybe see you tonight," he called over his shoulder.

"Later," Patrick called to his back.

Just as Mack pulled the door open, none other than Tyler Kang pushed it from the other side. Tyler held the door for Mack who nodded his thanks and stared briefly at Tyler as if trying to place him. He walked out.

Tyler began to walk towards the Drosniks at the back area of the bar, but stopped dead in his tracks when he saw Patrick. A storm cloud of silence enveloped the room.

"Well, well. Look who it is," Tyler said finally. His voice was quiet and affectless.

Patrick said nothing but held Tyler's eye defiantly. Tyler continued, this time in a snarling tone.

"I should have known they'd send you."

Patrick still said nothing.

"How were you planning to kill me?" he taunted. "Chopstick in the medulla?"

"Who says I was planning to kill you?" Patrick said finally.

Tyler spat air in a 'pah' sound. "Come off it. Hooper sent you here to shut me up."

"Only if you've really defected," Patrick said.

"I have."

"And you gave them those missile documents?"

"That's right. To Comrade Moon. He's the second-in-command here after Kim Jong-un."

"Why?"

"To prove I was sincere."

"In that case, I don't blame Hooper a bit for wanting to take you out," Patrick said bitterly. "What are you going to do, help these fuckers perfect their missiles so they can destroy the East Coast?"

"Oh relax, the stuff I gave Moon is no good. Typical Agency paranoia."

Patrick's eyes locked on Tyler's. "How do you know it's no good?"

"Because I'm a fucking aerospace engineer, that's how I know. I altered the data before I gave it to them. If they try to use any of it on one of their missiles, it'll blow up in their faces."

"Then why did you defect?"

"I'm sure you saw the statement I made."

"I did. And what was that bullshit about 'taking revenge against the people who have harmed me and the people I love'? Revenge against who?"

"Maybe a whole lot of people."

Patrick shook his head in disgust. "Jesus, spare me the mystery," he muttered.

A cryptic smile played about Tyler's lips. "Still want to shut me up?"

"I didn't come here to kill you."

"Much obliged."

Patrick picked up his full bottle of beer and began to chug, not even bothering with a glass.

Tyler snorted. "You can still put the shit away, can't you. Heard you drowned in the hard stuff back in the day. Back when you really did want to kill me."

"I came close to drowning in it," Patrick said, setting the bottle down. "And yes, it was when I still wanted to kill you."

"Because of my testimony at your court martial."

"You have a talent for the obvious."

"But now you're disobeying orders and not killing me." Tyler said this to himself as though puzzled. Then a light went on in his face. "Oh, now I remember," he said in an almost mocking tone. "You went all Buddhist and non-violent."

"That's right," Patrick said with a note of defensiveness in his voice.

Tyler's jaw tightened back into a scowl, creasing the sides of his mouth. "Well, a lot of good that'll do you in a place like North Korea."

Silence reigned for a long moment. Finally Tyler spoke again.

"Why did you come here, then, if not to kill me?"

"I think my fiancée is here. Ex-fiancée, I should say."

"Here? As in North Korea?"

"Yes."

Tyler laughed softly. "Seems to be the 'in' place these days. So what's she doing here? Don't tell me she's Agency too. Your backup in case you got cold feet when it came to taking me out?"

"She was kidnapped."

Tyler's head bolted back in disbelief. "Kidnapped? That's a good one. So where is she now?"

"No idea."

The disbelief faded from Tyler's face.

"I was hoping maybe you knew something about where she was," Patrick said.

"Me? How the hell would I know anything about that?"

Just then John Robert Drosnik and his son walked up from the back of the room.

"We're heading out to Andrew's gymnastics practice," the old man said. "Not even enough time to enjoy a drink in peace, ain't that a bitch?" he said in a southern accent, although his inflection sounded disjointed, no doubt from years of only speaking Korean. He avoided looking at Patrick. His son came up behind his father, glanced at Patrick with a blank expression, and then steered his father out the door. Tyler turned his back on Patrick and joined them as they exited.

CHAPTER 15

PYONGYANG
March 14

The four Americans who defected to North Korea in the 1960s were all subjected to a lengthy period of intense and often brutal ideological indoctrination aimed at replacing their corrupt American thought processes with "kimilsungsa" or "Kim Il-sung Thought". Tyler Kang, by virtue of the classified documents he had given to Comrade Moon, was spared any of this after his initial interrogation. Instead of the isolation the others endured for years, he was lodged in the guest house in downtown Pyongyang, as well as given a job in the Foreign Outreach Institute, summarizing passages from English-language academic and professional journals that had anything at all to do with the topic of missile technology.

Tyler's first weeks in his Pyongyang quarters had been spent on the usual stations-of-the-cross tours of factories as well as the capital's various monuments and museums dedicated to the Great Leader Kim Il-sung and his son. On his first day of actual work he was greeted by Mr. Yim, the functionary in charge of the engineering texts and journals.

"Good morning, Mr. Kang. I am hoping you slept well?" he asked.

"Very well, Mr. Yim, thank you," Tyler replied, also in English. He wanted to keep to himself his fluency in Korean in case he needed to eavesdrop on conversations he might be the subject of.

"Then let us start. This way please," Yim said leading Tyler to a back room that was to be his work space.

"Your desk. Tea pot is there, half spoon only please. Heater is not working today. Or tomorrow. You brought a sweater? Good. Please start by summarizing these." Yim swept his hand across an entire bookshelf overflowing with scientific journals.

"You've got to be kidding. That would take months!" Tyler protested.

"What is the problem? All you have to do is give us a general idea of the contents."

"The problem is that there's so much of it! And where do I start? Is there a particular journal your people are most interested in, or do I just pick one at random?"

Yim looked up at the bookshelf as if just realizing the magnitude of the task he had set for Tyler. "I suppose you could start at the top and work your way down. I'll be back after lunch," he said and darted out before Tyler could come up with any more objections.

Now Tyler was alone in a workroom with only a tall stack of scientific journals to keep him company. He shrugged resignedly, realizing it could have been far worse. John Robert Drosnik had told him with a tinge of bitterness in his voice that he and his fellow defectors from decades earlier had lived lives of the utmost deprivation for several years before being integrated into North Korean society as English teachers. Tyler had only been in the country for a short time and already he was advancing, which caused Drosnik no end of jealousy. Tyler resigned himself to the task at hand and took down a journal from the top shelf.

His tedious routine at the Foreign Outreach Institute varied little over the coming weeks. By the second week, Mr. Yim was no longer checking up on him every hour, and two days after his confrontation with Patrick, Tyler looked at his watch and decided to break early for lunch.

As he exited the Foreign Outreach Institute and began walking, Tyler was now truly alone for the first time since he had crossed over the DMZ. Even during his forays to the Koryo Hotel with the Drosniks he felt as though he was under surveillance of a sort. He took a deep breath, held it and released it, intoxicated by the freedom of being unmonitored. Blending in with all the other Koreans out walking to and from the nearby Puhung Metro Station, he wandered this way and that, taking in sights that were normally off-limits to foreigners. As he approached an intersection, his ear picked up on the sounds of play. He looked to the left and saw a small cul-de-sac in the middle of which a dozen or so young girls were practicing gymnastics routines. The crisp precision of their leaps and tumbles stopped him in his tracks, and he stood transfixed as they rolled without apparent ill effect on the concrete and sent each other flying through the air in group-vaulting maneuvers.

Struck as he was by the girls' athletic prowess, his breath caught in his throat when he beheld their coach, a delicately beautiful young woman in her early 30s who shouted directions and encouragement to her young charges.

"Hold your head high like this!" she shouted through a megaphone.

The girl she was speaking to immediately took on a regal air with her head raised high and proud.

"Your fingers have to be extended all the way! I know it's cold, but please try!"

And the girl, her face pinched by the cold, valiantly splayed her frozen fingers for just the right effect in the Tableau of Socialism she and her friends were working on for the Glorious Triumvirate Celebration set for May 1.

Plucked from the masses for their athletic potential, the girls of the squad had been lavished with an elite education and training in gymnastics at the Mangyongdae Children's Palace. Now students at the prestigious Hashin Public Elementary School, they wore the red kerchief of the Sarochong, the Party Youth, a month away from induction as full members. Pinned to their flat chests were badges reading "Always Ready".

"Alright, girls, good work today!" the coach said after another fifteen minutes. Her charges gathered around her.

"We are getting closer to our goal, but we still have a lot more to do. Be sure to get plenty of sleep tonight. Tomorrow morning we start again at 9 o'clock, so don't be late. That means you, Jin-ok."

The girls giggled as Jin-ok sheepishly hung her head. Before departing practice in groups of two and three, the girls clapped their hands once in unison after an exhortation by one of the girls to do their utmost for the Supreme Commander, Kim Jong-un. Coach Seo-mi stayed behind with the ever-tardy

Jin-ok who would collect the hoops and batons as mild punishment for being late again. As the coach wrote out a to-do list for the next day's practice, she sensed the eyes of someone upon her and looked up sharply.

Sure enough, at the entrance of the cul-de-sac stood a man gawking at her as if she were a being from another planet. She quickly turned her back to the man and made a show of concentrating on her notebook.

"Hurry it up, Jin-ok, it's getting late and we're both getting cold," she said.

Jin-ok was moving as quickly as she could, both to keep warm and to get the chore over with. She would be sure to arrive *early* at practice the next day to avoid any similar punishment as today's. After she had arranged all the hoops and batons in neat piles, she bowed to Coach Seo-mi and started home.

Coach Seo-mi hardened her face and continued to ignore the man as she placed a placard on the gymnastics equipment: "Hashin School Gymnastics Team". This would be enough to prevent any pilfering. Anyone stupid enough to make off with a single baton from a team preparing for the Mass Games could look forward to enjoying the next ten years in prison. So as to avoid coming any closer to the staring man, she started home down a side street, even though it meant doubling back once she got to the main thoroughfare. Tyler watched her leave with a mixture of awe and relief. Awe at the woman's beauty. Relief that he would be able to collect his thoughts before he saw her again. Tomorrow.

CHAPTER 16

PYONGYANG
March 15

In the weeks after his defection, Tyler's spirits had steadily deflated as the reality of his new life sank in: monotonous work, bad food, and little company except Mr. Yim and the Drosniks. The day after seeing the gymnastics coach, however, he bounded out of bed at the first trilling of his alarm clock and was off to the Foreign Outreach Institute around the corner from his guest house.

Instead of starting work right away, Mr. Yim had offered to personally take Tyler to the statues of Kim Il-sung and Kim Jong-Il at Mansu Hill, North Korea's Calvary and Tomb of the Resurrection rolled into one. They would buy flowers along the way to lay at the base of the statues.

"Morning, Mr. Yim," Tyler called out breezily as he entered the Institute. Mr. Yim didn't reply for a moment, accustomed as he was to Tyler's habitual black moods.

"Good morning, Mr. Kang. I can see you are very happy to go to our Leaders' wonderful monuments."

"I certainly am. Shall we go?"

"I thought we could perhaps have breakfast first, maybe at the Koryo Hotel?" Mr. Yim said.

Tyler had been given an allowance in U.S. dollars that allowed him to shop in hard-currency establishments, and he had treated Yim to coffee at the Koryo a few weeks back. Ever since, Yim had spoken of the place in tones of wonder.

"How about if we go now?" Tyler asked. "That way we can eat, buy the flowers and get to the statues before the crowds come."

"A wonderful plan, Mr. Kang." A smile stole across his face. "Do they still have those delicious donuts?" he whispered.

The first and last stop of the day's tour would be the statues of the Great and Dear Leaders on Mansu Hill, and so after breakfast they set out for the city center. At this hour of the day, only elderly pensioners and Chinese tourists were out and about in the area, and Tyler and Mr. Yim were able to quickly buy their flowers from the old lady who minded the kiosk, solemnly climb the steps leading to the base of the statue, lay the flowers in a pile with hundreds of others, bow, and leave. The bouquets they bought were bound with a ribbon printed with the words "On fire with unquenchable ardor," which Mr. Yim rendered into English for Tyler, although with his fluency in the language, he needed no translation.

After placing his flowers at the foot of the statues and bowing, Tyler commented with cream-like innocence, "Well, that was certainly a high point of my life."

Mr. Yim nodded approvingly.

"Yes, that is true for most people, even foreigners," Mr. Yim said. "Well, shall we go to some museums?"

"I am at your complete mercy, Mr. Yim. Whatever you say."

Their driver took them next to the Victorious Fatherland Liberation War Museum where they were greeted by a wall-sized mural depicting American soldiers gleefully skewering Korean infants on their bayonets. Then, it was on to the Korean Revolution Museum where those same bloodthirsty Americans were now decapitating peasants with blunt shovels.

An hour later, Tyler and Mr. Yim made their way back to the van.

"I am glad you had a chance to see more of my country's history, Mr. Kang. Did you enjoy yourself?"

"Immensely, Mr. Yim, thank you very much. Shall we go back to the Great and Dear Leaders' statues?"

Tyler sensed a momentary lapse in enthusiasm on the part of Mr. Yim, as if he might have had something more along the lines of the Koryo Hotel lunch menu in mind, but Yim soldiered on with the lifelong habit of forced enthusiasm known to all North Koreans.

"Of course! We must begin and end this day with tribute to the Leaders who made this country possible!"

The lady at the flower stand recognized them from their morning visit and had bouquets ready for them, identical to the ones they had bought just a few hours earlier. Mr. Yim as usual waited for Tyler to pay. Tyler and Mr. Yim took their bouquets over to the statues and placed one each at Kim Jong-il's feet, when Tyler suddenly grabbed his stomach.

"Are you alright, Mr. Kang?"

Tyler doubled over on the walkway, his breathing labored.

"I think I overdid it with the donuts, Mr. Yim." They had brought along a box after breakfast at the Koryo Hotel and had eaten them over the course of the morning. "Would you mind if I just went back to the guest house? I would hate to be sick on the Great Leader's shoes."

"Yes, yes of course, Mr. Kang!" He turned and signaled their driver who pulled up next to them and helped Tyler aboard the van.

"Thank you very much, gentlemen. I'm sorry to be so much trouble."

"No trouble at all, Mr. Kang. We shall take you back to the guest house right away. Perhaps you just need something to eat?"

"Oh no, that's the problem. I need to let my stomach rest."

Back in his room, Tyler brushed his teeth, shaved again, and picked up the flowers that had been meant for the Great Leader's statues. He took the emergency stairs down to the basement and exited onto Pulgun Street, making directly for the little cul-de-sac he had stumbled upon the day before.

Once there, he maneuvered himself so that he was behind the coach and her gymnasts as they warmed up. The pile of hoops and batons from the previous day's practice had as yet been untouched. After a quick recon of the area to make sure he hadn't been noticed, Tyler walked over to the hoops and propped the bouquet upright on top of the heap. Then he walked along the sidewalk past where the girls were practicing, not looking around until he was almost at the corner, whereupon he quickly turned to face the gymnastics team and saw that the coach was watching him, just as he had hoped.

Twenty minutes later the coach called for the noon break, and the girls all went over to where their lunch pails were neatly arranged near the pile of gymnastics equipment. The girl who had been late to practice the day before was in charge of soup distribution in recognition of her coming to practice early. The job had the benefit of an extra ration after everyone had been served. She ran over to where the large thermos had been placed near the hoops and batons. Curious, she picked up the flowers that Tyler had left and immediately took them to her coach.

"Coach Seo-mi, I think someone might have lost their flowers for the Great Leader!" she exclaimed excitedly.

The coach had been writing notes in her training log and looked up. She took the flowers from the girl and looked at the ribbon that held them together. "On fire with unquenchable ardor!" it read.

The next day Tyler came to work a little later than usual. He hadn't shaved, and he feigned a look of weariness and discomfort to reinforce the previous day's act.

"Mr. Kang, how are you feeling?" Mr. Yim asked with genuine concern as Tyler stepped into the office.

Tyler lifted his eyebrows and blew out his cheeks.

"Remind me never to have donuts at the Koryo Hotel again. I think I lost about two kilos during the night."

"I'm very sorry to hear that, Mr. Kang. It is strange, I had no such problem myself. And I had four donuts. You only had two."

"Maybe I just got a bad one. Anyway, if you don't mind, I'd like to take off after lunch for the day. I'm still feeling pretty weak."

Mr. Yim eyed him suspiciously. It was not uncommon for workers in North Korea to show up on the job site in order to avoid charges of absenteeism, but then claim illness in order to get permission to go home again. But Mr. Kang seemed genuinely green in the gills.

"Alright," Yim said and turned back to the paperwork on his desk.

After a lunch of rice covered with thin strips of seaweed, which Tyler made a show of eating sparingly, he bid Mr. Yim goodbye and left the office. He went back to the guest house where he shaved and changed into a suit. Then he was off again.

This time the gymnasts were already eating their lunches and Coach Seo-mi sat alone at her little table absentmindedly eating from a bowl of soup while reading her notes. Tyler noticed that the girls were all chattering happily among themselves and didn't seem to see him. He walked over to where Coach Seo-mi sat and cleared his throat.

The young woman looked up sharply from her lunch, clearly startled. Their eyes met and Tyler smiled, although his cheek muscles quivered with the fear that she might not only reject his overtures but report him to the authorities. She did neither.

Bowing in her seat slightly, she said, "Good afternoon" in accented but fully understandable English.

"Good afternoon," said Tyler with a more confident smile, although he wondered what in his appearance had given him away as a foreigner. By this time one of the girls was back at the soup thermos for seconds and happened to look up and see her coach speaking a strange language with a foreigner. A foreign *man*. Coach Seo-mi felt her stare and thought quickly.

"Girls, come over here, please!"

The girls' carefree banter suddenly turned to bewildered silence. They slowly walked over to Coach Seo-mi and Tyler. When all of them had assembled, their coach addressed them.

"Girls, we have a very important guest today. This is Mr....uh, Smith from Romania."

Tyler stifled a guffaw at the multiple incongruities of an obvious Korean supposedly being a Romanian named 'Smith', of all things.

"That is the country I told you about where the gymnasts are almost as good as ours. Mr. Smith is one of the coaches of their team. Let's give him a proper Korean welcome!"

The girls bowed en masse. "*Hwanggyong hamnida!*" they chorused in fluting soprano voices.

Tyler smiled and bowed back to the girls.

"Please finish your lunch and we will then give Mr. Smith a small demonstration of your skill." The girls all ran back to the lunch table, slurped the last of their bowls of soup and began stretching in preparation for the afternoon portion of the day's practice.

"But I know nothing about gymnastics," Tyler said sotto voce, as if the girls could understand English.

"It is not a problem. You should just watch and say that they are very good," Coach Seo-mi replied.

"Where did you learn English?" Tyler asked, as the girls assembled into formation.

"In college. I was an English major. But gymnastics was my real passion. That is how I became a coach."

Tyler nodded awkwardly, not knowing quite what to say next. Finally, he blurted out, "So are you practicing for the Mass Games?" knowing full well that they were.

"Yes, it is for the Glorious Triumvirate Celebration on May 1. It will celebrate the Great Leader Kim Il-sung and his son and grandson. You know about the Great Leader, of course?"

"Yes, of course. Yesterday I bought flowers for his statue. Twice." His eyes danced with mischief. Coach Seo-mi's darkened.

"So it was you who brought those flowers. Do you know that is a crime?" Her voice now had an edge of steel to it.

Tyler was taken aback. Here he had been making such progress with this young lovely and suddenly he's a criminal.

"I am very, very sorry. I didn't know it was a crime to take the flowers."

"It is a crime to give them to someone other than the Great Leader."

Tyler fell silent, his eyes cast down. Then he looked up and said in perfect Korean, "On fire with unquenchable ardor."

"So. You speak Korean," she said, her face even more stern.

"Yes," Tyler replied softly.

"Where did you learn it?"

"My parents were both born in Seoul. Please don't tell anyone about this. If you do, I will go to prison."

Coach Seo-mi tilted her head back and squinted. "I've seen you before."

Like a lock opening, her eyes suddenly widened in recognition. "Now I remember. You're the defector," she said.

"Yes."

"And your name is..." she looked down and to the side in an effort to remember.

"Tyler. Tyler Kang. And yours?"

"Seo-mi."

"'Seo-mi'. 'Beautiful snow'."

"Yes."

Suddenly the girls came running back and began peppering Coach Seo-mi with questions on the routines they had been running through.

"Girls, please! What is Mr. Smith from Romania going to think about our young Korean gymnasts who talk all at once!"

"Mr. Smith from Romania" came to the tail end of their practice every afternoon after work that week and the next. On the second Friday he helped Coach Seo-mi and some of the girls pile up the equipment for the weekend. The girls now smiled at him openly, suspicion erased from their faces. As Seo-mi directed the stacking of the hoops, she happened to glance up and see a man standing on the far corner of the side street. Tyler followed her eyes and saw the man duck into a doorway.

When the last of the girls had waved goodbye after practice, Tyler mustered the courage to ask Seo-mi if he could see her over the weekend.

"But that is forbidden!" she exclaimed, looking around to see if the man had reappeared. He hadn't, but he would the next day. "We are not allowed to have any non-official contact with foreign people. If anyone from State Security asked now, I could say I honestly thought you were a gymnastics coach. But practice is finished. I could get in trouble just for being with you now."

"Then how will I see you outside of practice?"

"It is impossible!" Seo-mi shook her head emphatically.

The following Wednesday he asked her again and the day after that as well. On the third Friday since he had first met her, he asked her yet again. She looked at him without shaking her head in refusal.

Getting closer, Tyler thought.

CHAPTER 17

PYONGYANG
March 19

Unlike tourists, who are forbidden to go off on their own or interact with North Korean citizens, foreigners with hard-currency business interests and the proper visa are allowed a certain degree of freedom of movement within Pyongyang without the usual minder dogging their every step. A daily runner and martial arts practitioner back home, Patrick rose early one cloudy morning and set out on a long jog along Otan Kangan Street, the thoroughfare fronting the Taedong River.

.After an hour, he headed back to the hotel. The sun had come out, and he sat on the steps fronting the Koryo Hotel and took out the paperback he was reading, "The Master of Go" by the Japanese novelist Yasunari Kawabata. *Go* was a board game he had dabbled in for several years. As he thumbed through its pages, he happened to look up and notice a group of young boys climbing over a wall near the hotel. They wore bags on their feet instead of shoes, and their clothes looked like old factory uniforms several sizes too big for them. They stopped when they saw his foreign face, uncertain as to what to do next.

Inspector Choy's life had been busy of late, and not just with his computer work for Comrade Moon. The anti-regime graffiti in the area of Kim Il-sung University had proliferated to the adjoining districts, and the youth gangs that made trouble on the banks of the Taedong River were getting more and more violent. Just the previous week one of the youths had lost a hand during a fight when his opponent came armed with a sharpened garden hoe. As he drove his battered Nissan Sentra along Sosong Avenue, his eye was caught by a group of adolescents congregating not far from a foreigner who was sitting on the steps fronting the Koryo Hotel. Gangs were clustering all over certain parts of the city, but near the hotels where the foreigners could see them? That was a first.

Choy pulled the Sentra over to the side of the street. The boys, ranging in age from nine to sixteen, instantly scattered to the wind when they saw the flashbar on top of his car. Just as well, Choy thought. *What the hell would I do with eight kids? Lock them up? Is being hungry now against the law, too?* Then he saw the foreigner and felt a surge of adrenaline in his gut. He reached into the glove box of his patrol car, examined the photo Pung had given him, and realized that the man in front of the hotel was the one Comrade Moon had ordered him to schmooze. He turned off the ignition and got out.

Patrick saw the plainclothes cop exit his patrol car and thought back to his JSOC training, a tenet of which held that some of the best prospects for turning are cops, especially in poor countries where they are usually underpaid and overworked. This one was as good a candidate as any. He nodded hello to the man with a smile.

Choy inclined his head in a quasi-bow. He had been an avid student of English at the Pyongyang Film Institute.

"How do you do?" he said.

"Fine, thank you, and you?" replied Patrick.

"Fine, thank you." An awkward pause ensued.

"I am sorry about our little kings and queens," Choy said finally as he walked closer, using a term for children that Kim Il-sung had often used, albeit ironically in this case.

"Who are they?" Patrick asked.

"We call them *kotjebi* which means 'flower-swallows'. 'Flower' because they're so young, 'swallow' because they're always hungry, just like the bird."

Patrick nodded. "Your English is very good," he said as the man stopped a few yards in front of him.

"Thank you, but not so good. I need more practice..."

"Would you like to practice over a cup of coffee?" Patrick asked.

"It would be a pleasure," Choy said beaming.

They both had the same thought but for different reasons: *contact initiated.*

Once they were seated at a circular banquette in the coffee shop off the lobby, they introduced themselves and made small talk as they waited for their coffee to arrive.

For the next ten minutes they chatted about sports and martial arts. Then Choy noticed the copy of "The Master of Go" that Patrick had placed on the seat beside him.

"You play *baduk*?" he asked

"Is that what it's called in Korean? I've always known it as *go*."

Choy snorted contemptuously. "That's the Japanese name."

Patrick hesitated before he spoke again. "Care for a game?" he asked. Choy looked at his watch and smiled.

Choy signaled the waitress over and asked for a *baduk* board and the bowls of black and white stones which she promptly brought to their banquette along with their coffee. Beneath the game's apparent simplicity of placing black and white stone discs on a board lies a ritualized simulacrum of war, with the stones advancing slow-motion across the cross-hatched wooden board as on a battlefield. The object of the game is to control a larger portion of the board than your opponent. Stones are captured and removed if a player is unable to prevent the opponent from surrounding a grouping. Placing the stones close to each other is a cautious defensive strategy that can aid in preventing them from being surrounded. Placing them far apart, on the other hand, is a more aggressive but potentially risky approach. Thus, the skilled player strikes a balance between strategic planning and tactical expedience, much as in combat.

With a blind choice of a black stone Choy got the first move. High-stakes games where money is involved are usually as silent as a requiem mass, but in social games casual banter is the norm. Choy and Patrick kept up a terse conversation, but one punctuated by silences of several minutes as they deliberated slowly and carefully on their next moves before answering. National honor was at stake, as well as an opportunity to size each other up.

"I hear that Canada is very large..." *Black begins game with corner-based opening*

"Yes, third largest country in the world...." *White answers with move on lower intersection of grids*

"Lots of places for criminals to hide...." *Black attempts cautious expansion of territory*

"If they don't mind freezing to death...." *White makes bold attack*

"Our criminals freeze to death all the time..." *Black checks with horizontal move*

"In Pyongyang...?" *White attempts an even more reckless attack*

"Not in Pyongyang. We send them away to the country...." *Black takes advantage of white's ill-advised attack and is one move away from victory*

Inspector Choy was about to place the winning disc on the board when their table was jostled by a member of a Chinese tour group.

"Getting crowded in here, don't you think?" he said.

"Yes, it is," Patrick replied. Choy looked at this watch.

"Perhaps we can play again soon. I must get back to work."

"That would be fine. Shall we meet here?"

"No. Not here." Choy shot daggers at the Chinese tourists. "We can play at my office. I will drive you there."

Patrick started to protest, but Choy cut him off. "It is no bother at all."

"In that case, I would enjoy it very much."

"Well, then, Mr. McGrail, it has been a pleasure to meet you. I will see you again soon."

"Goodbye, Inspector Choy. Till next time."

"Till next time."

CHAPTER 18

KORYO HOTEL BASEMENT BAR
The next evening

Patrick finally made contact with someone in the Ministry of Culture who gave him some snapshots of traditional Korean ink-brush paintings that he might find of value for his art export venture. He sat at a table in the Basement Bar, poring over the photos while eating a dinner of pork dumplings and rice. An hour later, Tyler walked in alone. He saw Patrick, who was engrossed in his work, and made his way to the bar without saying anything. Patrick happened to look up. On an impulse, he signaled to the barmaid that Tyler's drink was on him. A minute later Tyler carried the beer over to Patrick's table. He held up the bottle in thanks.

"I owe you a lap dance," he said and began to walk away.

"I'll take a rain check," Patrick said and nodded to one of the other chairs at the table. Tyler hesitated, then took a seat, the tightness in his eyes loosening. After an awkward pause, Patrick spoke again. "So how are you getting on in your new life?"

"Not bad, actually. Not bad at all," Tyler replied. He looked down as if suddenly interested in a coaster on the table, but Patrick noticed something almost glowing in his eyes.

"Don't tell me. They found you a woman."

Tyler looked up, blushed, and then looked back down at the coaster. "Nobody needs to find me a woman." His voice was steely, but his face was relaxed.

"Then you found one yourself."

Tyler nodded.

"Really? Well, congratulations! I'm glad for you."

"Now you *really* can't kill me," Tyler said.

Patrick ignored the comment. "Where did you meet her?"

"On the street."

Patrick frowned theatrically. Tyler snorted.

"Nothing like that, for God's sake. She's a gymnastics coach, has a team that practices down the block."

"The pretty one, about 30? Man, you're going to make a lot of alcoholic losers very jealous," Patrick said cocking his head toward the foreign regulars in the bar. "I never knew you to be the relationship type. What was it you used to say? 'A lot easier to get into the saddle than out'?"

Tyler's demeanor brightened. "This one's different. Before, whenever I got involved with a woman, I always felt like a porcupine that went down a rabbit hole and couldn't get back out again."

"Not exactly an image I would have chosen, but I get your drift."

They sat in silence as they drank and looked at yet another replay of the previous year's Mass Games on the TV. But their silence gradually lost its tension and became something close to companionable. After twenty minutes Tyler looked at his watch and emptied his glass.

"Ten o'clock already. Ain't that a bitch." He laughed to himself. "I guess I'm picking up old man Drosnik's speech patterns. Anyway, I'll be heading out. Thanks for the beer." He got up and started walking, then turned back. "See you around?"

"If I'm careless and you're lucky," Patrick said with a cautious approximation of a smile. The sides of Tyler's mouth lifted slightly, and he walked out the door.

Mack had entered the bar just before Tyler left. He sat down at Patrick's table, and Patrick raised his hand to Miss Ok for a round and some snacks.

"So, how's the art business coming along?" Mack asked, setting his scarf aside and nodding toward the snapshots on the table.

Patrick shrugged, then nodded thanks to the barmaid as she delivered their new round. "I think I might be making a bit of progress with these, but maybe they're just leading me on like you said."

Mack leveled an unblinking gaze at Patrick and then looked all around the room. He turned back and set down his beer.

"Who are you really?" he said in a low voice

Patrick stiffened. "Sorry?"

"I'm not buying the art dealer act. For one thing, you seemed to know that American defector pretty well. When I first mentioned him, you acted as if you'd barely heard of him."

Patrick chewed on his lower lip but tried to keep the rest of his face impassive while a fierce debate raged inside his head:

-I need allies, and allies have to know the truth...

-Sure, but how well do you know this guy?...

-Hardly at all, but what's the alternative?...

-Not saying anything, of course....

-But maybe he knows something about Yumi...

-And maybe he works for Moon...

-I have to take the chance...

-Don't say I didn't warn you...

-Thanks for the vote of confidence. Here goes nothing...

He leaned in toward Mack. "It's not about him. Or at least it isn't now. I'm here to find someone else."

"So. A garden-variety spy," Mack said leaning back in his chair, clearly unimpressed.

"In a sense. Not officially, though."

"Well, who are you trying to find if not the defector?" Mack said, sipping from his bottle.

"I'm looking for a Japanese woman who was taken here against her will. I have to locate her and extract her. I'm pretty sure she's being held by someone called Comrade Moon."

"Moon! Jesus Christ, she's probably in some gulag. You'd better watch your step. People just seem to disappear when they come in contact with that one. How do you plan to find this woman?"

"I thought maybe you'd be able to help since you seem to know everybody."

"Me? What would I know? I'm just a lowly language reviser. You need someone inside, and that's hard to find in any country, let alone in this godforsaken place."

"I know a cop."

Mack's set down his beer and widened his eyes. "Christ on a crutch, you don't waste any time, do you. Where'd you meet a cop?"

"Outside the hotel. I'm going to his office to play go, or *baduk*, as they call it. Guy's name is Choy. Middle-aged, stocky build...?"

"Drives a beat-up old Nissan? Chases punks off the street?"

Patrick nodded. "The very one. I just don't know if I can trust him. I thought maybe you might have some ideas. You seem to be the most knowledgeable of the foreigners here, anyway."

"Don't read too much into that." Mack looked musingly into the near distance and rubbed his beard. "Tell you what. I hardly know you, but sometimes you get a feeling about people. I've got a couple of chits I can call in. I'll see if I can find out anything about this Choy."

"How would you do that?"

Mack smiled tightly and shook his head. "One *hears* things. That's all I'll say. I'll be back in a bit. You owe me, mate."

Alone now, Patrick got up from the table with his dirty dishes and set them on the bar behind which Miss Ok who was polishing a good-luck amulet she usually kept under the counter out of sight. She glanced up as the image of a young man flashed on the TV screen: Kim Jong-un, son of the Dear Leader.

"*Choego salyeong-gwan,*" she said under her breath with a hint of mockery in her voice, not realizing that Patrick was watching and listening.

"*Supreme Commander?*" he said in English.

Miss Ok swung around and looked at him in shock. "You speak Korean?" she asked.Patrick nodded. Miss Ok turned back to the TV.

"He is supposed to be just like his father," she muttered and went back to polishing her amulet.

"Is that a good thing?" Patrick asked.

Miss Ok pretended not to hear him and continued her polishing.

After a moment, Patrick lifted his head in the direction of the amulet. "I thought that kind of thing fell into the category of superstition," he said. All forms of superstition were officially outlawed in North Korea.

"It is only superstition if you believe in it," she replied without hesitation, as if she had rehearsed her answer.

"Then why do you keep it if you don't believe in it?"

She thought for a moment, and then a self-satisfied smile came over her face.

"Because it works even if you do not believe in it."

A while later, Mack came back in. He walked over to Patrick and cocked his head for him to follow. They walked over to a deserted corner of the room.

"Your cop, Choy? He's good."

"You're sure?"

Mack nodded with his mouth set in certitude.

"Thanks, Mack. Beer's on me." He raised his hand in the direction of Miss Ok, but Mack cut him off.

"Next time. I'm going on vacation for a week and I've got an early flight in the morning." Mack grinned and left.

CHAPTER 19

PYONGYANG
April 2

After weeks of pestering Coach Seo-mi to meet him some place private, Tyler finally succeeded. They would meet secretly at the Martyr's Cemetery Park that evening which turned unseasonably warm.

Located on Mount Taesong in a virtually unpopulated section of Pyongyang, the Revolutionary Martyr's Cemetery is the final resting place for those who sacrificed their lives in the cause of *juche* socialism, a place so hallowed that even spying on citizens is forbidden in its immediate vicinity. Thus, the surrounding lush parkland is a favorite rendezvous point for couples craving North Korea's scarcest commodity: privacy.

Tyler knew the way there from a bus tour he had taken with Mr. Yim several weeks earlier. Dressed all in black with a woolen cap pulled low over his head, he rode the tram to the foot of Mount Taesong and made his way quickly to the park on the north side of the cemetery. He checked his watch. 7:45. He was early.

"Over here!" he heard a voice whisper. Seo-mi had arrived even earlier. She held a large bag that sagged at the bottom.

"Come with me," she said softly, walking toward a system of geometrically arranged hedgerows. Looking around once again, she took his hand. "This way," she said.

Once inside the hedgerows, they were completely cut off from prying eyes. "We are safe here," Seo-mi said and opened the bag she brought. She proceeded to take out and arrange two small thermoses and a pair of bowls for each of them, and began to fill the bowls with rice and soup.

After they had eaten in self-conscious silence for several moments, Seo-mi finally broke the ice. "It is Korean tradition. Our favorite pastime is having a picnic. Not usually at night, though." she said smiling. "Do you have picnics in Romania, Mr. Smith?" she asked, her smile broadening.

Tyler laughed softly. "Oh yes, picnics and vampires."

A puzzled look passed over Seo-mi's face. "What is that word?" she asked as she filled their bowls with seconds.

"A vampire?" he said, nodding thanks as she returned his bowl. "A vampire is someone who lives on the blood of human beings." He bared his front teeth and growled.

Seo-mi snorted slightly. "We have this in the DPRK, too," she said, spearing a carrot with her chopsticks. "But we don't say vampire. We say 'Kim Jong-il'. He lived off of our blood for many years."

Tyler stopped eating. "Don't talk like that, even here!"

"Don't worry," Seo-mi replied. "Everyone thinks this way, not just me. The Great Leader, Kim Il-sung, we respected. But Kim Jong-il...he was a vampire." Seo-mi looked away in thought as she spoke. Realizing that Tyler was staring at her, she turned and smiled weakly.

"I am sorry. Have some soju."

She poured out two small cups of the fiery vodka-like drink from one of the thermoses and passed one to him. He took a sip while holding her eye seductively— then began hacking his brains out, completely spoiling the moment.

"Nice bouquet!" he managed to croak, his eyes filling.

She laughed softly. They held each others' eyes. Simultaneously they set down their cups. She moved close to his side. Tyler brought her head close to his and lightly brushed her cheek with his lips. Seo-mi closed her eyes as her breathing quickened, her entire being filling with sensual delight. A guttural murmur escaped her throat as Tyler's hand found her breasts. His own breathing quickened and deepened, as if drinking her in. Within a few short fumbling moments, their clothes lay scattered on the ground around them. Tyler moved on top of her and her head rolled from side to side in delirious rapture. When at last he entered her, her entire body spasmed, the center of her brain a riotous explosion of shimmering light and color. With sharp cries of ecstasy, their breath gushed and shuddered into each other's faces. They were one being, flesh intertwined, spirits indistinguishable from each other.

A half hour later, as they lay nuzzled side by side, Seo-mi broke the blissful silence. "Have you seen that man who watches the girls at practice?"

"I've been too busy watching you," Tyler replied languidly as he stroked her hair. Seo-mi smiled but was instantly serious again.

"He worked for Kim Jong-il. Now he works for the 'Supreme Commander,' Kim Jong-un. He goes around the country looking for young girls for the 'Happy Corps.'"

Tyler's body became rigid, and he sat up. "'Happy Corps'? Do you mean...? But those kids are so young! Some of them can't be more than 12 years old!"

"All the better for their purposes. They have parties and everyone gets drunk. And then they take photographs of men when they're with the girls. That's all it takes to keep them 'loyal'."

Tyler watched her intently as she spoke. The way she turned her eyes to the side, as if remembering. . .

He put his arms around her and brought his face close to hers. His eyes bore into hers for a long moment.

"You were one of them, weren't you," he said softly.

Seo-mi took a deep breath and nodded.

"I never told anyone, but I'm sure everyone knew. It was such *han*, such shame." She began to sob. "They just take you away one day, and tell your parents that you're being sent to special military service or something. If the parents complain, they say that the girl is in service to the country, and that's the end of it. If they continue to complain, they are taken away. My father even worked for Kim Jong-il, but that wasn't enough to get me out of it."

"How long were you involved in this?"

"Until I was 19. After that you're past your prime. They give you money, but it's just to keep you quiet. I got a commendation from Kim Jong-il himself for 'service to the fatherland'. That gives me enough power to keep people away, like that man who comes to practice. He has his eye on the girl called Jin-ok who is an only child. It would break her parents' hearts if they took her, especially for something like that."

Seo-mi began to tremble with rage. "I would have given anything for *boksu*," she rasped from deep within her throat.

Tyler shook his head in incomprehension. It was a word he didn't know.

"*Retribution*," she hissed. "I would have given anything to kill that vampire Kim Jong-il. Now that he is dead, I would settle for killing his son."

Tyler held her tighter. Goose flesh that had nothing to do with the cold erupted on his back and scalp. After a long moment, he brought her head close to his and whispered in her ear.

CHAPTER 20

PYONGYANG
April 4

A few days later Choy picked up Patrick in his patrol car as they had arranged, and they met for several days in a row thereafter for marathon games of baduk in his office. By virtue of Choy's work with Comrade Moon at Bureau 39, his superiors didn't dare question why a foreigner was being brought into the People's Security precinct house on a daily basis and assumed that Patrick, with his vaguely Mediterranean features, was one of Moon's associates in Hezbollah or some other terrorist group. They had no idea that their own Inspector Choy had been instructed by Comrade Moon to 'schmooze' the foreigner.

Once inside Choy's office for the first time, they limited their conversation to game strategy as Patrick tried for quick victories two games running. Choy clucked in disapproval.

"You tried that same thing when we played at the hotel. Every time you attack right away like that, you give away your position. You have to lure your opponent into attacking you first. Haven't you ever heard of Sun-tzu? 'Read your enemy's mind and you can defeat him whenever you choose'. Let's start again."

Chastened, Patrick tried a different opening gambit and Choy paid him the ultimate compliment: he said nothing and just looked at the board with knitted brows. Then he counter-moved, and the game was on in earnest. Patrick still lost, but he had learned a valuable lesson.

By the end of the first week of daily games, Choy had opened up about his training at the Pyongyang Film Institute, and Patrick told of his study of sumi-e and calligraphy, although he substituted the name of a Canadian art college for Tokyo University of Fine Arts. As they neared the conclusion of a marathon game that had lasted through four daily afternoon sessions, they took a break. Choy leaned back in his seat and lit one his endless stream of foul-smelling cigarettes. Patrick by this time felt comfortable enough in the office to get up and pour them both a cup of tea.

As Patrick set down the cups on the table, Choy sighed in what seemed to be a mixture of satisfaction and wistfulness. "I wish my wife were here to meet you," he said.

"What does she do?" Patrick asked, taking a sip of tea.

Choy shook his head with a weak smile. "She died in the Arduous March. My son, too," he said, referring to the famine of the late 1990s.

"I'm sorry," Patrick said. Choy waved away the condolences. "It's been a long time." He paused. "How about you? Married?"

Patrick shook his head. "I was engaged, but it didn't work out."

"Another woman?" Choy asked with a mischievous smile.

"No. That might have been easier. For me, at least. No, I was in love with the idea of enlightenment."

"I don't know what that is."

"Meditation? Buddhism?"

"Ah. I've heard about that. Never made any sense to me. Something about 'life is nothing but suffering'— now go enjoy it."

Patrick chuckled. Choy spoke again.

"Speaking of which, you asked me about the camps when we first met at the hotel."

"Yes."

"Now *that's* suffering."

"Do you know anybody in the prisons?"

"Camps. We call them camps. *Kwaliso*. It means 'education camp'."

"Alright, 'camp' then. Do you know anybody who's being. . .'educated'?"

"Many people." Choy said nothing more for a full minute. He turned back to the game board where his stones were in danger of being surrounded. With a daring extension to his lineup, he brought off a brilliant maneuver that rescued his position and turned the tables on Patrick, placing him in mortal danger.

"Excellent," said Patrick in grudging admiration.

"You have no *hwallo*," Choy said with satisfaction in his voice.

"What is *hwallo*?" Patrick asked.

"I think 'escape route' or something like that in English." Patrick tried one last strategy and then conceded the game.

Choy leaned back in his chair and lit another cigarette, seemingly lost in thought.

"I know many people in the camps," he said again.

Patrick said nothing. Despite Mack's assurances about Choy, he was beginning to find it more than a little unsettling that a North Korean law enforcement officer was opening up to this degree about sensitive issues of national security. But at the same time, he didn't want to interrupt what might be a flow of potentially valuable information on Yumi's whereabouts. He was torn. He decided in the interest of personal safety to play his hand close to his vest until he was absolutely sure about this cop.

"In fact, I sent some of them there," Choy continued.

Patrick felt a knot forming deep in his stomach. Was this a warning? He nodded to Choy in acknowledgment but still said nothing.

"I sometimes feel...what is the word? We say *jwe* in Korean. Guilty? Yes, guilty. I sometimes feel guilty about them." Patrick sat stock still, willing Choy to continue but apprehensive about what was coming next.

"Do you know the movie 'The Godfather'?" Choy asked. "The opening scene of Don Corleone's daughter's wedding?"

"I seem to recall seeing it a long time ago."

"Well, one time I had to arrest a man on the day of his daughter's wedding. He had a Christian Bible that his neighbor knew about. He and the neighbor had been drinking buddies until this man got the Bible. I guess he became holy or something. Anyway, the neighbor hated him because he thought the man now looked down on him, and also because the man wouldn't lend him any more money for *soju*, since he was saving up for his daughter's wedding. So the son-of-a-bitch neighbor waited till the wedding day to turn him in about the Bible. I didn't have a choice, you have to make an arrest on the day something as serious as that is reported or it's your own head. I made the arrest and State Security took over from there. I often wonder what happened to that man..."

Choy's voice trailed off. He was leaning back against his chair, looking off into the distance and smoking.

"Who exactly do you work for, if you don't mind me asking?" Patrick asked in as innocent a tone as he could muster.

Choy looked at him as if he were weighing his words before speaking. "Basically, there are two kinds of police: *Inmin Boanseong*, or 'People's Security' in English, and *Kukga Bowibu*, or 'State Security'."

"What's the difference between them?"

"People's Security is the state police. That's who I work for. We're the ones who knock on your door in the middle of the night."

"And what about the other one, State Security?"

"They don't knock."

A shroud of silence enveloped the room. Finally, Choy shifted in his chair. "Tell me, Mr. McGrail, how much does a computer expert make in America? I mean Canada?"

"That depends," Patrick said with relief at the change of subject. "Certainly a lot more than a computer expert makes in North Korea."

Choy then veered in still another direction. "What do you believe, Mr. McGrail?"

Patrick was taken aback. He felt for a moment as though Choy were intentionally trying to rattle him with his disjointed line of questioning. "Believe?" he said finally.

"Yes. You said earlier that you practice meditation. Is that like praying or reading the Bible?"

"Not exactly. It's more like letting the mind settle. It's supposed to lead to some deep insights—which I haven't had— but it does calm me down. As for belief, well, I guess I believe in karma, that everything we do comes back to us. 'For every action there is an equal and opposite reaction'. You've heard of

Newton's First Law of Motion?"

"Actually, that's Newton's *Third* Law of Motion. We do know *some* things in the DPRK." Choy's face tightened in mock indignation. "So in karma do you come back in new lives and so on, as the Hindus believe?"

"That's what they say, but I have no idea. I suppose so," Patrick said, feeling flustered at his lack of answers to questions he had never really considered, despite his long practice of meditation.

"And so if you do evil things in one life, evil things are done to you in your next life?"

"I'm not in a position to know that one way or another," Patrick answered, again feeling flat-footed.

"But it would have to be that way," Choy insisted. "If every action has an equal and opposite reaction, and somebody does something evil but he dies before his 'equal and opposite' happens to him, then he would *have* to come back in a new life."

"Well, I suppose you have a point. Logically speaking, that is," Patrick said, trying not to come off as hopelessly obtuse. Choy just sat smoking, his eyes squinting into the middle distance. When he spoke next it was as if he were musing to himself.

"I wonder what we North Koreans did in our past lives to deserve being born here," he said softly. After a moment he continued on a metaphysical tack.

"Do you believe there's a God, Mr. McGrail?"

"I believe there's something more than this life, but beyond that I don't think it's possible to actually *know* anything like that for certain. That takes faith, and I've seen too much in my life to have a whole lot of that."

"But do you not believe that faith is a powerful thing?" Choy said.

"Oh, yes. Powerful enough to make someone give up his life for other people. But also powerful enough to make someone hijack a passenger jet and fly it into a building full of innocent people. Faith is one of the most powerful emotions a human being can have. It's just that it doesn't make *what* he believes in any more true." Patrick paused. "And what do *you* believe in, Inspector Choy?" he said after a moment.

A profound sadness seeped out of the edges of Choy's practiced smile.

"I believe that the future is the present before you know it, and then the present turns into the past. Unless you prepare for the future."

"You're being enigmatic," Patrick said, his own smile concealing more than it revealed.

Choy took a deep breath. "Life is for the living, Mr. McGrail. My wife and son are dead. I felt guilty about it, but now it's time to move on. I want to plan for the future." He looked at Patrick appraisingly for a long moment. "Let me show you something," he said finally.

He stubbed out his cigarette and walked over to his file cabinet. With a quick, jerking motion, he lifted the bottom drawer off its hinges and placed it on the floor. Then he reached his arm all the way in to his shoulder and came out with a bulging manila envelope. He looked inside and found a sheet of parchment of a type that Patrick had used back in his university days while studying with Professor Park. It was paper made expressly for ink-brush painting and calligraphy."Let me read this to you. It's a poem written by my grandfather." Choy held the paper almost reverently in both hands as he scanned the lines of calligraphy. Then he began to read with a quavering voice:

O name shattered to pieces,
O name vanished into the void.
O name without response,
O name I will be calling till death—
You are gone before I have said
What I have carved for you in my heart.
O my love,
O my love.
The sunset burns the western sky.
Even a herd of deer sadly weeps.
Your name I call
Up on a lonely hill.
I call till sorrow chokes me.
But my voice escapes into vast space
Between heaven and earth.

I will be calling your name till death
Even if I should turn to stone.
O my love,
O my love.

When Choy had finished reading, he continued looking at the calligraphy on the page.

"That's one of the most poignant things I've ever heard," Patrick said softly.

Choy nodded with his head down. Then he looked up.

"I once read something in a book that I found at the Film Institute. One of the participants in the International Film Festival was English, and he forgot the book in the theater. I don't recall the title, but I'll never forget a quote from it. It said, 'To know and love another human being is the beginning of all wisdom.' I had that wisdom once, Mr. McGrail. But then the two human beings I loved above all others were taken from me. I don't think I have that wisdom anymore."

Choy exhaled softly and smiled that same smile of unrelenting sadness. "Well," he said with forced chipperness after a moment. "I have told you things I have never told anyone else. Now it is your turn."

Patrick looked him straight in the eye. Despite Mack's assurance about Inspector Choy, Patrick felt an almost comical sense of irony that he would be putting his faith—and life—in the hands of a North Korean cop. He took a deep breath and began to speak— in Korean. Choy's eyes widened into saucers. . .

Fifteen minutes later, Patrick finished his explanation as to the real reason he had come to North Korea. He didn't get into anything about his CIA connection, or about Tyler Kang. Nor did he mention his real name. But he told Choy all about Yumi. Choy sat looking at him, his brow furrowed in concentration. If he had any intention of arresting me, Patrick thought, it would come right about now. Instead, Choy lit another cigarette, inhaled deeply, and looked up at the ceiling.

"Maybe I can help," he said in a quiet voice as he exhaled.

CHAPTER 21

THE WHITE HOUSE SITUATION ROOM
April 5

National Security Advisor Jonathan Barnes clicked on the first page of his PowerPoint presentation.

"Mr. President, these are the overnights from NSA," he began, referring to the infrared, Keyhole-class satellite photos the National Security Agency had taken the night before.

"This is the Reunification Highway that leads south from Pyongyang to Kaesong, which is the main city on their side of the DMZ. This other photo was taken two days ago. As you can see, it was empty then, and today it's crawling with all sorts of vehicles."

"What kind of vehicles?" the President asked.

"Mostly military transports."

"Can you pump up the image?"

Barnes fiddled with the remote and the image magnified to show tanks, armored personnel carriers, and artillery pieces making their way by the hundreds down the Reunification Highway toward Kaesong.

"Holy shit," the President murmured in a drawn-out voice.

"And did you notice the markings on this one, Mr. President?" Barnes asked excitedly, indicating with a pointer a truck in the vanguard of the cavalcade. "It says '1st Army'."

"General O's 1st Army Corps?"

"Exactly, sir."

"Get me General Merkin on the phone," he barked to an aide.

"Which one is he, sir?" the man asked.

"Our commandant at the DMZ, the one who wanted to turn North Korea into toast. I want to make sure he doesn't go nuts when he gets wind of this. At least not yet."

CHAPTER 22

PYONGYANG
April 6

"Maybe I can help," Choy said the last time he and Patrick met. Two days later, they met again in Choy's office.

"She is being held at a place called Senghori Prison. It's near Kaesong, down by the DMZ."

"But why did they kidnap her?"

"Her father stole something from Comrade Moon."

"Then why didn't they just go after her father?"

"They can't find him. He seems to be in hiding. They're probably using her as leverage."

Patrick paused in thought. "How can you be sure she's at this place?" he asked.

"I do weekly checks of the Bureau 39 computer system to make sure everything is running alright. I looked her up."

At last Patrick knew the reason Yumi had been abducted, but suspicion crowded out all other emotions in his mind. Choy picked up on it. He got up and checked to see that his office door was locked and then sat back down.

"You're wondering why a DPRK security agent is helping you," he said. "Now I will tell you." He lowered his voice to a whisper. "The last time we played *baduk*, you asked me what I believe in. I believe in *juche*, self-reliance. But the juche I believe in is *real* self-reliance, where people are free. I am unable to be free here, in this land of false juche. Mr. McGrail, I want to defect."

Patrick searched Choy's eyes but saw no sign of deceit. Either the man was completely sincere or was Oscar-caliber.

"But how?" Patrick asked. His pulse leapt into triple digits as Choy reached into his jacket pocket and took out a pair of handcuffs. Choy laughed.

"Relax! I will take you as my 'guest'," he said, playfully jingling the cuffs. "If anyone asks, I'll just say that I'm transporting a foreign spy to Kaesong for questioning. It sometimes happens. Besides, no one will question me about it. I have a double-Kim badge," he said, pointing to the lapel badge that everyone in North Korea is required to wear in public. The "double-Kim" features the images of the first two Kims, Great- and Dear Leader, and may only be worn by war heroes or those very high up in the bureaucracy. Choy was neither, but he had inherited it from his father.

"Once we're there, we'll go to Senghori Prison, find Yumi Takara and escape to the South through the tunnels."

"What tunnels?" Patrick asked.

"They're all over the place down there. I was stationed in Kaesong during my initial training. I know one tunnel that's not far at all from Kaesong. It's bound to be close to Senghori. We just need a guide who can bring us to the prison. We can't just wander around until we find it, it would look suspicious."

"So who's the guide?" Patrick asked.

"Do you remember those *kotjebi* flower-swallow kids, the ones at the hotel? The mother of the leader of the gang is at Senghori and so is his girlfriend's brother. The young girlfriend has secretly visited the place before. She will be our guide."

"A 12-year-old kid?" Patrick asked, wincing with skepticism.

"Believe me, these flower-swallows are able to get to all sorts of places that adults can't. It's like they have some kind of underground network. If we can get the girl to guide us the next time she goes to visit her brother, we should be able to find Yumi Takara."

Patrick searched Choy's eyes again. "Alright," he said finally, although a voice in his heart told him he was moving much too fast.

Bureau 39

Later in the day Comrade Moon met with Inspector Choy.

"Well? Is the American spy buying it?" Moon asked.

"Yes, Comrade," Choy replied. "I guess I'm a better actor than I thought. I'm arranging it so that he meets the girl at Senghori."

"How did you manage to win his confidence?"

"I just followed your advice, Comrade, and told him I wanted to defect. We'll be escaping through the tunnels to South Korea once he finds Yumi Takara." Choy said all this matter-of-factly.

Moon's face was serious at first. But then he slowly broke into a grin and wagged his finger at Choy. "You had me going. Anyway, when are you going to Senghori?"

"Tomorrow, Comrade. I'd like to do this as soon as possible before he has any second thoughts."

"Good idea. Get going, then."

Choy stood and left.

The next day, Choy guided Patrick by the elbow onto the local train to Kaesong. Flashing his badge to the conductor, he opened his jacket to reveal a Browning automatic pistol, whereupon the other passengers immediately parted to let them pass. It was not unheard of for these State Security types to arrest someone just for looking at them funny. *And this one! Transporting a foreigner, no less. Probably some filthy American spy.* Patrick walked with his hands cuffed in front of him, his head down, defeated. Once they were on the train in a special compartment reserved for those on official government business, they let down their guard.

"So where's the kid?" Patrick asked with a hint of skepticism.

"Her name is Sun-yi."

"Alright, so where's Sun-yi?"

"She's with Jebby, her boyfriend. They went ahead on a different train. They somehow got hold of travel permits. Probably at Mrs. Pae's."

"Who's that?"

"She runs a *jangmadang* [outdoor black market] not far from your hotel. She's the one who arranged for the kids to guide us in return for us helping them and their family members escape to the South."

The "family members" part was a new wrinkle. Choy had never said anything the day before about what was becoming an ever-growing defection party. But what good would it do to protest, now that the wheels were in motion? Besides, did he think the kids and Choy were helping him out of the goodness of their hearts? Still, it raised his level of alertness several notches that Choy had sprung this on him at the last minute. What else had he not told him?

Patrick's suspicions were allayed somewhat during the two-hour train ride to Kaesong, as Choy filled him in on some of the more arcane details of the North Korean regime, such as the workings of Bureau 39, including its siphoning off of billions for the top leadership, and its elaborate system of tunnels that ran under the streets of Pyongyang.

As the slow local pulled into Kaesong Station two hours later, Choy reached up to the rack above their seats and brought down an overnight bag containing a change of clothing for each of them as well as a thousand U.S. dollars and Patrick's passport. Jebby and Sun-yi were on the platform begging, and as Choy and Patrick got off, Jebby ran up to them.

"Can you help me, mister? I just need 10 chon to phone my mother," he pleaded pointing to a payphone just outside of the station.

"Beat it," Choy said gruffly, pushing Jebby to one side while forcibly guiding Patrick in the direction of the exit. Once outside, Choy paused, and while holding Patrick by the chain of his handcuffs, made a show of searching his pockets. A moment later he produced a piece of paper and studied it intently.

"I have to make a phone call," he said loudly in English to Patrick while patting his shoulder holster. Other passengers from the train stopped to gawk, but the dark look they got from Choy hastened them on their way. He went to the payphone, deposited a 10-chon coin and dialed his office number in Pyongyang. Pretending to wait for a pickup on the other end, his eyes wandered casually around the inside of the kiosk and settled on a couple of pencil marks Jebby had made on the side wall. That was enough. Choy cursed and hung up. Checking to see that the area around the phone booth was deserted, he spoke softly to Patrick.

"We head down Chongnyon Street in the direction of King Songmin's Tomb. Jebby and Sun-yi will meet us there." The road also led to a building that housed the local State Security, so an officer heading in that direction with someone in handcuffs would not have aroused inordinate suspicion.

Fifteen minutes later they caught sight of Jebby and Sun-yi who pretended not to see them and just shuffled along aimlessly, just another couple of homeless and hungry waifs. Foot traffic gradually thinned out the farther they got from the station, and when no one else was about on this stretch of Chongnyon Street, Jebby bent down to tie his shoe. Choy and Patrick were 30 yards away. In the blink of an eye, Jebby and Sun-yi disappeared into the undergrowth. When Choy and Patrick reached the spot they had last seen them, they heard a short whistle.

Choy squinted at a blank piece of paper in his hand and then turned this way and that, the picture of an out-of-towner trying to get his bearings. No one was about.

"Now," he whispered to Patrick, and the two of them ducked into the narrow opening in the foliage that Jebby and Sun-yi had just disappeared into. They were waiting for them. Choy took off Patrick's handcuffs.

"Sun-yi found this trail the last time she was here," Jebby whispered, beaming at his girlfriend who blushed and lowered her head. "It leads right to the prison," she said in a delicate, flute-like voice.

"It's perfect," Choy murmured to Patrick as they followed Jebby and Sun-yi along the trail leading up a mountain. "Did you notice that hill on the other side of Chongnyon Street? The entrance to the tunnel I told you about is on the far side of it behind a fence. That's our next stop after this."

Choy cached the overnight bag containing their changes of clothing and Patrick's money and passports behind a solitary birch tree, and tried to match pace with Jebby and Sun-yi up the increasingly steep trail. The youths moved deftly through the low-hanging brush, while the two adults constantly had to duck to avoid branches. Their breathing became more labored as the angle of the path became more and more severe.

Forty minutes later, silent except for Choy's smoker's wheeze, they reached the summit of the highest mountain west of Kaesong and came to a halt. Choy gasped with his hands on his knees, while Jebby and Sun-yi sat serenely on their heels. Patrick reconned the area to make sure they were alone and noticed a series of small mounds rising in the near distance. Walking over for a closer look, he stopped in revulsion. For scattered on and around the mounds were human remains that had been picked clean, probably by wild mountain pigs. They had stopped for their rest in the prison graveyard. Absolute silence reigned all around them. Not even a single bird, the emissaries of heaven in Korean culture, could be heard in this cold hell.

A few minutes later Choy had recovered. He shrugged inquiringly at Jebby and Sun-yi, and the girl pointed down into the valley below.

"Do you see that lone pine tree?" she asked in her tiny soprano voice. "That's where the main gate is. We can't go anywhere near that. We have to go around the back. This way," she said and began leading the way.

A quarter mile later the terrain flattened a bit, and Sun-yi again pointed, this time at a barbed wire fence, a section of which was covered in elephant grass. Jebby parted the grass with his hands, and a hole in the fence appeared. He looked back at Choy with a grin. Choy nodded.

Once the four of them were on the other side of the fence, Sun-yi held up her hand. Not fifteen feet away, a half dozen or so human shapes plodded from one low hut to another as if only semi-conscious. Jebby's head shot forward.

"My mother!" he exclaimed in an excited whisper. Choy clamped a warning hand on the boy's shoulder, but Jebby cupped his hands and blew air through his lips, stopping just short of a whistle. One of the walking cadavers stopped and began edging closer to where the four of them lay in the grass.

"Who is that with you?" his mother whispered into the grass while pretending to search for kindling.

"Friends from Pyongyang. Sun-yi guided us." Sun-yi raised her head.

"The girl I remember," Jebby's mother said. "Her brother is in here. Who are the others?"

"One of them is looking for someone in here from Japan."

"And the other one?"

120

"A policeman."

The woman stiffened and abruptly turned around.

"Wait, Mama!" Jebby called out in a loud whisper. "He's on our side! We're going to escape to the South!" His mother stopped and turned back in their direction.

"Where is the one looking for someone from Japan?"

Patrick pulled himself forward and raised his head so that she could see him. The woman's eyes widened. "A foreigner?" she asked. Patrick nodded.

"He speaks Korean, Mama," Jebby said.

"What is the name of the person you are looking for?" she asked.

"Yumi Takara."

The woman deliberated a moment before speaking again.

"Wait here," she said in a low voice and shuffled off unsteadily.

Patrick tapped Choy on the shoulder and shrugged. *Are we safe?* he asked with his eyes. Choy moved his head side to side noncommittally.

The next few minutes stretched into an eternity. Suddenly three prison guards with raised rifles came charging toward them from the direction that Jebby's mother had just gone. Choy, Jebby and Sun-yi immediately scuttled back into the dense undergrowth, but the guards made a beeline for Patrick, and he was quickly surrounded. He raised his hands in surrender, and as the guards grabbed hold of his arms, a volley of shots rang out from the direction that Choy, Jebby and Sun-yi had gone. The guards turned in the direction of the shots and then back at Patrick. The one closest to him rammed his rifle butt up into his chin.

Two of the guards dragged him senseless into the camp, the heels of his boots carving swales into the mud. The appalling stench that hovered like a toxic cloud over the camp jolted him back to consciousness, and his gut contracted violently, bringing up bile and acid that seared his throat and nauseated him further. The third guard who appeared to be in charge wielded a wooden club which he jabbed repeatedly into Patrick's ribs.

Several minutes later, the guards with their captive foreigner came to a halt in front of a building above which the North Korean flag drooped forlornly from a bamboo pole. The door opened and a tall, uniformed man with an oily complexion and acne scars strode out, the metal cleats on his heels tap-tapping a slow tattoo on the rough-hewn porch planks. He wiped at his nose with a dirty handkerchief and coughed drily as he slowly descended the stairs, his watery eyes never leaving Patrick's. He stopped in front of Patrick and stood expressionlessly for a long moment before speaking.

"Who are you?" he croaked in English.

Patrick said nothing. And what could he say?

-I'm a Canadian art dealer scouting for talent in North Korean prison camps.

-I'm an American spy sent to kill my old sniper partner.

-I'm here to rescue Yumi Takara from you sadistic sons of bitches.

The man came closer until his face was no more than an inch or two from Patrick's and he sniffed back a watery slug of snot. As he studied the wound that the guard's rifle butt had opened up on Patrick's chin, his fist suddenly shot up. Patrick's head exploded in pain, but a voice deep within told him that if he lost consciousness he might never regain it.

"I asked you a question," the man shouted.

Patrick forced himself to say nothing.

"Do you want to die today?"

Patrick still said nothing.

The man hawked and spit on the ground and turned with a disgusted look to the head guard with the club. After a few whispered a few words, he stomped back up the stairs. The head guard's eyes glinted as they bore into Patrick's, his breathing rapid as if in anticipation of something perversely erotic. The prisoners called him Bastard Cho.

He cocked his head to the right, and his two underlings dragged Patrick to a nearby building where the stench of death and disinfectant competed for dominance, with death the hands-down winner. A room-sized furnace dominated the building, and they forced Patrick inside, slamming its iron door behind him. In seconds the oxygen in his brain exhausted itself, and his mind broke free of his body. As he felt himself floating above the glowing coals at his feet, he was beyond all fear and knew that he could just let himself fall onto the coals and be done with it all. But before he could relinquish his hold on life, a pair of hands reached in and dragged him out.

"Who are you!!" Cho screamed again and again while clubbing Patrick furiously over his head and body. When Patrick still said nothing, Cho motioned to the two younger guards who dragged Patrick to an even more ominous section of the darkened building where the only light was a single flickering bulb. They bound Patrick hand and foot to a thick wooden pillar the size of a small tree that had been nailed and re-nailed into a depression in the floor. A horrifying realization broke through the fog of Patrick's mind as they tied his arms behind him: others before him had been made to suffer such an unendurable level of pain that they had actually uprooted the seemingly immoveable pillar from its moorings. Bastard Cho walked slowly over to where Patrick stood bound and immobilized. "The rest was just a preview," he hissed in Korean with lips that barely moved. He shouted sharply to the other guards. They turned Patrick around 180 degrees so that his back faced Cho and tore off his shirt.

Footfalls from behind Patrick gradually increased in speed and suddenly stopped as Cho dug in his heels and brought the full extension of the whip onto Patrick's upper back. The steel tip bit first into his left shoulder blade, ripping the flesh out to a depth of half an inch. Patrick's last thought before passing out was that it wouldn't have mattered if he had told them who he was. This had all been for sport.

CHAPTER 23

At the very moment Patrick passed out, the tall, uniformed man with the acne scars and runny nose, known to the prisoners as the Rat Catcher, was on the phone in his office waiting for his connection to Pyongyang to go through, giddy at the imminent prospect of getting out of Senghori Prison. When he was first assigned there two years earlier, he had been promised a civilian career track if he proved himself worthy as a camp superintendant, and what could be more worthy than capturing a foreign spy? As he waited, he fantasized of a future as a high school English teacher in the capital, perhaps. He had picked up a working knowledge of the language from books. Or maybe he could be a chauffeur to someone important, maybe even Comrade Moon himself, with whom he waited to speak. Finally, Moon came on the line, and the Rat Catcher greeted him with the news that he had caught an enemy spy, someone who... *What's that? Oh yes, of course, Comrade Moon, his description. Tall white man, green eyes, hair that is going gray...*"

The Rat Catcher had ordered Cho to keep the foreigner alive during questioning, but Bastard Cho had blocked out everything that stood between him and his ultimate trophy. He slowed his breathing, eyed his target one last time, and began his bounding approach. He got to within five feet of Patrick when the door flung open.

"Stop!" the Rat Catcher screamed in panic. Bastard Cho's momentum carried him forward a full ten feet past Patrick, and he turned in rage toward the Rat Catcher who had just ruined his shot at homicidal glory.

When Patrick regained partial consciousness hours later, he was lying on a filthy mattress with an IV bag that had been used a hundred times or more hanging from a hook above his arm. His back was numb from a coating of lidocaine. The IV drip he guessed to be antibiotics and some sort of opiate solution, judging from the dopey sensation in his head of floating a finger's breadth above the mattress. A man in a soiled smock came over to him as he opened his eyes and shoved a thermometer into his mouth. He looked at it, frowned, and injected the contents of a hypodermic needle into the IV bag. Patrick felt himself drifting slowly away until he was enveloped in a morphine cocoon.

Two days later, he was well enough to be relocated to a small building on the outskirts of the camp. The Rat Catcher himself visited and told him that he owed his survival to the benevolence of the Supreme Commander Kim Jong-un and Comrade Moon. He would be held there until his trial for espionage.

"When will they come for me?" Patrick slurred, his tongue an inch thick from dehydration.

The Rat Catcher shrugged and blew his nose into his handkerchief. "Comrade Moon will send for you when he is ready. You must be a very important spy. Cho has killed many with that whip. You and I are both very lucky I came back when I did."

"Why is Comrade Moon taking a personal interest in me?"

The Rat Catcher shrugged again as he lit a cigarette. "You will have a fair trial and then shot. Better than the whip, don't you think?"

Patrick said nothing. The Rat Catcher continued. "I don't think Bill Clinton will take you home. No one in America even knows you are here."

Patrick remained silent and felt himself drifting back into the arms of Morpheus. But not before he wondered, *How did he know that I'm not Canadian?*

Hours later Patrick's eyes opened by fractions, and he found himself lying in the dark, confused and disoriented by the morphine. The moon was low in the sky, more early morning than late night. Nauseous from lack of food, his back burning as though it had been painted with acid, he turned over on his side and began to raise himself up until he felt the IV tugging at the skin of his forearm. He clenched his jaw and yanked it out. Pulling on the metal bar that surrounded the bed, he was gradually able to bring himself into a standing position. He was dressed in an old pair of pajamas, and his clothes were nowhere in sight. As quietly as possible he crept his way to the door and pressed his ear to its frosted glass window. A loud snoring sound came from the other side.

The pain of simply moving shot adrenaline through his system and helped clear it of the drugs they had been pumping into him for two days. In the near total darkness, he steadied himself on a table that sat next to the only window in the room. He felt for a latch on the window. It was sealed shut. But as he drew back, still clutching the table for balance, his hand brushed against the hypodermic needle that had been used to fill his IV bag. He shook it and heard a faint sloshing sound. Was it the drug that had kept him under, or just an antibiotic or saline solution? The watch of the man snoring outside beeped the hour. Time to move.

Looping his thumb through the plunger of the syringe, Patrick made a gagging sound from deep in his throat, coughing and choking as if desperately trying to fill his lungs with air. Sure enough, the snoring on the other side of the door stopped, replaced by the sound of a metal chair sliding across the floor. A light went on outside the door accompanied by a frantic jangling of keys. The lock clicked and the door flew open. As the guard hurried inside, Patrick cupped his hand tightly over his mouth, and plunged the syringe into his neck. After a moment a bewildered look came over the man's face. As he lost motor control, Patrick guided his body down onto the floor. The guard's breathing weakened and his eyelids fluttered closed. He would be out for hours. Patrick stripped him of his uniform and changed into it. It was much too small but would have to do. He relieved the guard of his flashlight and covered all but a thin strip of its lens with the black electrical tape that had been used to hold his IV catheter in place.

Once outside the infirmary, he paused to allow his eyes to adjust to the darkness and searched for something, anything, that might aid in determining which way to go next. The camp stretched for kilometers in either direction but was divided into sub-compounds of four to six huts each, depending on the work unit of the prisoners housed there. The question was, which sub-compound was Yumi housed in? Looking around in all directions, his eyes settled on a hill rising above the camp which he recognized as the location of the cemetery he had seen on the way in with Choy and the young kids. Walking slowly in its direction, he saw the four tiny huts behind which they had waited for Jebby's mother to return. Surer of his bearings now, he quickened his pace and within a minute had covered the distance to the huts.

He crept along the side of the first one and squinted through a space between the slats. Shining the guard's flashlight inside, he could just barely make out six people sleeping inside, their bodies spectral in the faint light. All of them were men, which suggested that the huts were segregated by sex, and that the women's dwelling was one of the other three. The faintest tincture of indigo diluted the blackness of the horizon. A single bird chirped tentatively in its nest. Time was growing short. He moved on to the next hut.

Lifting a wooden latch out of its socket, he gingerly eased open the door. As he slowly panned the room with the flashlight, his hand jumped at the sound of a truck engine turning over nearby, probably some of the guards preparing for another day of casual sadism. Again, the people in this hut were all men, and he padded more quickly over to the third hut. Another truck engine started up closer down the road. If this was the wrong hut, it was unlikely he'd have time to check the last of the four. Still another truck started. This was no time to be timid.

He took a deep breath and lifted the latch of the third hut, tiptoed inside and gently shook one of the sleeping figures. It was an old woman who moaned softly, turned away, and went back to sleep. But at least he had found one of the women's quarters. Moving on to the next cot, he tugged at the ragged blanket. Too young, only a teenager. Just then, another woman suddenly jerked up out of sleep, and Patrick stopped dead in his tracks. The rumble of approaching trucks grew louder.

With her eyes never leaving Patrick, the woman pulled herself and began shaking the person sleeping next to her. That woman coughed once and bolted straight up. Patrick had not seen Yumi in well over a year, but in spite of her matted hair and the rags which barely covered her, her eyes gave her away. The same eyes that had melted into his as they made love. Unmistakable. Tears welled up in his eyes at the thought of what she had gone through during the weeks of her imprisonment.

"What are you doing here?" Yumi hissed, instantly panic-stricken. "If they find you here, they'll kill us all!"

"I've come for you," Patrick whispered urgently.

"No! No!" Yumi exclaimed under her breath, her head shaking vehemently. "These people saved my life! If I go, they'll be tortured and killed. I'm not leaving them!"

Just then one of the work trucks squealed to a halt in front of the first hut Patrick had checked. Yumi's eyes followed the sound of guards pounding on doors and yelling for people in the four huts to pile onto the trucks for their work detail. Mere seconds remained until they would start throwing open doors and violently rousting the laggards.

Yumi's face twisted in fear. "Go now!"

Her fellow prisoners were shuffling numbly toward the door.

"Not without you!" Patrick insisted.

"I told you, I'm not going!" Her whisper was at once frantic and resolved.

"Then tell me where your father is! If they know where he is, they'll let you go!"

"If they know where he is, they'll kill him and then they'll kill me!"

By now Yumi was shaking uncontrollably. Tears spurted from her eyes, and she struggled desperately to keep from sobbing out loud. Patrick fought the instinct to simply snap her up in his arms and spirit her away from this place of evil forever, but he knew that she would never forgive him for what would then surely happen to her friends.

Yumi stabbed a finger at the back door. "Wait outside till they take us away. Then go!"

Patrick's jaw trembled, and the most profound pity he had ever felt for a human being welled up from the depths of his heart. He took her head in his hands and brought her face close to his. "I swear to you, I'll come back for you. I swear it!"

Yumi grabbed his hand and led him quickly to the back door of the hut. Patrick turned to face her one more time and started to speak. Yumi held up her hand.

"Go *now!*" she commanded. But Patrick couldn't just leave her like this. As he again took hold of her arm, the latch of the front door began to lift, and a guard yelled furiously that a good whipping awaited any prisoner not in the work truck in ten seconds. In the split second before he flung open the door and made good on his threat, Yumi shook off Patrick's arm.

"Dragon Mountain," she whispered. "I just remembered about it this morning, it's the only thing I can think of." Then she pushed him out the back door.

CHAPTER 24

OUTSIDE OF SENGHORI PRISON
April 9

Once down the trail leading to and from Senghori Prison, Patrick located the tree where Choy had cached their money, changes of clothes, and Patrick's passport. As he changed out of the ill-fitting uniform of a North Korean prison guard, his mind went back to the volley of shots he had heard when he was captured. The fact that Choy hadn't gotten to the cache first was a near-certain indication that he, Jebby and Sun-yi had been cut down as they tried to escape down the hill. Sad as that thought was, Patrick forced himself to concentrate on his own escape across the border.

The tunnel that Choy had spoken of lay on the far side of a hill just across Chongnyon Street, the main road they had come in on. A ten-foot-high fence surrounded it. Patrick removed a thin metal band that he kept secreted in the lining of his shoe at all times and picked the lock on the fence. He was through the dank two-mile length of the tunnel in less than an hour, thanks to the infirmary guard's flashlight that flickered out just as he neared the end. Emerging from the tunnel just outside of the village of Daeseong-dong in South Korea, he waited till mid-morning and bluffed his way onto one of the DMZ tour buses, telling them he had wandered off from the previous tour group and been left behind. Once back in Seoul, he took the next flight back to Tokyo. When he arrived back in Kamakura, he collapsed onto his futon. Yumi's face flickered through his mind as he drifted off.

The next morning broke cold and clear, and at 5 a.m., Patrick donned his leather jacket over a thick sweater, pulled his leather cap down over his ears, and began the motorcycle ride down to the town of Mishima at the foot of Mount Fuji, for once in his life observing speed limits. He doubled back several times along the way to spot anyone who might be following him. Satisfied that he was on his own, he crossed the city limits two hours later and sped up a steep incline at the top of which was a Zen monastery called "Ryusanji." The Dragon Mountain Temple. Years before he had spent weeks at a time at the monastery during intensive retreats. He stopped the bike for a moment at the main gate, closed his eyes, and allowed a tide of nostalgia to wash over him from the tolling of the low gongs signaling the beginning of the monks' work period in the fields.

Instead of turning into the main gate, he pulled his leather cap down low over his head and coasted along a back road in search of a tiny house that a former abbot had used for solitary meditation retreats years earlier. After Goro Takara, Yumi's father, developed ulcers from the stress of running his pachinko parlor/drug transshipment point, Yumi urged him to take up zazen, which he did, finding a modicum of relief from his stomach pain. He began attending week-long retreats and was even granted, on account of his age and medical condition, permission to sleep in the old abbot's meditation house instead of in the temple proper with the rest of the retreat participants. If Mr. Takara was anywhere in the vicinity of the temple, Patrick figured, it would be at this little house.

As the house came into view, he dismounted from his Road King and began to chant the "Dai-hi-shin" *dharani*, a sutra said to offer protection from worldly danger. He remembered that Mr. Takara had a special devotion to that particular *dharani* owing to his perilous line of work, and within seconds a wizened face appeared at the window. Patrick walked up to the house, and the door was opened a crack. Looking around the area one last time to see if he had been followed, he quickly slipped in.

Yumi's father, clad in a faded brown monk's robe stained with the detritus of recent meals, cowered behind the door, his eyes cratered with sleeplessness and anxiety. Patrick at first didn't recognize him, since he appeared to have aged at least a decade since the last time they had met.

"Did anyone see you come up here?" Mr. Takara asked in a dry, rattling whisper.

"No, I was very careful."

Despite Patrick's assurance, the old man peered out the window before turning back to Patrick.

"Have you seen Yumi?" he asked, in a voice filled with dread at any answer Patrick might give.

"Yes. She is being held in a prison camp in North Korea."

Like the sound of someone being impaled, a visceral moan erupted from the old man's gut. He stared at the ground and shook his head from side to side. "It is all my fault. I will never forgive myself for what has happened to her." His body began to spasm with sobs. Patrick lay a hand on his shoulder. His own feelings had been much the same when he left Yumi at Senghori. But the empathy he felt for the man was superseded by a need to know exactly what had led to Yumi's abduction.

"What did you take from them? Why was it so valuable that you would put your only daughter in this kind of danger?"

"I didn't know they would go looking for her!" Takara howled in protest. Gradually his wails diminished into whimpers, and he sobbed out the story in halting, staccato bursts. How he had been recruited into a yakuza family with ties to North Korea. How he had allowed them to use his pachinko parlor to stockpile their drugs.

"But then Mr. Pung came to my place of business. He's Comrade Moon's right-hand man. We had done business together for many years. This time I could tell he was on the run from the cops by the way he kept looking out the window. He had a small suitcase which he said he would come back for the following day. As always, I was told not to open anything, and he said that if the police came, I should give them any drugs I had stashed away and say they were mine. But in no case were they to find out about that suitcase." Mr. Takara's voice grew scratchy in the telling of his story, and Patrick brought him a glass of water which he gulped down completely before continuing.

"After Mr. Pung left, I heard sirens outside and went down to the cellar to hide the suitcase in a space behind a false wall I have down there. But as I was carrying it, I could hear something clanging around inside. I was feeling really bad about the drugs I had gotten onto the street, and the only thing I could think about was the terrible thing Mr. Pung must have had in the suitcase that he was willing to sacrifice a big drug shipment for it. He warned me that if the suitcase was tampered with, it would blow the whole place sky-high, but I tried to feel what was inside it anyway. There were two containers inside, and my mind went back to that poison gas attack in the Tokyo subway in 1995. All I knew was that if even one person was harmed by it, I would never forgive myself, and it looked like it could harm a lot more than one person. I know the drugs I helped them hide over the years killed people too, but this..." His voice trailed off and then rose again in a plaintive wail. "And now, my Yumi, my precious Yumi!"

"Where is the suitcase now?" Patrick asked.

"Now do you understand why I did what I did? My life has been a living hell, I tell you, hell!"

The old man's self-absorption was too much to take. Patrick shook him by the shoulders. "This isn't about you, dammit, tell me where the fucking suitcase is!"

Mr. Takara's lip quivered, but he got up and walked unsteadily to the window. Seeing no one, he motioned Patrick to follow him out the back door. They walked a short distance along a footpath, and then Mr. Takara led the way through a waist-high briar-patch leading down the side of a hill. In a matter of moments they were completely invisible to anyone above. Or so they thought.

Mr. Takara continued walking to a cave whose entrance was inexpertly concealed with tree branches and uprooted bushes. When they reached the entrance, he pointed inside. Patrick quickly kicked the bushes out of the way and entered. After giving his eyes a moment to adjust, he was gradually able to make out a small mound covered by a blue plastic tarpaulin in the far corner. He walked over and pulled it off. A softshell suitcase lay on its side on the ground. Remembering what the old man had said about it possibly being booby-trapped, he lifted it up slowly by the handle.

As he transported it to the mouth of the cave with small, light steps, he called out to Yumi's father. No reply. He set the suitcase back down and crept forward. He called again. Still nothing. As he inched his way out of the cave, something heavy and hard crashed down on his head, but his leather cap absorbed some of its force. As he fell, a man wearing a black ski mask dashed into the cave and grabbed the suitcase. From his position on the ground, Patrick was able to hook a leg around the man's knee, but the man kicked free and delivered a perfect taekwondo knee-extension to Patrick's face, dropping him momentarily.

Seeing his opening, Patrick's assailant dashed to the mouth of the cave with the suitcase, but Patrick reached out and grabbed hold of one of his legs. From out of his belt the man produced a foot-long metallic object which, with the press of a button, immediately turned into a three-foot-long metallic object which he plunged like a jousting lance into Patrick's solar plexus. Patrick gasped from deep in his throat, struggling without success to re-inflate his lungs. The world bled of color as he fell to his knees, and the man then followed up with a vicious kick to the temple behind the eye, the softest part of the skull. Patrick went down hard and stayed down.

His assailant drew a silenced pistol and aimed at Patrick's head. With one ounce of pressure to go on the trigger, he turned at the sound of approaching voices. Racing out of the cave, the man brandished the pistol at four monks who had coming running in from the fields. They held up their hands, and the man fled with the suitcase. When he was gone, the monks beheld with horror the double murder that had defiled sacred ground.

PYONGYANG
April 13

"Good news, Comrade Moon. We got the package back."

Moon looked up from his desk at Pung. A broad smile spread over his face. The news couldn't have come at a better time. He had just received word from the Commission that their patience with his plan was nearing an end. And when the Commission's patience ended, so did lives. A wave of relief washed over him as he offered Pung a Cuban from a box on his desk.

"What happened to the father?" Moon asked as he lit Pung's cigar. Pung blew a plume of smoke up at the ceiling.

"Dead."

"And the American?"

Pung drew another contented puff. "Dead too, of course. Our man is a professional."

Moon sighed audibly and allowed his body to slump back in his chair. After so many hindrances, his plan was back on track. Now he would have some good news to tell the Commission.

After a respectful pause, Pung asked, "What shall we do about Takara's daughter at Senghori Prison? Kill her?"

Moon thought a moment as he puffed on his cigar.

"No," he said, casually musing on Yumi's fate. "We might as well get some use out of her. Have her sent to Special Unit 14, Dr. Lee's place. It's not far from where she is now." Pung turned to leave.

"Oh, and bring me the package," Moon called after him.

Pung bowed again and left.

Moon stubbed out his cigar and his face turned grim again. He went back to the spreadsheet from Bureau 39 that indicated a series of incremental depletions of its cash holdings in Macau's Eastern Star Bank. The Bureau's head accountant assured him it was merely a clerical error on the bank's part, but Moon would not rest easy until the money was accounted for down to the last chon. The door opened and his secretary poked her head in tentatively, afraid she might be disturbing him.

"He's here," she said in a tiny voice.

"Send him in." He put the spreadsheet in a desk drawer.

A moment later a man strode confidently into the room. His fluency in Korean was belied by his Caucasian features. "You sent for me, Comrade Moon?"

"Yes, thank you for coming. Please have a seat."

The man sat down in the chair facing Moon and met his eye without blinking.

"I have a matter of the utmost urgency and importance to the state," Moon began. "As you know, the Supreme Commander, Kim Jong-un, has many enemies in the world, people who are envious of the love his people hold for him, people such as yourself."

"I have the utmost respect and love for the Supreme Commander, Comrade Moon. I always regarded his father as my own father as well."

"And the Supreme Commander understands that. That is why in times of great need, he is compelled to call upon people such as yourself to make the ultimate sacrifice for the good of the fatherland."

At the words "ultimate sacrifice" the man's eyes widened slightly but nothing else in his demeanor suggested anything approaching fear.

"I place myself entirely in his hands, Comrade Moon. If he decides that I should walk through hell itself for the sake of the fatherland, he can be sure I will do so without hesitation."

"Then you will help him?"

"I am ready to make the ultimate sacrifice, Comrade, I have already said so."

Moon took measure of the man. Such an idealist. Such a devotee of Kim Jong-il and now Kim Jong-un. Such a fool. But a useful fool.

"The mission we have chosen you for involves traveling to Kaesong right before the Glorious Triumvirate Celebration. Once in Kaesong you will set in motion an event that will start a war with the southern puppets. There are many details to the mission."

"I am totally at your service, Comrade Moon."

"Good." Moon pressed a buzzer on his desk.

Pung came back into the room. He was holding a softshell suitcase.

CHAPTER 25

MISHIMA HOSPITAL
April 16

"Is he conscious yet?"

"No."

"But it's been three days."

"Give him time. His constitution is strong."

"Is there a chance he might not make it?"

The surgeon measured his words before he spoke. "One never knows in cases like this. But the blow was to the most delicate part of the skull," he said, indicating a point just behind his right eye.

The surgeon then left the room where Patrick lay in a coma. The abbot of the Dragon Mountain Temple placed his hand gently on Patrick's head, as if to take his injury upon himself. He stayed by his side for two more days, but Patrick remained unresponsive. Finally, the abbot gave up hope and returned to his temple.

-Dad, is that you?

-Looks like you took a pretty bad knock on the head.

-I'm getting rusty. I should have had him. Is Mom there, too?

-She didn't want to see you like this.

-Am I here for good?

-No. It's not your time yet. Someone needs you here.

Two days later

"He just moved his eyelid! Get the doctor!"

A week later Patrick was eating baby food and hobbling about unaided. The only evidence of his injuries was the cut in his scalp from when he had fallen in the attack in the cave. It had been sutured closed and bandaged. The stitches had been removed when he was unconscious and his salt-and-pepper hair was already growing back over it, but with a bit more salt to the mix than before.

As he tried to piece together the dream he had had of his father, the neurologist came into the room.

"You're a very lucky man. Another blow like the last one, and you probably won't get up again."

"But that's what they were saying a week ago. I saw my medical chart."

"All I'm saying is don't press your luck," the doctor chided. "You're not a cat. And you're no samurai either, otherwise your attacker would have gone down, not you."

"You really know how to hurt a guy."

"From what I've heard, so do you."

A further week of recovery later, Patrick returned home to Kamakura.

KAMAKURA
April 25

Patrick sat cross-legged on the tatami floor of his cabin sipping tea and mulling over the events of the past several weeks. The common denominator in just about everything that had happened to him in North Korea was Comrade Moon. Moon, Moon, Moon. Everywhere he turned, he kept coming back to that name. It gnawed at his brain like a half-remembered melody.

Then he remembered Yumi's face, gaunt from starvation and unspeakable abuse, and a deep sense of remorse for having left her there welled up in his heart, even though it had been she who forced him to leave. His resolve to return and free her from Senghori had become an unshakeable commitment.

And based on all he had experienced in North Korea the first time, he now realized without a doubt that lethal force was inevitable when he returned. But how could he, a would-be Buddhist monk, take the life of another human being? On the other hand, if killing was the only way to save Yumi, how could he not? He needed answers, and every moment he waited was a moment that Yumi withered away further in the dark circle of hell known as Senghori Prison.

A thin cloud of incense wafted through a Kamakura alleyway at the end of which stood Eiwa-ji, the Temple of Eternal Peace, rising imposingly on ancient oak pylons. Patrick shut off his motorcycle and felt as though drawn by an unseen hand as he walked down the narrow lane toward the temple gate. When he reached the *genkan* entrance he removed his muddy boots and stepped up onto the tatami matting of the meditation hall, his footfalls echoing through the cloistral hush of the temple. He padded barefoot to the back of the meditation hall and knocked gently on a pinewood door at the rear of the temple.

"*Gomen kudasai*," he called out softly, apologizing in advance for any disturbance.

"*Dare desu ka?*" a voice called out. *Who's there?*

"Patrick *desu.*"

"*Doozo.*" *Come in.*

"*Hisashiburi*," Yasuhara Roshi wheezed as Patrick entered. *It's been a long time.* He struggled to raise himself up on the futon bed, and Patrick rushed over to help him.

"Please excuse my rudeness in not coming sooner. I've been traveling," he said while propping a pillow under the Roshi's head. The old man, now more comfortable, kept hold of Patrick's arm. His grip was still strong.

"You have been doing zazen?" he asked.

"Not so much lately, I'm sorry to say. I feel as though I need a week-long retreat. Maybe later in the year. Right now, though, I'm just too busy. But I wanted to come by and see how you were doing."

"Thank you for thinking of me. It's just a bad cold. I can tell from your eyes, though, that this is more than a social visit." As always, the Roshi cut through to the essential.

Patrick held the old man's probing gaze. Then he nodded.

"I am sorry to be so direct, but there isn't much time. I've come to ask you an important question."

The Roshi said nothing but continued to look into Patrick's eyes. Patrick couldn't help but notice how much the old man had aged in the few months since he had last seen him. His eyes, once so expressive and lively, were now clouded over with cataracts.

"What is your question?"

Patrick paused to consider how he would frame his dilemma and then began. "After evening meditation we chant, 'Life and death is the Great Matter. . .'"

"Yes."

"I've come to ask you if it is ever permissible for a monk to take a life. A human life."

The old man's eyes narrowed as if trying to see into Patrick's soul.

"But you're not a monk."

"I hope to be someday soon. That's why I need to know if it's ever permissible for a monk to kill."

"You mean in your past? I know you were a soldier of some kind..."

"No. My future. My near future."

"Is this about Yumi?"

"Yes."

"Is she still...missing?"

"Yes and no. That's why I've come to ask you this question."

The old teacher was silent for a long moment, then gestured for Patrick to let him fall back on the pillow. After he had settled into a comfortable position, he pointed a bony finger at a small desk on the other side of the room.

"Third drawer," he said.

Patrick went over to the desk and opened the drawer. The only object inside was a rectangular cedarwood box of a type used to hold calligraphy implements. He removed it from the drawer and brought it over to Yasuhara Roshi.

"Open it," the old teacher said. When Patrick did so, he found inside, not calligraphy implements, but rather a stack of sepia-tinted photographs, their perforated edges crumbling into confetti. Yasuhara Roshi gestured for Patrick to pass them to him. With trembling hands, he took the photos and began thumbing through half a dozen of them until he got to one near the bottom. He brought it close to his eyes and held it up for Patrick to see. Two teenagers dressed in uniforms of the Imperial Japanese Army, their arms draped around each other's shoulders, grinned back at the camera.

"Is that you on the left, Roshi?" Patrick asked. The old man nodded.

"And who is the other boy?"

"That was my best friend, Taizo Miura." As the old man spoke the name, his eyes went distant and he began hacking from deep in his lungs, a long, desperate spasm that brought a look of alarm to his face. After a moment, he managed a deep breath and looked again at the photo in his hand.

"That was taken in China in 1944. Have you ever heard about that time?"

Patrick nodded.

"Taizo Miura, Taizo Miura..." the old man said, repeating his friend's name over and over as though conjuring his spirit. "He once rescued a puppy that some of the others wanted to cook for dinner, and fed it from his own rations. He would even step out of the way of bugs crawling on the ground. I never knew a gentler person in my life." He stared at the photo as if in a trance. "I killed him." Patrick's breath caught in his throat. The Roshi continued.

"We had just been drafted into the Army out of high school. They sent us to China and had us train using our bayonets on haystacks. Then one day they announced we weren't using haystacks anymore. Taizo and I hid in the back of our platoon. I looked over at him. He looked like a ghost, his face completely white. The others at the front of the platoon were coming back covered head to foot with blood, and when Taizo saw them he ran into the trees."

Yasuhara Roshi again paused and looked at the photo as a single tear formed in his eye. "Some of the bigger draftees caught him and dragged him forward. They fixed a bayonet on the end of his rifle and pointed in the direction of the next victim, a young Chinese boy maybe fourteen years old. Taizo was literally shaking. The others laughed and started taunting and pushing him. I'll never forget that, all these guys covered with blood laughing at Taizo because he wouldn't kill a young kid.

"All of a sudden Taizo yelled out, 'Kill me instead! Someone please kill me instead!' In the commotion I had taken cover behind a small berm. I took a deep breath, aimed my rifle at his heart and fired. He went down instantly. Then I killed the sergeant and three corporals who were supervising the executions. The men in the platoon either thought it was some kind of divine intervention, since Taizo had just asked to be killed, or they thought the Chinese resistance was attacking. At any rate, they all dispersed and took up defensive positions. The young Chinese kid who was next in line to die was able to run away. Who knows, maybe he was caught and murdered later. But I like to think I saved his life that day. I saved his life by taking the life of the best friend I ever had."

Yasuhara Roshi looked one last time at the photo of Taizo Miura and then lovingly replaced it in the calligraphy box and closed the lid. He looked up at Patrick.

"You asked me if killing is ever justified."

Patrick nodded but wished he had never asked the question. He started to rise from his seat, but the Roshi spoke again.

"The older I get, the lonelier I am, Patrick. But that is the life I chose as a monk."

Patrick sat back down and waited for the old man to continue.

"But you, Patrick, you are not a real monk."

Patrick opened his mouth to protest. Yasuhara Roshi held up his hand. "I am talking about temperament. For me, wisdom of a sort has come from a life devoted to meditation and reflection. For you, though, that wisdom must come from somewhere else."

"Where?" Patrick said in a tight voice, confused and more than a little hurt.

"From love."

Patrick was taken aback. He had never heard the Roshi even use that word before. Compassion, yes, but not love. "But I've promised myself that I will attain the way of the Buddha, I must reach satori first. After that I can think about love all I like."

The Roshi shook his head and spoke in a gentle whisper. "But don't you understand? Love *is* satori. Everything you say or do is satori. You just don't realize that yet. You think, here is satori, and here is *real* life. Nothing could be further from the truth. We say, 'This very place is the Lotus Land, this very body is the Buddha.' Never forget that. It's not just nice-sounding words. You can love, you can work, you can paint, you can do *anything* and become enlightened. It's a matter of *forgetting* yourself, not becoming *more* involved with yourself. That's what a lot of monks do these days, you know. A monk's life is an escape for them. And I'm afraid that you have fallen into the same self-centered trap. But you are not like those other monks. You must stay in this world. And the best way for you to forget yourself in the midst of the world is to love someone. This is the most important lesson I can give you."

Patrick was thunderstruck. Yasuhara Roshi paused as if weighing what he was about to say next.

"We are all looking to become complete, to become part of a humanity that sometimes wants no part of us. I killed my best friend and for years I felt I had removed myself from civilized society. The others I killed that day I've never regretted for a second, but Taizo? Not a day goes by that I don't think of him. And I dealt with this problem in a way that has worked for me, by becoming a monk and praying for him in order to connect myself back to humanity. For you, though...I don't know what happened with you and Yumi, but I do know you will never be complete on your own. You need her for your completion, just as she needs you. You once told me about losing yourself in her. What else are you looking for? That is the whole point, to lose yourself. That is the only real wisdom there is, in Buddhism or anywhere else."

As the Roshi said this last part, Patrick struggled mightily against tears that were being wrung from his heart by a single question: *But what if she's already dead?* Not wanting to completely break down in his teacher's presence, he bowed in his seat and got up to leave. But then the old man's firm grip turned him around. Without a word, the flinty old Zen master who had saved him from himself all those years ago had him wrapped in a tight embrace. Patrick let the floodgate burst open and held onto the old man as if for life itself. His sobs of guilt for his self-centeredness toward Yumi tore through the night. Now he would atone for that self-centeredness. Right then and there, he made a solemn vow to himself to spirit her out of Senghori Prison even if it cost him his life.

The next morning he awoke before dawn with stinging eyes but a firm resolve in his heart. He rose, walked down the steps of his cabin, and returned to a familiar place in the forest.

After lowering himself down the steep hill to where the ground leveled off, he paced off two hundred yards and came to the small shed that held his weapons locker. Inside was his M5 Sabre Tactical rifle, his father's Colt .45 1911A, and ammunition and silencers for both weapons. As he prepared for his shooting *kata* he thought back to the dream he had had of his father when he lay in Mishima Hospital. *Someone needs you here*, his father had said. *But had it really been a dream?* he wondered, ramming a magazine into the M5. Then he was brought back to reality. What was inarguably real was that Yumi was dying in a North Korean prison camp. That is, if they hadn't already killed her.

A sense of urgency quickened his step as he walked up to the firing line and then let loose with over 50 silenced rounds in quick succession. Then he fired five mags with the Colt at a target 30 yards away. Every round found its mark. He replaced the rifle in the locker, tucked his father's Colt into his waistband, and walked out of the forest with unblinking eyes.

PART THREE

CHAPTER 26

April 26

Later in the day it began to rain heavily, and instead of riding his motorcycle, Patrick took the train to Tokyo and began walking to the American Embassy in the Akasaka district. There was a man he needed to see, and a block from the embassy, he saw him.

"Fitz!" he called out and began waving madly to a tall, thin, bearded man walking down the opposite side of the street. The man turned and peered intently in Patrick's direction. His jaw dropped.

"Patrick?" the man called out in disbelief.

Jack Fitzroy, the Agency's oldest hand and top spycraft developer in Asia, waved Patrick over. "I can't believe you're here. They've been searching the whole country for you. What happened?"

It took Patrick a full ten minutes to relate the details of what had happened since the last time he had seen Fitz.

"And now I have to go back," Patrick said.

Fitzroy's head snapped back. "Are you out of your mind? After all that?"

"I told you, Yumi's being held in a prison camp. You need to help me."

"But it would be insane for you to go back! I'm not helping you commit suicide, for God's sake. Hooper would have my head if he knew I let you go back."

Patrick folded his arms across his chest and held Fitz's eye. "Then don't tell him."

"Did you hear what I said? You can't go back," Fitz shouted.

Patrick didn't respond.

"You. Can't. Go. Back!" Fitz shouted even louder.

Patrick didn't respond.

Fitz's mouth tightened. He sighed loudly. "Shit. Follow me," he said.

They continued to the far end of the alley, where Fitzroy took a palm-sized plastic box from his pocket and waved it at a thick steel door. The door opened and they walked inside.

"You must have a goddam death wish. But I can tell there's no stopping you," Fitz said. His eyes shifted back and forth in thought. "You might as well have a fighting chance," he mumbled. "And for God's sakes, don't ever tell Hooper I did this," he said in a louder voice.

He walked over to a closet, unlocked it and emerged with an item he held up for Patrick to see. "It's a long shot, but if you don't mind being a guinea pig..."

Patrick face screwed up in bewilderment. "Batman?" he asked.

"Try Superman. Batman can't fly."

Patrick took the object and weighed it in his hands. "Light."

"A lot lighter than when we first started working on it. Try it on. It's our latest in bio-mimetics."

Fitzroy helped Patrick harness on a delta-wing that felt no heavier than a third grader's half-empty backpack. Then he picked up what looked to be two foot-long lengths of exhaust pipe. "It'll be a bit heavier with the rockets on, but you won't need those until just before you jump."

"Rockets? Jump? What the hell is this thing?"

"I wanted to call it the 'Dragonfly' but Langley decided on the Griffin1-A. You'll be able to HAHO [high altitude, high opening] on the friendly side of the DMZ and then...you fly. That is, if it even works. We've done some preliminary tests, but not in the field."

"What about North Korean radar?"

"Shouldn't be a problem. The signature's not nearly as big as falling the whole way with a parachute on, and you can deploy a mini-drogue chute once you're under their radar. Here, try the helmet on."

Patrick pulled the feather-light polymer helmet down over his head. Inside the faceplate was a glowing array of holographic indicators.

"Those displays you're seeing will give you the navigation data you'll need. When you go in for your approach, you fire up the jets..." Fitzroy held up the small pipes, "...and you can even boost up over hills in terrain-following mode. When you're ready to touch down, you pop the drogue, and release the Griffin so that it hits the ground first. Once you exit the plane on the South Korean side, you've got a range of about 100 miles." Fitz paused. "Are you sure you want to go through with this?"

Patrick folded his arms again. Fitz took out his cell phone. "Alright. Give me a minute. I'm going to arrange for your... test flight."

Fitzroy spoke softly into the phone, powered off, and motioned with his head for Patrick to follow him. They came to a walk-in closet holding hundreds of articles of clothing, including the chameleon suit Patrick had seen the last time.

"Take your pick," Fitzroy said, handing Patrick a small backpack. "It's all coated with Shear Thickening Fluid, the stuff I showed you last time that hardens on impact with a bullet before it can do any real damage."

Patrick filled the backpack with STF-coated clothing as well as an extra bottle of the fluid and followed Fitzroy to the steel door they had come in through.

"There's a car out back," Fitzroy said, tossing Patrick a set of keys. "Atsugi Naval Air Base. They'll be waiting for you. When you get to the gate, you'll be met by one of the people we work with in development. Now get going, you've got a plane to catch. And don't dare blame me when you're doing a life sentence in some gulag."

"Don't worry, Fitz."

But Fitz had already gone back inside.

Before pulling onto the highway, Patrick stopped at Akasaka Station, bought a prepaid cell phone at a kiosk and made a call to Professor Park, his mentor in Korean art during his university days.

NORTH KOREA
Special Unit 14
April 27

As Patrick prepared for his return to North Korea, Yumi was being moved to a barracks-like building at Special Unit 14, a facility not far from Senghori Prison. Ostensibly a synthetic fiber factory, Special Unit 14 was actually a proving ground for chemical weapons. The rats that the Rat Catcher had trapped at Senghori Prison were used to measure the effects of various mixtures of gases until the scientist in charge, Dr. Lee Eun-bae, was ready to begin human trials. That time had come, and the trials were to be conducted on anyone even suspected of being part of the democracy underground.

Hundreds of dissidents had been taken to Unit 14 where they were forced into individual aluminum boxes the size of coffins. Each box was covered with a heavy lid with a round, plexiglass window built into it at face-level. Dr. Lee's every waking hour went into refining the mix of chemicals that went into the precise formulation of what he called Beulsun-X, or "tainted blood X", a form of nerve gas. The poison was tremendously expensive to manufacture, and Comrade Moon had instructed him to ascertain exactly how much of the substance was needed to kill an average human being as cost-effectively as possible. From there he would be able to calculate how much Beulsun-X was needed to wipe out every South Korean man, woman and child from the DMZ to Seoul. When Yumi arrived at Special Unit 14, all of the aluminum boxes were occupied by dissidents whose reactions to being slowly gassed to death were being meticulously recorded. The following day one of the boxes would become available and it would be Yumi's turn.

Yumi's health took a dramatic turn for the worse when she was separated from her fellow prisoners at Senghori. Despite the horrendous conditions they were forced to endure, they were able to find a measure of comfort in each other's company. Alone now, Yumi curled up in a ball on the floor of the barracks, overcome with despair and regret that she hadn't gone with Patrick when he had come for her.

"I feel so alone so alone so alone so alone," she moaned over and over again. As she lay curled up on the floor of Special Unit 14, her thoughts turned back to Patrick. She remembered his face at Senghori when he came for her. Then she remembered the afternoon when they decided to get married. Lying in bliss after making love, she spoke to him softly just to make sure he was real, and he answered for the same reason. It was as if they were one being, with no "I" or "you", just oneness calling and answering itself: I love you/I love you too.

"Let's stay here forever", Patrick had said, holding her tightly with his face nuzzled in her ear.

"We can't just make the rest of the world go away," Yumi said gently.

"We can try."

They made love. Their engagement began that day.

In the coming months he had dropped hints that he had had a change of heart. Like telling her about the state of deeply absorbed meditation called samadhi and how it gave him the feeling of "I need nothing". She felt that he was telling her that he didn't need her anymore. Then when he finally announced that he wanted to become a monk, she had felt an aching void in her head and heart, as if she had been eviscerated and was just a hollow encasement of flesh with nothing vital to encase. She wanted to go back and take him in her arms as she always did after an argument, kiss him, and restore the almost electric connection that had melded their souls for so long. She wanted to go to that place where her breathing was his breathing to the extent that the universe emptied itself of all else, and...

Just then a truck rumbling by outside her barracks jolted her back to the hopeless present.

CHAPTER 27

April 28

That night Patrick exited a De Havilland DHC-3 Super Otter at 30,000 feet over the south side of the DMZ. It was 4:17 a.m. and the first traces of dawn tinted the eastern horizon. In free fall to the earth, the wind rushed by his ears with hurricane force, but when he deployed the wings of the Griffin 1-A, he found himself suspended in the stratosphere, describing arcs and circles as he desired. It had been years since he last jumped, and when he left the Super Otter his feet instinctively felt for terra firma below them, but once his brain's gyroscope adjusted to the idea of flight, the gentle downward glide was all giddy delight. He looked up and was captivated by the spectacle of an ice ring surrounding the moon against a backdrop of stars mounted like multi-faceted diamonds mounted on an infinity of blackness.

With a tug on the aileron controls, the trailing edge of the right wing rose while that of the left wing lowered, creating a lazy roll like a falcon at play. He instinctively stifled a laugh, then realized that at six miles up not even the most sophisticated listening devices could pick him up anyway, and he let out a gut-busting guffaw into his oxygen mask. After weeks of anguish both physical and mental from his near-death at Senghori and his anxiety over whether Yumi would ever survive her imprisonment there, he felt temporarily liberated from even gravity, and part of him wished he could stay in this realm of unfettered freedom forever.

Turning south, Seoul's nightshine beamed the city's perpetual vitality into the sky even this close to dawn. But when he inclined the Griffin's wings northward, only a smattering of meager lights here and there punctuated the bleakness. Directly below him lay the city of Kaesong, and he tried in vain to pick out any landmarks that might give some indication as to the location of Senghori Prison. Nothing. But it wasn't time to go back there yet anyway. He would be as useless as he had been the last time. No, he had a rendezvous first with someone who might be able to help him. He fired the Griffin's two small rockets to propel him closer to a mountainous region between Kaesong and the DMZ.

As Patrick fired the rockets, a 32-year-old Korean man with matted hair and newly-graying beard bolted upright from his bed of rags and straw and hurried to the lip of his cave. With his night vision impaired by a diet low in carotene, he winced from a sharp pain behind his eyes as he willed them to take in more than blackness. Finally, he was just barely able to make out the silhouette of mountains in the burgeoning purple of dawn. His name was Nahm Myong-dae, leader of the dissident group, Rising Tide. He had been a wanted man for as long as he had lived in hiding with his followers in this warren of caves fifteen miles from Kaesong, and that sound he had heard could only mean one thing: someone unknown was approaching.

For a full ten minutes he rotated his head in probing arcs for a source of the sound but saw nothing. Finally, as the sky tinted into a faint pink of pearl, the shadows of false dawn became distinct objects, developing by degrees like a photograph in a darkroom. And then he caught sight of something high above, something falling slowly this way and that, like a feather suspended on a whisper.

Nahm took from his coat a pair of binoculars of a similar vintage as his M2 rifle. Locking onto the object gliding overhead, he positioned himself behind a granite outcropping as a canopy opened. He focused on the man's face as he descended in an arcing pendulum. Caucasian. Incredible. Nahm had zeroed the M2 just the day before for a distance of 400 meters. The white man who had just descended into his territory was easily within that range, and Nahm's eyes never left his target as he chambered a round to the sound of precisely machined metal locking tight against metal.

Patrick had shot an azimuth on the way down to a promontory in the distance, and he now made a final adjustment in its direction. During his phone call to Professor Park before driving to Atsugi Naval Air Base, his old mentor from college gave him detailed instructions for making contact with people he could trust in this area. He maneuvered the parachute toward the hill, but a sudden gust of wind blew him off course. A moment later his feet touched the earth. He rolled and did a lightning-fast scan in all directions. Nothing. At least nothing that he could see.

Nahm listened carefully to the sound of the intruder hacking his way through the thick underbrush. A half hour later, he saw the white man cut through the last swath of entanglement and come to the clearing 50 yards in front of where Nahm had positioned himself.

Patrick studied the topo map he had drawn based on Professor Park's dictated instructions. As he did so, Nahm aimed. Patrick central nervous system registered a clicking sound faster than his ears could, and he dropped to the earth. Nahm pulled the trigger and instantly chambered another four-inch bullet during the tenth of a second of recoil. He aimed again. The first shot was for effect. The next was for blood.

Patrick's heart raced uncontrollably. After the serenity of his free-fall through the heavens, he found himself suddenly thrust back into the earth-bound world of arbitrary and capricious violence. Burying his head into the undergrowth he shouted, "Day of days!" in Korean, the phrase Professor Park had said would be his contact code.

Nahm squinted suspiciously and waited a full minute. Then he called out in a menacing, guttural rasp for Patrick to turn around with his hands on his head. Then he closed the distance between them, his rifle raised. Once he had patted Patrick down thoroughly and been given the rest of the coded message from Professor Park, he relaxed and propped his rifle up against the granite outcropping. Half an hour later, they sat across from each other at the mouth of his cave eating a cold breakfast of goat meat and millet. A stone jug of tea steeped by the side of the fire pit just inside the cave.

Not a word passed between them throughout the simple meal. When they had finished eating and Nahm reached over to pour from the tea jug, Patrick broke the tense silence.

"*Yeogi-seo honja itteu yo?* [You are alone here?]," he asked, hoping he didn't sound too surprised—or disappointed.

"For the time being," Nahm replied without elaborating, focusing on the metal cup in his hand. Another five minutes passed. Then Nahm fixed Patrick with a penetrating stare. "Actually, there are thousands of us. Rising Tide is about to crest. Come with me."

They set down their cups and climbed to the top of the hill above the cave system. Nahm pointed to a column of white smoke rising from a village he said was called Darang-ri that lay far below where they stood. The smoke was from ceremonial fires burning all around the country in memory of relatives, many of whom had perished during the famine known as the Arduous March.

Nahm turned to Patrick.

"*That* is Rising Tide. I and others like me are just catalysts for what is to happen very soon. We will either succeed, or the streets of Pyongyang will run like rivers with our blood. Either way, the time for waiting has come to an end."

Nahm motioned with his head, and they walked half a mile to another cave which Nahm entered after requesting that Patrick wait outside. A few minutes later Nahm emerged dragging a long wooden crate by an ancient moldy rope. On the crate was stamped "U.S. Army" in faded green letters. Nahm smiled and set the crate in front of Patrick. "Open it."

Lifting the lid, Patrick picked up an M2 rifle of a similar vintage as the one Nahm had strapped to his back. It was almost perfectly preserved. Professor Park had bored him at college with his endless war stories, one of which held that his father had cached rifles in these very caves during the waning weeks of the Korean War. Now here was the actual evidence.

"Your father was a great friend of the Korean people," Nahm said still smiling.

Patrick cradled the M2 reverently, a sense of awe and pride welling up in his heart as he contemplated the very real possibility that the last hands to hold this rifle were his father's. A thrill rushed up his spine and out the top of his head like a spirit passing through him. Then he came back to the present moment.

"They don't still fire, do they?"

"Let's find out," Nahm said with grin, and he handed Patrick two more rifles and took three himself. He produced several cartons of shells from one of his inside pockets, and he led the way higher up into the mountains until they reached a box canyon where the villagers of Darang-ri hunted for wild boar with the small-gauge shotguns the government allowed them to own. Their gunfire would not stand out, and besides, the villagers were uniformly Rising Tide sympathizers.

For the rest of the afternoon they fired round after round at a target Nahm set up for them a quarter mile across a clearing with the mountain as a backstop. Even after six decades, the only adjustment the rifles needed was to their minute of angle, compensation for the bullet's downward deviation due to gravity and air resistance. At the end of the session, Patrick sat down on the ground and let exhaustion and exhilaration wash over him.

"These will work just fine for Rising Tide," he said, beaming at Nahm.

"We're not going to use them," Nahm said who didn't smile back.

Patrick's eyebrows shot up. "You have others?"

Nahm shook his head. "These were for the last Korean War, the one that's been going on for almost seventy years. This time we will use a different strategy."

Patrick was speechless for a second. "But how the hell do you expect to go up against the Korean People's Army? It'll be Tiananmen Square all over again."

"There is no way we could possibly win a shooting war against the People's Army," Nahm said softly, as though explaining simple addition to a child. "Tiananmen Square only had a few thousand demonstrators. We will have half a million. Not even the People's Army could prevail against those numbers."

"Half a million! Where are you possibly going to get that many people?"

"As I said, the time for waiting is over. I didn't just mean for the members of Rising Tide. Have patience, you'll see for yourself."

Patrick hid his skepticism. Is this what he was allying himself with, a bunch of starry-eyed idealists who were going to pull a Gandhi on the most murderous regime on earth?

That night as they ate, Patrick dropped a bombshell of his own as he told Nahm of his plan to rescue Yumi.

"From Senghori Prison?!" Nahm exclaimed. "It would be insane to attempt that on your own. Wait till the country is liberated, then you'll have more help than you'll need."

"I don't know if she'll last *that* long," Patrick said with more than a tinge of sarcasm.

"It won't be that long," Nahm said, ignoring the barb. "All of our cells will converge on Pyongyang for the Glorious Triumvirate Celebration this coming Tuesday. The only thing people have been waiting for is leadership and strength in numbers. I grew up here, and believe me, I know how much the people hate this regime. They just need a spark, and then all these years of anger and frustration that they've lived with will be our firepower. The army wouldn't dare attack. Besides, the foreign news groups will be broadcasting live around the world."

Nahm's eyes narrowed onto a small stone on the ground. He picked it up and began smoothing it with his thumb. "So if you can wait until Tuesday, we'll burn Senghori to the ground," he said, tossing the stone into a nearby puddle with concentric circles rippling outward.

"I'm not sure I can wait even that long," Patrick replied. "I'd like to go to Pyongyang and see if I can get help from some people I know there."

"Pyongyang's in the opposite direction of Senghori," Nahm said.

"I know, but it's only an hour away by car. There's a few people in Pyongyang who might be able to get me back to Senghori. I can't wait any longer to try and find Yumi."

A look of disappointment crossed Nahm's face, but he shrugged. "If that's what your heart tells you to do," he said without enthusiasm.

The next morning they set off on foot down the mountain through a dense pine forest that gave way to oak and maple as they reached the lower elevations. Two hours later, Nahm held up his hand and pointed. Patrick followed his finger and saw in the distance a gray ribbon of concrete cutting a swath of green through the forest.

"Do you see that maple tree that was struck by lightning? That's where this trail joins the Reunification Highway. From there you can go all the way to Pyongyang."

Nahm walked a little further along the trail and stopped at a collective shed used by the farmers of the area. He went inside and emerged a minute later pushing an ancient North Korean-made Bugang motorcycle. Compared to Patrick's Harley Road King at home, the bike was only marginally better than the one-speed Schwinn he had as a kid. He stifled a snort of derision.

"It's on its last legs, but it should be able to make one final trip to Pyongyang," Nahm said. "Don't worry about getting it back to us. And you'll definitely need these." He handed Patrick a helmet with a tinted visor and the uniform of a North Korean soldier. "There aren't a lot of foreigners out riding that highway." Patrick changed into the uniform, stowed his own clothes in the rear storage compartment, and climbed on.

"Once you get there, find a woman named Mrs. Pae who runs a jangmadang market near the Koryo Hotel."

"I've heard about her."

"She's one of ours. Tell her to get word to the northern provinces that we're on for Tuesday. And if you need anything, she's the one to ask."

"I'll tell her. Thank you for all your help."

"I have a feeling you'll be returning the favor before long."

Patrick brought his full weight down on the kick starter. Nothing. But on the fifth kick the bike finally coughed to life and then growled like an irritated bear awakened from an extended hibernation. The two new friends shook hands and Patrick began the descent down the trail leading to the Reunification Highway. Destination: Pyongyang.

CHAPTER 28

PYONGYANG
April 29

As Patrick approached the outskirts of the capital, he steered the decrepit Bugang onto a narrow pathway used by farmers as a shortcut to and from their fields. No one was about. He shut off the muttering engine and sat stock still on the bike searching for any sign that he had been spotted. Satisfied that he was alone, he climbed off the bike and pushed it into the high grass that bordered the path. He then stripped off the army uniform Nahm had given him and changed back into his own clothes.

From the lowering sun, he judged it to be at least 4 o'clock. He walked back to the highway, poked his head out of the little pathway and looked in both directions. No traffic. Emerging from the high grass, he headed in the direction of the capital. A hundred yards down the road, a car approached from the opposite direction, and Patrick's pulse surged in his ears at it got closer. The two men inside appeared to be officials of some type, judging from their dark blue suits and neckties. It was too late to jump off the road into the trees that lined the highway. Thinking fast, he urgently held up his hand. The vehicle slowed to a stop.

"Pyongyang? Pyongyang?" he said in a panicky voice he didn't need to feign. The men gawked at him with wide open mouths. Then the driver ever so slowly nodded his head.

"Pyongyang," he said and tossed his head back over his shoulder in the direction Patrick had been heading. They then drove off, wondering what the People's Republic was coming to with all these disgusting foreigners in town for the Glorious Triumvirate Celebration. And this one, traipsing about on the highway on his own without even a minder!

Half an hour of walking later, the Arch of Reunification marking the official city limits came into view. He had arrived.

He jogged over to a tram stop where a group of queued-up North Koreans stood agog at the sight of a man with Caucasian features coming their way. No one dared even whisper a word, fearing that anything negative they might say could be construed as an affront to the wisdom of the leadership which had decreed Pyongyang an open city for the week before and after the Glorious Triumvirate Celebration, with public transportation free to all for that time period. Still, a number of them drew back in fear. "They" all carry AIDS, they had been told. One couldn't be too careful.

He took the tram to the city center and walked in the direction of the Koryo Hotel. Mack, the "Mayor of Pyongyang", approached him in the opposite direction, a suitcase in his hand.

"Where have you been?" Mack asked. "It's been weeks since I last saw you. You've lost a lot of weight."

"I had to go back to Japan for awhile," Patrick said without elaborating. "Not staying for the big celebration?" he asked, changing the subject.

"I'm getting out of her while I still can," Mack replied grimly. A look of barely controlled terror filled his eyes. Patrick noticed flecks of gray in his beard he had not seen before. "There's a plane to Beijing at 7 p.m. I should just make it."

"What are you talking about?" Patrick asked.

"I have it on good authority that Comrade Moon is planning a coup for the day of the Glorious Triumvirate Celebration. Kim Jong-un will be assassinated, and there'll be a simultaneous attack of some kind at the DMZ."

"That's insane! How do you know this?"

"I have connections. The guy I heard it from is with the government. Or at least, he was. It looks like they've taken him in for questioning. I need to get out of here in case he mentions my name. If I were you, I'd be on that plane, too," he said and hurried off.

Patrick watched as Mack made his way to the hotel's taxi stand. He pulled the hood of his sweatshirt over his head and mingled with a group of other foreigners. They had come early for the Glorious Triumvirate Celebration and now just milled up and down the streets aimlessly, painfully aware of how deadly boring Pyongyang could be at night.

People's Security agents patrolling the streets on foot glowered hostilely at the foreigners whom they had always been taught were dirty and disease-ridden. As a pair of them swaggered by, Patrick canted his head up at the skyline and turned around and around as if lost in tourist wonderment in case any of them were from Choy's precinct and had seen him at their headquarters for the marathon games of baduk.

His first stop was the *jangmadang* black market near the Koryo Hotel. He walked up to the proprietress, Mrs. Pae, and introduced himself, and she motioned for him to follow. When they reached the stairwell of a surrounding building, Patrick whispered the news that Rising Tide was in its final stages of mobilization before converging on Pyongyang for the Glorious Triumvirate Celebration. Glancing around cautiously, he let his jacket fall open to reveal his father's Colt .45 pistol.

"Any chance you can hold onto some things for me?"

"Of course," she said, nonchalantly scanning the marketplace outside for security agents. She held out a cloth bag and Patrick deposited his gun, two spare magazines, and his passport, hoping the whole time that Professor Park and Nahm Myung-dae were right about her. Patrick thanked her and was off again.

The entire area shook with the rumbling of trucks and tanks moving into place for the military parade that would open the Glorious Triumvirate Celebration. Patrick walked two blocks down a side street leading from the *jangmadang* to a one-story building with a sign over its doorway reading "Foreign Outreach Institute". No light came from inside the front of the Institute, so Patrick circled around the back to what looked to be a service entrance. He slowly turned the doorknob. The door opened onto a dimly illuminated anteroom, on the opposite side of which led a stairway to a lower level. Easing off his boots, he tiptoed down the stairs in his socks, just barely able to make out a conversation coming from below: two voices, one high, one low. The voices became more distinct the lower he descended: a man and a woman. At the bottom of the stairs, a narrow band of light seeped from beneath a door. Recognizing one of the voices, he abandoned any semblance of noise discipline and gave a sharp rap on the door.

The conversation became agitated and then suddenly silent. A moment later, the male voice growled in Korean, "Who the hell is it?"

"Patrick."

The two voices rose in volume, the woman protesting something, the man conciliatory but insistent.

The door opened a crack to reveal the man with a look of alarm and confusion on his face. The woman wielded a pistol-like object and dashed behind a table stacked high with booklets of some kind. Patrick crouched instinctively, his eyes never leaving her hand.

"Relax for God's sakes, it's a staple gun," Tyler Kang said. "And that's Seo-mi, my fiancée."

Patrick's jaw dropped. *Tyler Kang engaged? God help her. God help the world, for that matter.* He walked quickly up to Tyler and pulled him into a two-man huddle facing away from his fiancée.

"Listen, there isn't much time," Patrick said in a low voice. "There's a plot on to assassinate Kim Jong-un on Tuesday and launch some kind of attack down at the DMZ."

Tyler's face registered no surprise. "I know all about the assassination."

Patrick's head jerked back. "You? How could you possibly know anything about that?"

"Because I'm the one who's going to do it"

"What?"

"Seems only fair, don't you think? Kim Jong-il's son for my parents?"

Patrick shook his head from side to side in utter bafflement. "Your *parents*? What the hell do your parents have to do with anything?"

The half-moon creases around Tyler's lips deepened. "I didn't come here to defect. Like I told you before, I came for revenge."

"Sorry, I'm still not getting any of this," Patrick said, annoyance at Tyler's cryptic statements rising in his voice.

"Then try this on for size. My parents were living in Saudi Arabia in 1988 and I was going to school in Seoul. I hadn't seen them in a year and they were coming to visit me in Seoul. But then their plane blew up, thanks to the 'Dear Leader' who wanted to sabotage the Seoul Olympics. I vowed I'd kill the motherfucker who killed my parents, except he died before I got the chance to nail his ass. So the son will have to do."

Patrick's face went slack and his shoulders slumped. "Oh Christ, Tyler.

Suddenly, Seo-mi jumped in. "You must not try to stop him! Kim Jong-un must die, and Tyler will end this vampire dynasty!"

With a look of utter disbelief on his face, Patrick turned back to Tyler.

"Tyler, this whole thing is beyond insane!"

"Comrade Moon will save our country!" Seo-mi shouted even louder. "He will be our Great Leader when all the bloodsucker Kims are gone!"

Patrick's head fell to his chest as he exhaled loudly from the back of his throat. "Come here," he said and dragged Tyler to the opposite side of the room while Seo-mi folded her arms and fumed silently. He pulled Tyler's face close to his.

"Listen and listen good, Kohai," he hissed in a whisper. "Moon's killed thousands of people in the concentration camps, one of whom might be someone very close to me if I haven't gotten back here in time. You think he's the savior of this country? Think again! He's the one responsible for just about everything that goes wrong here." Patrick's breath came in rapid spurts, and Tyler looked into his eyes, suddenly thoughtful. Patrick's intensity had clearly made an impression.

Tyler said nothing, but his face betrayed a flicker of doubt as he turned back to Seo-mi. She could see the uncertainty in his eyes, and she swore furiously as she stormed out of the room. Tyler followed and closed the door behind him. A few moments of silence were followed, inevitably, by Seo-mi screaming in rage. Feeling helpless and still in shock from what Tyler had revealed of his cockamamie revenge plot, Patrick picked up one of the booklets Seo-mi had been stapling and began thumbing through its pages one after the other in nervous energy. Each page had a patriotic inscription on top and a series of diagrams and numbers printed in the bottom portion. Not knowing what it was but having a feeling it might be tied up with the assassination plot, he stuffed one of the booklets into his jacket.

Ten minutes of shouting back and forth later, Seo-mi led the way back in, her arms folded and her head held high in triumph. Tyler walked with his head down over to Patrick and spoke in a low voice.

"Sorry, Sempai, I gotta go with the woman I love, and she thinks you're full of shit about Moon."

"And what do you think, Tyler? Or does she do all your thinking for you?"

Disgusted and running out of time, Patrick took no time at all to decide that rescuing Yumi was infinitely more important than preventing Tyler from pulling the trigger on North Korea's newest dictator.

"I never thought I'd live to see Tyler Kang pussy-whipped," he called out as he raced up the stairs and out of the building.

CHAPTER 29

THE WHITE HOUSE SITUATION ROOM
April 30

A military aide poked his head into the Situation room. "Mr. President, we've tried calling the DMZ command in South Korea and still haven't been able to raise General Merkin on the secure line," he informed President Dillard.

"Dammit, where the hell is he?" the President exploded. "That guy's liable to start a nuclear war if he finds out about General O's mobilization at the DMZ. I gave orders for him to be in contact 24/7. "

"Sorry, sir, I don't know. I spoke to his second-in-command, a Colonel Lawrence, and he can't find him."

"Jesus," the President muttered darkly. "Let me know as soon as you hear anything from him. No matter what I'm doing, that takes priority."

"Yes, sir."

"Goddamn fucking cowboy!" The President spat out the words as he stormed out of the Situation Room.

CHAPTER 30

PYONGYANG
April 29

When he had been captured at Senghori Prison, Patrick heard shots ring out a moment after Choy and the two young kids ran back down the mountain trail. Was that proof that they were dead? No. But at this point he was desperate and completely without allies, now that Tyler had thrown in with the plot to kill Kim Jong-un. He needed to get back to Senghori. That was all that mattered. And if there was a chance, however remote, that Choy was somehow still alive, there might also be a chance, even more remote, that he might be willing to go back and help rescue Yumi.

Patrick darted in and out of the groups of foreigners that were growing in size practically by the hour as their charter flights disgorged them into the capital ever since the unprecedented easing of visa restrictions for the Glorious Triumvirate Celebration. Normally a fifteen-minute walk, he reached his destination half an hour later.

The light in Choy's office glowed softly, the same office where he and Choy had faced off in several dozen *baduk* games and had engrossed themselves in deep and revealing conversations about faith, belief and love. Any other time, the building would have been crawling with security officers, but on this night the bulk of them were out patrolling the streets that teemed with foreigners.

His options dwindling by the minute, Patrick entered the building, bounded up the stairs, and put his ear to Choy's door. The only sound from within was the usual radio propaganda that not even People's Security was permitted to turn off all the way. A deep breath and a knock on the door later, the sound of a chair being pushed back was followed by footsteps. Patrick braced himself, at wit's end as to what to do if it wasn't Choy that answered. He had no Plan B. The door opened and a face poked out.

Mirror images of incredulity stared back at each other. At that exact moment, a door in the back of Choy's office opened. Choy turned to see who it was and then turned back to Patrick--- and buried a fist in his gut. Patrick had actually seen the punch coming and had managed to pull back from it a bit, but the pain was substantial nonetheless. He fell to his knees and doubled over. Standing in the back doorway was Comrade Moon, his lips parted in wonderment.

"Well, well," he said softly as he entered the office. His lower eyelids rose and covered the bottom of his eyes in a half-squint.

"Pung, would you mind coming in here, please," he half-sang in a voice pitched high in mock politeness. Pung trundled his squat frame through the back door, stopped, and stared fixedly at Patrick, his face a study in confusion. Moon pointed in Patrick's direction.

"Now Pung, take a good look. Is this, or is this not, the man you assured me had been taken care of at that temple in Japan?" Pung just nodded his head in mute bafflement. Moon walked up to Patrick and lifted his head up by the hair.

"It looks as though some people just can't get enough of our socialist paradise." He threw back Patrick's head and turned to Choy. "This time I'll leave it up to you. Pung is in disgrace."

Pung's face reddened, and he shuffled back and forth on his feet like a little boy who needed to pee.Choy hoisted Patrick to his feet, forced his arms behind him, and clicked a pair of handcuffs extra-tightly onto his wrists. "What shall I do with him, Comrade Moon?"

Moon leaned back against the wall, rested his chin in his hand, and rocked his head from side to side like a gourmand torn between the Oysters Rockefeller and the sheep's brains.

"Hmm," he murmured ruminatively. "How about we send him to his girlfriend. They can declare their final vows together at Special Unit 14. Take him down to Kaesong. Dr. Lee will take it from there."

Moon turned on his heel, followed by Pung who hung his head and trotted behind like an abused but ever-loyal bulldog.

Boarding the minivan for the trip down to Kaesong, with Special Unit 14 as Patrick's very final destination, Choy shackled Patrick into the back and took the shotgun seat while Sergeant Eun, one of Moon's most dependably sadistic minions, settled in behind the wheel. Patrick snuck a look at Choy's watch: midnight. The start of a new day to the rest of the world, but, from all appearances, Patrick's last.

Ten minutes into the drive, Choy turned around in his seat with a sneer on his lips. "Looks like you have no *hwallo*," he taunted in Korean, using the baduk term for escape route.

"He speaks our language?!" Eun asked incredulously.

"Probably better than you," Choy replied. "The CIA prepares its people well."

Eun took the opportunity to spend the next several minutes of the drive lecturing his prisoner.

"They should send *all* American bastards to where you're going. First you fucking Americans invade our country and now you come over as spies."

"When did America ever invade your country?" Patrick asked.

"In 1950, you idiot!"

"Kim Il-sung invaded the South. And you're the idiot for believing anything else."

Eun gripped the steering wheel so tightly that the backs of his hands were visibly white even in the moonlight.

"More American propaganda! Everyone in my country knows the truth about what happened!"

"Everyone in your country has been brainwashed, just like you," Patrick replied evenly. He was relishing the exchange. Who knows, if he got Eun so agitated that he ran off the road, he might have a fighting chance against him and Choy instead of going to Special Unit 14 like a lamb to slaughter.

"Yeah, you're all just a bunch of brainwashed zombies," he continued, calmly baiting Eun.

"Shut your mouth, you fucking imperialist! You're the ones who are zombies. We don't worship money, and we have something a lot more valuable," Eun shouted.

"What, a government that takes care of you? Where was your government when three million people starved to death? I bet you knew some of them, didn't you?"

"The Arduous March was the result of you Americans! You *wanted* as many of us to die as possible, so that you could come in and bleed us dry!"

"Then why didn't your pig of a 'Dear Leader' do something to save the people he was supposed to love so much? You know why? He couldn't. Because North Korea is the most backward country in the world."

"How dare you say that!" Eun screamed, spittle forming at the sides of his mouth, and the minivan veering precariously across the empty highway. "We are the most cultivated and civilized people on the face of the earth! America is hell on earth!"

"Alright, if it's hell on earth, then why not just send me back there as punishment?"

Choy put a steadying hand on the steering wheel, but otherwise did nothing to rein Eun in.

They arrived at Senghori Prison at 3 a.m. Choy had Eun wait in the minivan with Patrick while he checked in with the superintendant of the prison and got an escort to Special Unit 14.

"Leave some of him for Dr. Lee," Choy said with a grin at Eun as he set off for the superintendant's office. As soon as Choy was out of the car, Eun reached back and began pummeling Patrick who sat handcuffed.

Choy strode past the sentry post with his State Security ID held up high for the young, pimply private to admire. The soldier made a sleepy salute and indicated superfluously the main building that Choy was already well on his way toward.

Climbing the steps two at a time, he knocked on the door and opened it. The night clerk, a soldier only a little older than the one at the sentry post, looked up. "Don't you people believe in waiting for permission to enter?"

Choy's chest puffed out. "People's Security has the authority to enter any building in the country at any time. Where's the Superintendant? I have a new prisoner for Special Unit 14. My direct superior is Comrade Moon. Perhaps you've heard of him."

Upon hearing Moon's name, the soldier blanched and practically knocked over the phone in a feverish attempt at making a call to the Rat Catcher.

"Superintendant, an important guest has arrived from Pyongyang!" he squeaked into the phone. Then he smiled unctuously at Choy. "May I offer you some tea, Officer?"

"It's Inspector. And no tea."

The back door of the office flew open, and a tall, uniformed man with acne scars and bed-head hair emerged from a back room. His expression was angry. The clerk began to address the Superintendant, known to the prisoners of the camp as the Rat Catcher, but Choy cut him off.

"Special delivery from Comrade Moon. I have a new one for the Special Unit."

The Rat Catcher's eyes stayed fixed on Choy. He said nothing for a moment. Then with a toss of his head indicated that Choy should follow him into his inner sanctum.

"Who is this new prisoner?" he asked taking a seat behind his desk and pointing to a chair. Choy sat down.

"An American spy. He's been here before." Choy pushed an official document across the Rat Catcher's desk.

"The one we allowed to escape?" he said as he read the document. "He's *back*?"

Choy chuckled. "Comrade Moon had the exact same reaction. Yes, he's back, and this time he's to end his days at the Special Unit."

The Rat Catcher nodded. He picked up his phone and barked an order into it.

"They'll be here for you in a minute," he said after hanging up.

A few minutes later a truck pulled up in front of the Rat Catcher's office. Choy went back to the minivan and got in. Eun sat grinning. Patrick sat bleeding. The driver of the truck called out for Eun to follow him.

"I told him to shut up, but he just wouldn't listen," Eun said with a look of feigned innocence as he started the engine. Choy laughed. "That's nothing compared to what Dr. Lee has in store for him. Fall in behind that truck."

After taking a right-hand turn out of the main gate, the two vehicles drove for several uneventful miles, whereupon the truck slowed and the driver made another right onto an unpaved road that wound through miles of thick forest. Eun followed close behind.

"This place gives me the creeps," Eun said as the forest closed in around them.

"Shut up and drive," Choy said. "I want to get to Special Unit 14 sometime this month."

After ten miles of dizzying curves, the truck stopped and the driver walked over to Choy's minivan.

"This is it. Bring your prisoner over to this building on the right. Hey," he said looking into the car more closely. "They didn't say he was a foreigner."

"That's right. American spy," Choy responded.

"Well, this place'll teach him good."

"I don't suppose you get a lot of night deliveries."

"Oh, all the time. We're used to it. Right this way."

Choy nodded to Eun who hauled Patrick out of the back seat by his handcuffs and roughly pushed him in the direction of a long, whitewashed building that dominated the compound. The assistant had gone ahead to unlock the door and stood waiting for them.

"We call this the 'capsule hotel', like those places in Japan," he said pointing inside the building. Row upon row of horizontal boxes filled the room, each the size of a freezer with a large round window on top. As Patrick was being shoved into the room by Eun, he noticed human hands moving inside several of the capsules. A surging wave of foreboding filled his gut, not so much for his imminent fate, but for the fact that the hands he had just seen might well have been Yumi's.

The assistant walked ahead to the far corner of the room and opened one of the capsules. "I hope the esteemed guest will find the accommodations acceptable," he said to Patrick with an exaggerated bow. "Here, help me load him in," he said to Eun. Choy took Patrick's other arm.

"Shit, this guy's heavy!" said Eun. "Can't you just drug him first? No way is he going in willingly."

"Sorry, Dr. Lee's orders are that all new guests of the facility be fully conscious so that we can accurately gauge the effects of the gas."

The three of them took Patrick by his arms and legs, forced him inside the aluminum capsule, and clanged the heavy lid shut. A moment later, a high-pitched hissing sound filled the capsule, and Patrick's face contorted involuntarily from the insecticide-like smell of the gas.

Choy, Eun, and the assistant stood back with folded arms and watched the spectacle. Inside, Patrick tried in vain to push open the heavy lid as the stench of Beulsun-X permeated the capsule. His head began to spin violently, and his lungs burned from the bottom up, as if filling with something flammable. As the assistant started walking over to the master locking system to seal Patrick in for good, Choy sniffed. Traces of the poison gas lingered in the air.

"Son of a bitch, that shit is *foul*!" he exclaimed taking out a pack of cigarettes. The assistant stopped in mid-step and walked back when he noticed they appeared to be real Marlboros. Choy held up the pack for him and Eun.

"Try one of these, comrades. Might help get rid of the stench."

Both men now had cigarettes dangling from their lips. As the noxious smell grew stronger, Choy produced a lighter from his pocket and held the flame under their cigarettes. Their eyes rolled back in a nicotine buzz so blissful that they failed to notice Choy reaching into his other pocket. In a literal flash, the assistant was missing half of his head. Eun's eyes squinched in confusion as the man's body crumpled to the floor. Eun turned back to Choy questioningly, and Choy answered with another round from his Browning .45, this one blowing off the entire right side of Eun's face. His body rolled twice on the ground before stopping.

Choy immediately pulled open the heavy lid of the capsule and grabbed Patrick who emerged sputtering, a deep purging cough exploding from the bottom of his lungs. Gagging all the while, he half-rolled onto the floor like a drunk on a bender and tried to stand, vomiting everything in his stomach and then dry-heaving for another few minutes. Even the relatively small amount of Beulsun-X he had been exposed to was enough to send his system into near total collapse.

"That was a bit too convincing," he panted in a wispy voice, his hands on his knees.

"'Keep your friends close and your enemies closer,'" Choy said, quoting from "The Godfather" and placing a hand on Patrick's shoulder.

Patrick retched for several more minutes and then bolted upright. "We need to see if Yumi's here," he shouted, his body and mind suddenly jump-started with frantic, desperate energy. "You start on that end, I'll start over there."

Without a word, Choy ran and Patrick staggered to opposite ends of the room and began peering into the windows of the capsules.

"All men so far," Choy called out. "Some moving but mostly dead from the looks of it."

Patrick said nothing. All of his focus was on the forms inside the capsules. They were all men on his side of the room, too, most of them dead as well. Judging from the meters on the lids of their capsules, the prisoners had been given varying amounts of the poison, no doubt to determine precisely how much of the staggeringly expensive substance was needed to end a human life over particular spans of time. Patrick prayed that Yumi, if she was there, had been given one of the lighter doses.

From the other side of the room Choy let out a yell. "A woman!"

Patrick stumbled over on rubber legs to the capsule where Choy had stopped.

"She's still moving!" Choy cried out.

"It's locked!" Patrick screamed after trying to force the lid open.

"Check that guy's pockets for a key!"

Adrenaline giving new life to his legs, Patrick jumped down to an open area between the capsules where the assistant had fallen and began fishing through his pockets. Nothing. *How the hell do you open these th...*" Before he had a chance to finish the thought, a shot rang out through the building, and Choy instinctively curled into a ball and rolled under one of the capsules while Patrick stood exposed in the middle of the floor. With the reverberation created by the metal walls of the building, it was all but impossible to tell which direction the shot had come from, so Patrick flattened himself onto the floor and began tried to crawl under the nearest capsule. Before he could make any real progress, another bullet whizzed by his ear and ricocheted off a metal I-beam behind him. Footsteps hurried toward him, and he tumbled across the floor to an alcove raised a few steps off the ground, in the middle of which sat a bulky metal cube that resembled an industrial air-conditioning compressor.

With a bounding leap, he threw himself up onto the alcove and took cover behind the cube just as another bullet whizzed by his head. Still another shot followed a split second later, but this one slammed into the center of the cube. With that, the hiss of gas flowing to the capsules ceased, and the slightly-built shooter, whom Patrick could now see from behind the cube, began running from capsule to capsule, a look of panic in his eyes. For his last shot had penetrated the Beulsun-X delivery system. So preoccupied was the man that he never noticed Choy behind him until the Inspector jabbed the barrel of his Browning into his back.

"Your choice, Dr. Lee, drop it or die."

Dr. Lee dropped the gun as if he couldn't be bothered with it anymore and raced up onto the alcove towards the cube, oblivious to Patrick.

"Ruined," he said under his breath. "Ruined, ruined, ruined!" He ran his hand along the surface of the cube as if he had lost his best friend.

Patrick spun him around and shouted in his face, "Where's the locking mechanism?"

But it was as if Lee were in another world. Patrick grabbed him violently by the shoulders and began shaking. "I said, where's the locking mechanism?" he screamed furiously.

The intensity of Patrick's shaking rattled Dr. Lee back to the here and now, but a glint of defiance flashed in his eyes. Patrick dragged him bodily down the stairs and across the room to the capsule that had imprisoned him all too recently. He gave Choy a curt nod and together they lifted Lee up and in. The insecticide-like smell nauseated Patrick all over again, and he fought the urge to retch as he reeled Lee in by his necktie until they were face to face.

"Last chance, scumbag, where's the fucking locking mechanism?"

Dr. Lee gave nothing up in words, but Patrick caught a lightning-fast twitch of his eyes to the left. He slammed down the heavy lid of the capsule and ran in the direction that Lee's eyes had traveled, searching for anything that looked like a central control device. His eyes came to rest on a panel of five buttons at eye-level in the far corner of the room. He swallowed hard and pressed the button on the left. A deafening alarm erupted throughout the entire building. What would the next button cause? A lockdown of the entire facility until help arrived from Senghori? No alternative. He pressed the remaining four buttons in quick succession.

The alarm stopped as suddenly as it had started, and a series of clicking sounds echoed off the metal walls of the building. When the clicking stopped, the only sound in the room was Dr. Lee's muffled voice screaming frantically to be let out of the capsule. *Rot in hell, motherfucker,* Patrick thought as he raced back to the coffin he was sure held Yumi and lifted the lid. His intuition had been right. He reached in and lifted her head up and saw that her skin was completely blue. Cyanosis. The final stage of oxygen starvation. Choy ran over and raised one of her eyelids with his thumb. A pinprick for a pupil. Together they hoisted her out of the capsule, carried her out of the killing room by her hands and feet, and lay her on the cold, wet grass. Choy took off his coat and spread it over her while Patrick frantically began mouth-to-mouth resuscitation.

Five minutes later, Yumi's color gradually lost a bit of its bluish tinge. Choy held both eyelids open this time. One pupil had widened, but the other was still pinned out, and she was completely unresponsive. Death from systemic shock could take her any moment. That or a massive stroke. They began rubbing her extremities in an effort at restoring circulation and raising her body temperature. Then they carried her inside the administration building and lay her in an armchair where they continued to apply warming friction to her hands and feet.

Back in the killing room Dr. Lee's shot had dealt an unwitting bull's eye to the brains of the compressor and cut off the flow of Beulsun-X to the capsules. The prisoners who had been administered the lightest experimental doses revived first. Their hands, numb at first, instinctively pushed up against the lids that trapped them, and unlike in their previous futile attempts when they were first sealed in, this time the lids opened. One by one they found the strength to lift themselves up and out, and before long six of them staggered around the room in total disorientation. As they gradually regained their equilibrium by small measures, they began to open the other capsules, and their fellow prisoners who had been given heavier doses but who were still alive began to stir. Soon another four joined the growing fraternity of the undead. Silently they moved around the capsules, the only sound being the zombie-like shuffling of their stiffened feet along the concrete floor. Then one of them caught sight of a capsule that held a fresh subject. He grunted for his fellows to come over and together they beheld the monster who had tried to end their lives in unspeakable agony. Dr. Lee mutely entreated them with his eyes to open the lid of his capsule. They were only too happy to oblige. As Dr. Lee raised himself into a sitting position, he had twenty eager hands at his assistance...

An hour later, Yumi regained a semblance of consciousness. Her face was still paper-white, but at least the cyanosis had abated. Patrick supported her head as she drank some juice from a can of peaches Choy had found. Just handing the can back to Patrick seemed to overextend her.

"Have some more," Patrick urged.

"I need to rest," she said in a feeble whisper, her first words since emerging from the capsule. Patrick and Choy lifted her out of the chair, lay her down on a sofa, and covered her with a heavy blanket they found in a closet. She fell asleep immediately. A haggard-looking Choy pantomimed that he was going out for a smoke. Fifteen minutes later, after making sure that Yumi's breathing was regular and her airway clear, Patrick joined Choy outside.

"What now?" Choy asked in a fatigue-depleted voice as they sat on the stairs at the entrance of the building. Patrick had his legs drawn up and was resting his head on his knees. He didn't look up as he responded.

"I have to get her out of here before anything else. You've heard of the group called Rising Tide?"

"Of course."

"I know where they're hiding. I'm going to take her there."

"Where is it?"

"Up in the hills. Not all that far from here."

"And what then?"

Patrick lifted his head wearily. "Do you know anything about an attack of some kind that Moon is engineering at the DMZ on Tuesday?"

Choy shrugged. "I overheard bits and pieces about something like that. No real details, though."

"I have to try and stop it."

"Why be a hero? It's not even your country."

"It's not a question of being a hero. I'm not doing it for myself."

Choy crushed his cigarette butt under his heel and motioned for Patrick to follow him. "I found something you might be interested in."

Choy led the way into Dr. Lee's office. On a table sat a computer and a printer. The icon on the desktop indicated an active internet connection, one of only a handful in the country.

"I booted this up while you were looking after Yumi. The password was on a piece of paper in the drawer." Choy sat down at the terminal and clicked open the browser. He interlaced his fingers and cracked his knuckles.

"Anyplace you'd like to go?"

Patrick's eyes widened. With Choy's hacking skills, the possibilities were almost endless.

CHAPTER 31

SPECIAL UNIT 14
April 30

Choy looked up from the computer screen.

"Looks like I got into the office of the Secretary of State," he said with only a hint of surprise, as if he had stumbled across a 10-chon coin in the street. Patrick laughed. He had suggested the Secretary's office based on her reputation as being lax on security.

"See if you can find anything on the situation at the DMZ."

Choy's fingers flew across the keys. A minute later he stopped.

"I think I found something. It's an email memorandum from a few hours ago marked 'urgent' that says that a General Merkin isn't taking calls from the White House and that he's preparing something called War Plan 5027. It's not even encrypted."

"Does it say what that is?" Patrick leaned over Choy's shoulder and scanned the page Choy had opened. His eyes fell to a footnote on the page. *War Plan 5027: the complete annihilation of North Korea.*

"Good Christ," he muttered under his breath. He looked at a clock on the wall: 6:43 a.m. The attack was a day away. Time was dwindling.

Patrick looked up from the screen and cocked his head to one side. A rogue blast of wind rushing down from the surrounding mountains and through the stand of pine trees outside had created a sound not unlike that of a solid object moving up the road to Unit 14, a truck perhaps. It was an auditory illusion brought on by exhaustion, but it brought back to Patrick's mind the danger they still faced.

"We've got to get out of here," Patrick said urgently. "It's only a matter of time before someone from Senghori comes up here," Patrick said. "What if Dr. Lee missed a commo check or sounded an alarm before he came after us? Speaking of whom, I'm going to go over and make sure he's snug. If we ever get out of this shit alive, I'm going to come back and make sure that son of a bitch stands trial for crimes against humanity. Lend me your gun in case he gets restless."

As Patrick entered the Beulsun-X killing room, his first olfactory impression was not the insecticide stench as it had been the last time, but rather the meaty reek of an abattoir that almost knocked him over. A dozen or more wet, maroon footprints splotching in the direction of the rear door stained the concrete. Not a sound came from inside the facility, and Patrick was on his guard as he edged his way toward the capsule that held Dr. Lee. From behind a corner, he leapt out with Choy's pistol raised in a firing position...and immediately fought the urge to vomit. Lying in the middle of the floor was Dr. Lee's dismembered body with a fire-ax buried into its torso. From the looks of it, the prisoners who had still been alive had escaped their capsules after the central locking mechanism was disabled and had put the ax to use in methodically lopping off Lee's fingers joint by joint, then his hands, then his forearms, then his toes, feet, legs, all the way until he was a literal basket case. His eyes were open, his mouth frozen in agony around a bloody gag that had muffled his screams. His digits, limbs and joint sockets were black with feasting flies, and Patrick again fought the urge to retch. Just as he was about to turn and run out the front door, however, he noticed the tiniest of movements in Lee's lips. He walked over, leaned down, and saw that his eyes were not completely sightless. With a single shot from Choy's pistol he put Dr. Lee out of North Korea's misery for all time.

Best break that bastard ever caught, he thought to himself and walked back to the administration building where Yumi lay fighting for her life.

Yumi's head began spinning as soon as she tried to stand, so Patrick picked her up and carried her to the minivan that Choy had brought around to the front entrance. Patrick's concern deepened as he carried her; it was as though her bones were filled with air instead of marrow. Together he and Choy gently eased her down on the back seat and covered her with a blanket. She lay back and closed her eyes.

"Well, what now?" Choy asked as they got into the front seats.

"I'm going to take her to the Rising Tide camp in the mountains. She'll be safe there." He hesitated before speaking again. "Then I have to go to the DMZ to see if there's any way to stop Moon's attack tomorrow. What are you going to do?"

Choy looked over at Patrick as he shifted the van into gear. "I'm going to get out of this country once and for all. You can be the hero."

From the back of the van came a sharp intake of breath and a scream. Patrick turned around with alarm but then relaxed when he realized that Yumi was having a nightmare. She woke up briefly and then allowed her eyes to close. In an instant a thin, dry sound like corn rustling in the wind rose rhythmically from her throat. Patrick reached back and lightly brushed her cheek. Then he faced forward and looked vacantly out the window as Choy drove. An awkward silence descended over them. There was something Patrick needed to know and Choy sensed it.

"Were you always on my side?"

Choy turned to face him and then looked back at the road. He scratched his head and set his lips.

"To be honest, no. Moon said that if I got you to Senghori that first time and you led them to Yumi's father, I wouldn't have to be a cop anymore, not even part-time. I would be his full-time computer specialist."

"So what happened? Why did you turn against him?"

"Jebby and Sun-yi, the two kids who guided us in," Choy said without hesitation. "The guards shot them on the way down the trail after they captured you. I knew they were waiting and I tried to stop them, but they just laughed and told me to go back to Pyongyang. When I saw what they would do to a couple of twelve-year-old kids. . ."

Choy's voice broke slightly and he coughed to disguise it. "I promised myself at that moment that I'd do everything I could to stop that son of a bitch Moon." Choy's fingers tightened into a vise-grip around the steering wheel.

"I was going to wait for the right moment and just shoot him when I got back to Pyongyang, but. . .well, as I said, I'm no hero. All the heroes in North Korea are dead. Anyway, Moon offered me a new apartment of my own and a big raise if I set you up. It's what I always wanted. The status, the respect, the sense that I'd finally made something of my life. I didn't know you except for a few games of baduk. I felt bad about your situation, but in North Korea feeling bad for someone usually leads to no good. So I decided to go along with Moon's plan. I'm very sorry."

Patrick sat silently for a moment. Then he reached over and patted Choy once on the shoulder.

Choy drove in the direction of Kaesong Central Station where they would ditch the minivan and take the next local to the stop closest to Rising Tide's mountain redoubt: the village of Darang-ri. Fifteen minutes later Choy pulled the van into the Kaesong Central parking lot. Patrick tied Yumi's hands behind her and had Choy handcuff him. Choy opened the door and gruffly ordered them out. Yumi was the epitome of starving prisoner of the state. Patrick hung his foreign head in defeat for the benefit of anyone watching.

In a miracle of punctuality for the North Korean train system, the next local pulled up within ten minutes, a mere two hours behind schedule. The train slowed to a crawl, and the throng of waiting passengers on the platform followed the doors at a trot, hoping for a coveted seat instead of having to stand in the aisles.

"State Security!" Choy called out authoritatively as the train ground to a halt, and the disappointed crowd waiting for the doors to open stood back reluctantly out of lifelong habit. When the conductor came up to object, Choy insisted that, since he was transporting two very dangerous criminals, he must be allowed a separate compartment to segregate them from law-abiding citizens. The conductor's face contorted, but he relented in the end. He had tried arguing with these State Security agents about this sort of thing before and all it ever gotten him were threats of a beating or worse. So while the conductor got an earful of grief from the bumped passengers who would have to wait another two hours for the next train, Choy and his prisoners got their own compartment.

When they had settled into the compartment, Choy helped them unbind their hands.

"Make sure you keep them around your wrists in case that conductor comes in. Put them under your jackets or something," Choy cautioned.

Yumi immediately slumped down low in her seat. Patrick looked over at her with concern.

"Don't worry," Yumi said. "I survived hell." In an instant she was fast asleep.

"You should sleep, too," Choy said to Patrick who hadn't had any real rest in a day and a half, and within seconds he felt himself hovering lightly on the edges of consciousness, unbound, for the moment at least, from the cares of this world.

His first dream was filled with grotesque images of Dr. Lee's disassembled body spread out in parts on the floor of Special Unit 14. Impossibly, the phantasmagorical images then melted into a sunlit meadow in Kamakura where he and Yumi had often picnicked in warm weather. In the next dream sequence, a hawk hovered over him and grew wide as the sky and then morphed into a people-mover at Narita Airport that was heading toward the departure gates. As Patrick stood on the moving track, someone glided effortlessly toward him from the opposite direction. *But how could that be?* he wondered in his sleep. *It's impossible to go backwards on these things, at least not without running.* But as the apparition got closer, Patrick began to recognize its facial features.

His father reached out his hand. *"Time to move, son."*

Patrick opened his dream-mouth to reply, but the people-mover then contracted into a boat rocking to and fro on a storm-tossed sea. He awoke with a start to Choy roughly shaking him. Drifting halfway between sleep and wakefulness, he tried to recapture that last segment of his dream. His father's hand had been outstretched, as if inviting him to go with him. Or was he literally reaching out to shake his hand? What could it have meant?

"This is too early for Darang-ri," Choy said forebodingly, and Patrick was jolted back to consciousness by the alarm in his voice. The train was coasting to a stop.

"Maybe it's just a problem with the power line," Patrick croaked in a voice made rough and low-pitched by his brief sleep. Yumi stirred in her seats and then woke.

"Not likely. The engine is still running."

Any further speculation was put to rest by the army truck speeding toward the train across a muddy field. It was packed with guards from Senghori, with Bastard Cho, the club-wielding head guard, craning his neck forward in the shotgun seat.

"Let's get the hell out of here," Choy growled, pulling the pistol from his shoulder holster while motioning for them to exit the compartment and walk toward the back of the train. Outside, the soldiers jumped off the truck and began boarding from the front.

"Quick, out this way," Choy ordered. They were in the caboose, and the train had stopped adjacent to a densely wooded area. "We'll have to make a run for it."

As he spoke, the soldiers had already made it to the car directly in front of the caboose and were smashing open toilet doors and searching faces. A woman in her early 40s was pulled from her seat and one of the soldiers shouted, "Escapee!" The woman had been missing from Senghori for a week.

Meanwhile, with two solid kicks, Choy dislodged the gate on the back of the caboose, and he and Patrick jumped off, with Yumi in Patrick's arms. They began running, and after about thirty meters, they realized that the soldiers weren't in hot pursuit. They turned to face the train and saw the escapee climbing up on its roof. Patrick felt Yumi's abdominal muscles contract in preparation for a scream, but he clapped his hand over her mouth and carried her into the trees.

"I know her!" Yumi cried through the hand over her mouth. Tears formed in her eyes.

Choy was there waiting for them among the trees.

"They're so busy with the woman they've forgotten about us. Come on, we can make it to the tunnels from here!" he said in a loud whisper and started wheezing his way south. Patrick was too busy restraining Yumi to reply.

By this time the woman was halfway up the side of the train, and as she climbed, she contorted her face and screamed an unearthly incantation that stopped the guards in their tracks.

"She's a witch!" one of them shouted. They looked to Bastard Cho for direction, but his blood was as curdled as theirs. When the woman caught sight of him, she screamed the incantation until her face was a bright crimson with pent-up hatred for a man even the other guards secretly despised.

Yumi pushed against Patrick's grip, tears of panic and helplessness coursing down her cheeks when she realized what the woman was about to do. But Patrick dragged her bodily deeper into the woods. A profound, moaning sob spread through her entire being.

The woman was now at the very top of the train, and a demented look came into her eyes as she stared at Bastard Cho. Slowly she extended a trembling hand toward him.

"Come down now," Bastard Cho shouted up to her, although a fair measure of authority had gone missing from his voice.

The woman's lips curled into a smile her eyes had no part of.

"But...You...Must...Help...Me," she rasped in an otherworldly voice. Bastard Cho shifted his weight from heels to soles and back again as realized that his guards were waiting for him to do something, anything.

"Wait there," he called to the woman, as if she might fly away, and he began to ascend the rusty ladder, the slightest of tremors evident in his hands as he pulled himself up.

Patrick and Yumi lay hidden in the woods, wanting desperately to turn away from the unfolding scene, but simply unable to. Patrick turned to where he had last seen Choy and saw no sign of him. Something sour in his stomach rose up into his throat. A sudden gasp from Yumi brought him back to the train. He cupped his hand more tightly over her mouth to stifle a wail breaking loose from her heart. She seemed to know exactly what was coming. As soon as Bastard Cho reached the top of the caboose, he paused, looked down at his men, and raised himself to his full height. Five feet away the woman extended her hand toward him while swaying back and forth, the demonic smile broadening across her face.

"Help me down," she moaned in a suddenly weak voice that was belied by unblinking eyes. Bastard Cho inched forward and held out his hand.

Yumi could watch no longer. She buried her head into Patrick's shoulder, and he felt her body tremble uncontrollably like a newborn hummingbird that had fallen from its nest.

At the exact moment Bastard Cho's hand was a foot in front of her, the woman reached out and grabbed hold of it with all her might. A scream of triumph burst from her lips as her left hand shot up to the sputtering electric cable running above the train. Instantly, the two of them were shaking uncontrollably, but the woman's hand had fused with the cable and the current passed directly through her, stopping her heart. Cho, who was the endpoint of the current, screamed in horror as he fell off the train with his hair on fire and blood pouring out of his eyes.

As the guards milled in shock about Bastard Cho's body, Patrick rushed deeper into the forest with Yumi over his shoulder in a fireman's carry. A quarter mile in, he set Yumi down on the grass.

"I knew her," she murmured over and over in a voice emptied of life. "She fed me when I got back from being tortured."

Patrick held her and stroked her hair helplessly.

As they lay on the grass, utterly spent, the faint scent of pinewood smoke drifted over them. Patrick shinnied halfway up a tree and scanned the surrounding area. A few hundred yards away a broken, wispy plume spiraled into the windless sky.

"Can I leave you for a little while?" he asked. Yumi nodded almost imperceptibly, her gaze inward.

Patrick sprinted in the direction of the smoke and a few minutes later came upon a tiny hamlet. No one was about. It was a holiday in preparation for the Glorious Triumvirate Celebration, and the villagers were no doubt enjoying one of their rare opportunities to sleep in. Still, Patrick took no chances as he edged closer to the outlying buildings. Leaning against one of them was an ancient motorcycle that was missing a kickstand and appeared to have been assembled from junkyard parts. He rolled it away from the building and brought his full weight down on the kick starter, popped the clutch, and steered the bike back to where he had left Yumi.

Ten minutes later, with Yumi slumped over his shoulders, Patrick rode down the Reunification Highway until he spied his landmark: the maple tree that had been hollowed out and blackened by lightning. He turned off the highway and onto the dirt track he had taken on the way down from the Rising Tide encampment. When the hill reached an incline of 30 degrees, the bike rebelled. Patrick lifted Yumi up and piggy-backed her up the mountain trail, but within five minutes, even as emaciated as she was, she felt heavy as a sackful of coal.

A torturous mile later, they came onto the clearing where he had glided in on the Griffin 1-A. Before leaving the last time, he and Nahm had arranged an emergency signal in the event either of them ran into trouble. Cupping his hands and whistling three times the call of a hawk, he stopped and listened. Nothing. Yumi lay motionless but alive on the ground, her system failing. Patrick was about to succumb to despair when he heard it: the muted hooting of an owl three times from higher up the mountain.

When Patrick and Yumi reached the Rising Tide encampment, Nahm had two of his followers lead them to a cave where a bed of straw and rags had been set out. As soon as Yumi lay down on the buckwheat husk pillow, her chest began to rise and fall rhythmically.

"You need to rest, too," Nahm said to Patrick. Patrick made him promise to wake him in six hours, not a minute later. Nahm nodded and left them alone. Patrick settled in beside Yumi, the first time they had lain side by side in well over a year. He tucked a thick blanket around her cadaverous form and tried in vain to get his mind to turn off. Finally, after twenty fitful minutes, he called upon his training from his sniper days and literally willed his mind to let go.

When he awoke, Yumi had thrown off the blanket in her sleep, and she lay curled in a fetal crouch on the makeshift bedding. Her skin had the translucent pallor of malnutrition and dehydration. Patrick listened for her breathing, the most vital of vital signs. It was regular and unobstructed. Finally, she stirred and turned this way and that around the cave, a puzzled look of disorientation on her face. When she remembered where she was, she weakly lifted herself up off the bedding. Nahm was at the cave entrance a few minutes later with cups of wild ginseng tea. He was clean-shaven, his hair had been cut, and he was dressed like an ordinary office worker on a day off. It took Patrick a minute to recognize him.

"You have a good internal clock. It's almost exactly six hours," Nahm said smiling. "Here, drink this, and then come have something to eat."

He led the way to an open area where a dozen men and women were filling bowls from a communal pot that sat simmering over a firepit.

"It's our specialty. Pig stew, mountain vegetables, and barley. Every vitamin and mineral you need and a lot of protein, which you, Miss, have gone without for too long. But stick mostly with the broth for now, you don't want to overload your system. Have a seat, both of you."

Patrick guided Yumi by the elbow to where the others were eating. After they had finished, Nahm came over eyeing his watch. He took Patrick aside.

"We'll be going up to Pyongyang tonight. All the Rising Tide cells have been activated for the Glorious Triumvirate Celebration tomorrow."

"What about the authorities, won't they be suspicious seeing so many of you?"

Nahm shook his head. "Half of Kaesong will be going up. We'll blend in with them." He paused as though deliberating his next question. "Will you be coming, too?"

Patrick told him what he had learned since the last time he'd seen him. Some sort of attack was going to take place the following morning at the DMZ. Nahm's face turned pale.

"Is it certain to happen?"

"I don't know."

"Maybe we should change our plans and go with you instead," he said.

Patrick shook his head. "I'm better off going alone."

Nahm called over one of his men. Patrick looked at Yumi who was staring off into the distance, apparently contented from the food and the sleep she had just had.

"Yumi, I have something very important to do near Kaesong. I'd like you to go with these people. I'll join you all tomorrow." He wondered if he would be able— or alive— to keep that promise.

She smiled weakly. "I'll be fine."

Just then, one of Nahm's men rolled an old but sturdy-looking dirt bike out of a cave.

"This time I don't think a Bugang is quite up to the job," Nahm said smiling.

Patrick thanked him. Then he remembered something. He reached into the inside pocket of his jacket and took out the booklet he had taken from Seo-mi's pile at the Foreign Outreach Institute.

"I don't know what this is," he said, pressing the booklet into Yumi's hands, "but I have a feeling it has something to do with tomorrow. Maybe you can figure it out."

"I'll try." She paused and looked into his eyes. "Thank you, Patrick. Thank you for coming back for me."

He took her in his arms and held her for a long moment. Then he kissed her on the forehead, shook Nahm's hand, climbed on the bike and was off. This time he proceeded more cautiously down the trail, as a mist had come rolling in off the mountaintops and hung over the woodlands like a gray linen shroud.

Lying five miles from the Demilitarized Zone, Kaesong is a city of over 300,000 with low-rise buildings, broad boulevards and very little traffic. As Patrick slowly rode down the rain-puddled thoroughfare of Tongil ("Unification") Street, a helmet hiding his foreignness, he was struck by how deserted the city appeared at five o'clock in the afternoon. The residents were no doubt using the evening before the Glorious Triumvirate Celebration for that most precious commodity a North Korean can have—time to oneself, with no criticism sessions, no political cadre meetings, nothing. Just blessed respite from the political burdens of everyday life.

Perhaps they were spending the time relaxing and enjoying the unprecedented round-the-clock coverage of the preparations for tomorrow's festivities. A wide-screen TV had been set up in a minuscule triangular park, and several citizens sat on the grass watching, oblivious to the drizzle. Patrick kept his helmet visor down and coasted over to the area. The screen was filled variously with gymnasts and tanks, acrobats and truck-loaded missiles. Suddenly, the announcer said that they were going live to Kaesong, and there on the screen was General O's 1st Army Corps. The rows and rows of tanks and artillery pieces reminded Patrick of *baduk* stones. The announcer spoke in an emotion-filled voice.

"The Supreme Commander has dispatched General O Jun-suh to repel any aggressive actions by the Americans on the day of our Glorious Triumvirate Celebration. . ."

As Patrick watched, the wheels of his mind turned. He thought back to his early games of baduk with Choy which he had lost after overly aggressive opening moves that led him into the trap Choy had set. *What if Moon. . .?*

Suddenly, it was as though a chandelier had been turned on inside a room that had previously been lit by a single candle. *Of course!*

187

PART FOUR

CHAPTER 32

DMZ HEADQUARTERS OF GENERAL CARL MERKIN
May 1, 5:10 a.m.

Major General Carl Merkin paced the balcony of his headquarters that overlooked the desolation of the DMZ. The full moon, ringed with phosphorescence, glowered intermittently from behind a scrim of rain clouds, just enough to illuminate the two-mile expanse that, in Merkin's mind, separated civilization from barbarity. Turning his head to the left, he could just barely make out the Bridge of No Return where prisoners of war had been exchanged sixty years earlier. Turning to the right, he could see the dam where the North had unleashed a torrent of water in 2009 killing 12 South Koreans. *And what did the South do?* he thought. *Not a goddamn thing. Same as when their battleship was torpedoed, same as when Yeonpyong Island was shelled yet again in 2015. Fucking pussies!* His mind ran through the catalog of North Korean perfidy over the years— axe murders of GIs, assassinations of South Korean political figures, constant provocations of war. Then his thoughts went to his commander-in-chief's parting words: "A preemptive nuclear move on our part is not in the cards unless I give a direct order."

Fat chance of an order from him happening in time, Merkin thought disgustedly. *Sonofabitch has already moved 85% of my men to the Mideast. What the hell am I supposed to defend with if General O attacks, for God's sakes? By the time that idiot gets his thumb out of his ass, O and his army will have overrun my position, killing all these fine young boys.* Merkin's thoughts went to his outfit, the 7th Cavalry, the famed and much-decorated "Garryowen", inherited down through the generations from another American facing similar odds, the Boy General himself, George Armstrong Custer.

Merkin blew out his cheeks and shook his head ruefully. There was not a doubt in his mind that General O of the Korean People's Army was at that very moment hunched over a topo map in a field tent two miles away, refining his plan of attack. For an attack was coming, that much was clear. You don't amass that many troops, tanks, and artillery pieces in one place unless you intend to use them. The only question was whether O would lead with his artillery or order his men to come in through the underground tunnels, which could allow 30,000 KPA soldiers an hour into the South right under Merkin's headquarters. And here he was, tethered and talonless after his recent encounter with the so-called "Leader of the Free World".

He went inside and called for Yung-shik, his Korean valet, to bring a fresh bottle of bourbon. The valet entered a short while later, set the bottle on the table, bowed and left. Merkin poured himself two fingers of Jim Beam, sat down at his desk, and studied the oil portrait hanging above the fireplace. Douglas MacArthur's eyes seemed to twinkle back at him with something approaching mischief. During the Korean War, MacArthur had lobbied hard to launch low-emission nukes from artillery pieces—"atomic cannons", the press called them— which would have taken out the Chicoms on the other side of the Yalu River. *And Mac was dead right*, Merkin thought, taking a sip of brown booze. *Only he got second-guessed by another spineless politician 12,000 miles away.*

Merkin set down his glass, picked up his phone and called his executive officer, Colonel Lawrence, and told him to hold all communication coming in from Washington.

"But sir..."

"Just do it, Ray. Tell them I'm in the field."

He thought again of his briefing at the White House. His lips tightened with resolve and bitterness as he remembered his unspoken words to the President.

And fuck you too, sir. No way in hell do I let my men get massacred.

DMZ HEADQUARTERS OF GENERAL O JUN-SUH
May 1, 5:33 a.m.

The nighttime mist had tightened into bundles of low-lying clouds, and a stuttering rain now splattered all across the DMZ. Dawn was breaking uncertainly on the day of the Glorious Triumvirate Celebration. General O opened the flap of his command tent and beheld his forces assembled all around the countryside. His sleep had been on a creaky bamboo-strutted army cot instead of the teakwood four-poster enjoyed by his counterpart across the border. Dandelion tea had softened his dreams, not Jim Beam. And instead of a life-sized oil portrait of MacArthur, he communed with his treasured miniature image of Ulji Mundok, the legendary leader of Korea's Koguryo kingdom, who 1,300 years earlier had decimated China's invading force by luring them into a floodplain and then breaching the dikes. And now it seemed the time had come to smite a more recent enemy with similarly overawing force.

With a close-cropped, bullet-shaped head atop a tall, muscular body, the 59-year-old commander had once been one of Kim Jong-il's most ardent supporters. But despite all his talk over the years of turning the South into a sea of fire, in his heart of hearts General O couldn't abide the notion of killing even a single fellow Korean, however politically misguided they might be. For the Korean bloodline, he was convinced, was unsullied and its people endowed with an infinitely greater measure of toughness, tenacity and brains than the lesser races of mankind. The capitalistic, race-mixing American mongrels, on the other hand, had willfully contaminated the gene-pool in South Korea in an obvious attempt at dragging the Koryo people down to their level. He would have no compunction whatsoever about dispatching every last one of them to hell.

On this gray morning at the DMZ, however, he had to wonder. Was Moon telling him the truth? Had orders to repel an American sneak attack actually come from Supreme Commander Kim Jong-un? Such were the thoughts that went through his head as he stood outside his tent proudly beholding his 1st Army Corps: four infantry divisions of 12,000 men each, a light infantry brigade, an armor brigade, two artillery brigades, an anti-aircraft regiment, and two mortar regiments. Over 100,000 men, not a single one of whom he would sacrifice needlessly. He folded his arms and turned to go back into his tent. He would be calling the shots here, not Moon. At that moment a junior aide rushed breathlessly to his tent.

"General O, another urgent message has arrived from Comrade Moon's office..."

O's reply was unhesitating. "Tell him you can't find me."

After bivouacking the night in the woods under a thin blanket, Patrick forced his stiff and tired muscles into action and climbed wearily on his motorcycle at dawn. Burying its tachometer needle into the red zone brought him back to life, and soon he was tearing through the muddy countryside near the DMZ, coming to a halt near the top of a bluff. Adrenalin sent his heart and brain surging. For down below was the largest concentration of militarized humanity he had ever seen. And they appeared to be mobilizing for an attack. As he was looking across the DMZ at the skeleton-crew American forces, two North Korean sentries suddenly appeared. They snicked off the safeties of their rifles and took aim at his head.

DMZ HEADQUARTERS OF GENERAL CARL MERKIN
May 1, 6:33 a.m.

"I'm sorry, General, but there's something about this whole thing that just doesn't smell right," said Colonel Raymond Lawrence. Lawrence was Merkin's executive officer in charge of the tactical nuclear weapons Merkin had as his only defense against what looked to be a looming enemy attack from across the DMZ.

"Dammit, Ray, we're dealing with General O and his whole fucking 1st Army Corps not two miles from where we're standing. If we wait, it's over, we're all dead. I'm not going to stand by and do nothing while that dickless fool in the White House twiddles his thumbs."

"But what if that 'dickless fool', known in some circles as our 'Commander-in-Chief', is trying to contact you now? You've given orders not to take any commo from Washington."

"You got that right, from now on this goes my way."

Colonel Lawrence shook his head. "Part of me doesn't blame you one bit, sir. It's just that the timing is plain wrong. They've got that Glorious Triumvirate Celebration scheduled to happen today. Why would they launch an attack now, of all times?"

"And I'm supposed to wait and find out? What if you're wrong? What if Kim Jong-un wants to show the world that he's as loony as his old man? And what if General O is crazy enough to strike first on his own? He knows we have tactical nukes. What if he's going to try and take us out before we have a chance to use them? I can't take the chance of risking any of our boys' lives. Besides, we can end seventy years of this bullshit right here and now and be done with it."

"Begging the General's pardon, sir, but that's not your call to make."

"And whose is it?" Merkin shot back. "Our intrepid Commander-in-Chief's? MacArthur had the right idea, Ray, but he waited for Truman to make the call. And Truman said no. So now we're still technically at war with these idiots seven decades later. *That's* what doesn't smell right to me. Prepare two low-yield tactical devices for artillery deployment. That's an order."

"Sir, my orders for the nukes are to come directly from the President, but..."

"I'm not going to ask you again, Ray."

"Dammit, sir, hear me out!" Lawrence was breathing hard both from his insubordinate outburst as well as the exertion of having kept his tongue in check for so long around his fire-breathing commander.

Merkin stared at Lawrence with his jaw clenching and unclenching.

"Sir, I have full trust in you, and I know that you have the welfare of our men foremost in mind. But we're talking nuclear war here, and I want to make absolutely sure we're not overreacting."

Merkin exhaled slowly. "So what are you proposing?"

"I'm proposing that we wait for some clear indication that they're planning to attack."

"Christ, what more do you need? What if they're infiltrating the tunnels right now? Or what if it starts with a blitzkrieg artillery attack?"

"I understand all that, sir," Lawrence replied, his voice matching Merkin's in volume. "But the alternative is lobbing four kilotons of radioactive explosive into enemy territory with the whole world watching. You thought the invasion of Iraq was a mistake? Just watch what happens with something like this. We need to be absolutely certain that we're *counter*attacking."

Merkin was silent for a moment with his lips pursed and his eyes never leaving Lawrence's. "Alright," he said finally. "Here's what I'll do. The morning satellite pass for this area isn't due for three hours, but I've got a guy in the NSA who I can get to tweak the trajectory of one of the China satellites so that it's directly overhead in forty minutes. It's Keyhole-class, so it'll be able to see right through the cloud cover. He'll stovepipe me the images direct, rather than through Washington. That'll give us a clear indication of what they're up to over there. Then we give Washington a chance to respond appropriately. And if they don't, I move ahead with my original plan. Fair enough?"

Colonel Lawrence chewed the inside of his cheek. "Fair enough, sir," he said finally. "I don't trust the desk jockeys in Washington any more than you do, but we at least have to establish that we alerted them first. If they don't give a green light in the face of a probable attack, then I'll back you up all the way. They can hang us together."

North side of the DMZ

General O sat in his tent, his eyes contracted in absorption as he studied a topographical map of the DMZ. An urgent voice came from outside.

"General O, we have captured a foreign spy!"

O emerged from his tent and saw Patrick standing with his hands cuffed behind his back, his nose and mouth bloodied from the beating the sentries had given him. He had gotten in several solid blows of his own, and the left eye of one of the sentries had swollen into a multicolored egg.

"Who are you?" he asked in English above the steady slash of the rain. "How did you get here?"

"I'm an American. There is a plot to destroy you and your army."

"Plot?" O said incredulously, waving his hand in the direction of the DMZ. "Right across that border is an American general named Merkin who would like to incinerate me with nuclear weapons. That's not a plot. That's a plan of attack by your country on mine."

Patrick shook his head vehemently. "Comrade Moon wants you to attack the Americans so that they will counterattack with nuclear weapons and destroy you and your army. He wants you out of the way because he plans to kill Kim Jong-un and take over as leader."

General O just looked at Patrick, his eyes revealing nothing. He had long suspected something of the sort from Moon. But the details of the plot coming from an American spy who just suddenly appears on North Korean soil?

"How do you know any of this?" he said finally.

"General, if even one word of what I say is true and you proceed with an invasion, the blood of your men will be on your hands. There's no time to debate this. You have to let me go over to this General Merkin and let him know that this whole thing is a setup engineered by Comrade Moon."

"Let you cross the DMZ? Are you insane? I have no idea who you really are."

Patrick swallowed hard. Time was running out. He had to take a chance.

"Rising Tide..." he began. Five minutes later, General O granted him permission to cross the DMZ.

Patrick recklessly powered the motorcycle down the wet road, sending giant rooster tails of mud skyward. The rainstorm was now in full force. Lightning burst in the sky above him like trellises of electric snakes, and the acrid smell of ozone permeated the atmosphere.

His destination was the site of the signing of the armistice in 1953: Panmunjom. Almost anytime a story on North-South tensions appears in the media, its row of boxy blue buildings leads the visuals. Soldiers on either side of a literal line in the sand had faced off against each other there for well over sixty years, and the stand-off resumed immediately after the ballyhooed but fruitless border meeting between President Dillard and Kim Jong-un. Those on the North Korean side had been ordered by General O to grant Patrick safe passage. It was the other side of the line that had him worried.

Despite the weather, South Korean and American troops stood guard behind mirrored sunglasses, glaring threateningly at their North Korean counterparts. But when they suddenly caught sight of a Caucasian face speeding toward them from the Northern side, their lips parted, their brows furrowed, and their rifles were brought up into firing position. Patrick revved the motorcycle, popped the clutch and thundered past them across the border. They leveled their rifles at him as he passed, awaiting an order to fire, but as soon as he was in South Korean territory, he 360ed the bike around and jumped off into the mud.

"Don't shoot!" he screamed as he ran toward them with his hands held high. "I'm an American! I have to see General Merkin immediately!"

A squad of guards advanced on him with their rifles at the ready for point-blank head shots, but their sergeant pushed through them and into Patrick's face.

"Alright, asshole, you got one second! Who the fuck are you?"

Patrick's words poured out one on top of the other. "My name is Patrick Featherstone! I'm an American working for the CIA, check for yourself!"

The sergeant got Col. Lawrence's people on his shoulder radio and told them to do just that.

"I have to see General Merkin *now*!" Patrick shouted frantically. "The North Koreans are getting ready to attack and he's the only one who can stop it!"

"An American general is the only one who can stop a Nork attack? What kind of bullshit is that?" the sergeant screamed, his rifle coming ever closer to Patrick's head. He chambered a round with a double metallic click.

"No, wait! Their General O is convinced that Merkin is going to attack first with nukes. O's attack would be preemptive."

The sergeant's eye went to the metal sight blade on top of his barrel and his finger tightened around the trigger.

"If General Merkin did anything, it would be a pre-emp of our own! That's a whole shitload of pre-emps wouldn't you say, dead man?"

Just then a jeep pulled up. A tall man in his late 50s with two stars on his collar jumped out and swaggered over on long legs to where Patrick was about two seconds away from having his brains blown back across the border.

"Start talking," he said.

"This guy hasn't stopped talking since he got here, General! Something about only you can stop the North Koreans from attacking."

Merkin fixed the sergeant with a withering look. "I'm fully capable of asking my own questions, Sergeant. Lower your rifle." He turned back to Patrick.

"This better be good."

Patrick identified himself and gave Merkin the details of Moon's plan to use the American army to annihilate General O and his army so that he could take over the North Korean regime.

Merkin's eyes tightened into an ever-deepening squint of incredulity when his executive officer, Colonel Lawrence, rushed to the scene from the intel office.

"General, this guy says he's with the CIA and we checked him out. For some reason, his name is familiar to me, but they say they have no idea who the hell he is."

"That's because I'm NOC, non-official cover!" Patrick shouted in frustration. "I went to the North to find that guy who defected, Tyler Kang, and then my ex-fiancée got kidnapped after her father stole something from Comrade Moon and..." His voice petered out as he saw the expression on Merkin's and Lawrence's faces. "Look," he said, "I know this must sound farfetched..."

"Son, you've got a gift for understatement," Merkin replied.

Patrick's guts churned in desperation. What if General O thought that everything Patrick had told him was just a ploy to buy time so that he could warn the Americans to attack first? He could very well be ordering the opening artillery salvo at any second.

"General," Patrick blurted out. "You absolutely *must* trust me! Let me go back to General O before he orders an attack. I can get him to meet with you so that you can clear up this. . . misunderstanding."

"*Misunderstanding*?" Merkin thundered. "O has 100,000 troops ready to spill over the DMZ to wipe up anything his artillery doesn't get first, and you call it a *misunderstanding*? What do you think this is, a fucking sensitivity workshop?"

"General, I'm going back *now* to meet with O again. I'll tell him that you'll be in the middle of the bridge down the road in ten minutes."

General Merkin stood with his mouth agape. *The balls on this man*! He looked one way and then the other and then up at the sky, as if searching the clouds for an appropriate response to this alleged undercover CIA agent with his ridiculous story about a plot. Then he looked around him: two thousand of the best soldiers America has ever produced up against 100,000 North Koreans hell-bent on their destruction. If there was even a minuscule chance of saving a single one of them. . . He cut his head to one side in thought and shrugged his shoulders.

"Let him go," he said finally.

"But sir, he's...!" the sergeant blurted out.

"I said let him go, godammit!"

Without waiting for Merkin to change his mind, Patrick vaulted onto the motorcycle and sped back to the North Korean side. In less than a minute he was back at General O's tent. O was waiting outside with his mouth set and his arms folded in front of him.

"I have wonderful news, General," Patrick began, with a palsied smile on his face and a desperate hope in his heart that his quaking legs wouldn't give him away. "General Merkin says he would be most honored to meet with you to discuss the current unfortunate situation. May I suggest the Bridge of No Return?"

But what neither Patrick nor General O nor General Merkin nor anyone else knew was that Moon had an ace in the hole even if his plan to destroy O and his army was initially thwarted. The man who had volunteered to make the "ultimate sacrifice" for Kim Jong-un and who was now in possession of the weapon Yumi's father had stolen was now not two miles away from the Bridge of No Return setting up position for an ultimate sea of fire.

CHAPTER 33

THE BRIDGE OF NO RETURN
May 1, 8:13 a.m.

In 1953, after the cessation of hostilities that masqueraded as an end to the Korean War, prisoners taken on either side of the 38th parallel were repatriated via a bridge they were told they would never cross again. Hence, the Bridge of No Return. The only ground link, other than Panmunjom, between North and South Korea, the bridge is a lonely outpost in the loneliest place on earth.

An entourage of military vehicles pulled to a halt on either side of the bridge, as the rain marched in sheets across its narrow span. Patrick eased his motorcycle behind a guard shack and stayed on the North Korean side to avoid being a distraction to the historic meeting. General Carl Merkin got out of his jeep, adjusted his sodden beret, and strode with a purposeful gait that concealed the trepidation in his heart. For all his talk of a preemptive nuclear strike on General O's army, he knew that he would do any honorable thing to avert a clash if it meant sparing the lives of his men.

General O alighted from his military truck and stared imperiously at his opposite number standing in a ramrod-stiff posture of defiance. He walked slowly but resolutely to his end of the bridge, paused slightly, and then took the first step toward the line in the middle. As he did so, Merkin closed the distance between them. When they reached the center, they held each other's eyes and Merkin broke the silence.

"Why are you massing your army?" he said in a voice raised in anger.

"The Korean People's Army has the right to defend itself!" O shouted back in English.

"*Defend*? I've got two thousand men over here, and you have fifty times that many, not to mention artillery, tanks and all the rest of it. If anyone's on the defensive, it's me. And just so you know, I have a couple of 2-kiloton tactical devices all ready to go. It's my defense against *you!*"

Suddenly, Colonel Lawrence rushed to the center of the bridge with a handful of photos. He urgently took Merkin to one side but in his excitement spoke loud enough for O to hear. "General, we have the Keyhole images you ordered. They show some guy in the vicinity of the Kumgang Mountain Dam over on their side with what looks to be a satchel charge of some kind. And sir..." Colonel Lawrence leaned in and whispered. "Sir, he's wearing American BDUs [battle dress uniform, top and bottom]."

Merkin turned to Lawrence and whispered, "Have the images forwarded immediately to Washington. Tell them I want to know what their response is within fifteen minutes. And be sure to tell them that it's an NK soldier wearing one of our uniforms."

"Yes, sir." Lawrence trotted quickly back to the American side.

Merkin turned to O and spoke in a raised voice. "Well, General, I'm sure you heard most of that. It appears that one of your people is preparing to breach the Kumgang Dam."

General O shook his head vehemently. "This is not one of my people! I know absolutely nothing about this!"

When Patrick heard the sincere profession of innocence in O's voice, a shockwave rippled through his entire body. Of course! Like a *baduk* grand master, Moon had a deadly backup strategy up his sleeve. If for any reason O wouldn't attack, Moon himself would provoke the American nuclear response by having his man breach the dam and send billions of tons of water rushing across the DMZ. Merkin's last act on earth would be to launch the nukes against General O. And with his man on the dam dressed like an American GI, Moon could still blame the Americans for the total annihilation of O and his 1st Army Corps.

Half a mile away, the lone figure in an American army uniform was nearing the top of the stairs on the eastern side of the Kumgang Mountain Dam.

Strapped to his back was a standard-issue rucksack bulging with the weapon that had been recovered from Yumi's father. Despite its size, the weapon was more than capable of bringing down a mere dam. A TNW, or Tactical Nuclear Weapon, it had a yield of 12 kilotons, the same as the much larger bomb that had leveled Hiroshima.

The man's guts churned. It was his last day on earth. Comrade Moon had laid it all out for him when they met. His final mission would immortalize him as a shining example of selfless sacrifice for the Democratic People's Republic of Korea. His pulse raced, and yet he somehow welcomed death. It would be his way of paying back the god/man who had done so much for him—Kim Jong-il. The best father a man could have ever had. As he readied himself for his final act, he swore he would prove himself to be as much a son to the departed Dear Leader as the Supreme Commander himself.

O and Merkin continued to stare each other down, neither of them certain of what to do next. Finally Merkin spoke.

"Prepare a mortar strike for the top of that dam," he ordered Colonel Lawrence.

"No!" O shouted angrily. "I would regard that as an attack on my country!"

"I'm not going to just stand here and wait for that guy to breach the dam. He'll kill us all!" Merkin shouted back. "If you won't take care of this, I will!"

The two generals stood face to face on the bridge, their breath exiting their mouths in rapid jets of steam.

"Wait!" Patrick cried out. He started out onto the bridge but was pushed back at rifle point by a North Korean sentry. He stood his ground and shouted to Merkin. "A mortar would just blow the dam up! I'm a JSOC-qualified sniper, I can take the guy out with one shot."

Colonel Lawrence's eyes widened. "Wait a minute, now I know where I heard this guy's name before. He was one of JSOC's top operators back in the mid-90s. Had a kill list as long as my arm." He called out to Patrick. "What were the names of the Iraqis who tried to take out H.W. Bush?"

"Abdul Karim al-Nasir and Narji Salman," Patrick shouted back without hesitation. They were names he would never forget. His first kills.

Colonel Lawrence turned to Merkin. "He was in my division back then, General. I'll vouch for him."

Having exhausted all other options and relying on Lawrence's recommendation, the two generals reluctantly agreed to give Patrick exactly one hour to try and take out the man on the dam. That is, if the man didn't breach the dam first. With O's permission, Patrick crossed to the American side where, on Merkin's orders, he was issued a Remington M24 sniper rifle, the most accurate in their arsenal, and a Kevlar vest. He ran back to the North Korean side, jumped on his motorcycle and was off.

A quarter mile away from the base of the dam, he ditched the motorcycle and started in on foot. The area where he walked inclined sharply and was strewn with a haphazard of boulder-sized scree made slippery by the rain, limiting his progress to slow, tentative steps. The rain fell more lightly than before, but at this altitude, enfolded by clouds, he was lucky to be able to see 100 feet in front of him.

The eleven-pound M24 strapped to his back dug into the wounds Bastard Cho's whip had inflicted, and he brought the rifle into shooting position. Detaching the 10X scope from the barrel rail, he focused it all around and on the dam. No movement at all. He clicked the scope back in place, brought the rifle up to port arms, and proceeded forward, his eyes in constant search of any movement in the area. About fifty yards from the base of the dam, he was brought up short by a faint melodic sound coming from above. *Birdsong?* he wondered. No. This was human. As he canted his head forward and up, he began to make out words:

"Our General born on Mount Paektu
guides our beautiful land.
Our Great General, who is hailed by us all
And cheered throughout the land.
He leads our people, the Sun's cause he carries on
Long Live General Kim Jong-il"!

From somewhere up on the dam, a resonant baritone was singing "The Song of General Kim Jong-il", an anthem that everyone in North Korea was required to memorize and sing en masse at public celebrations when the former leader was still alive. Patrick's eyes narrowed at the utter incongruity of hearing it under these circumstances, but it meant that he had reached the base of the dam undetected. Tilting his head straight up, he saw the enormity of the danger he and everyone in the vicinity faced. The dam was at least three hundred feet high and almost half a mile long. The volume of water it held back had to run into the billions of tons. With one last look for any sign of movement, he broke into a run toward a stairway on the eastern side of the dam that wound its way to the very top.

General Merkin returned to his HQ to wait out the hour and sat alone again in front of MacArthur's portrait. His mind, long trained in approaching problems from every angle, methodically calculated his options. In mid-rumination, there was a knock at the door, and Yung-shik, his valet, announced the arrival of Colonel Lawrence.

"Send him in," Merkin muttered in a detached voice.

Lawrence strode in, waited for the valet to close the door behind him and then turned to Merkin who was lost in thought under the MacArthur portrait.

"General, I got a call back from the White House. They saw the satellite images we sent of that guy on the Kumgang Dam. And they're saying that under no circumstances are you to engage the North Koreans. They're also ordering me to relieve you of command if you refuse."

Merkin took a deep breath, his eyes locked onto MacArthur's. "Well?" he said, slowly turning to face his executive officer. "What are you going to do, Ray?"

Colonel Lawrence stood silently for a long moment. When he finally spoke there was a glint in his eye. "I told them the connection was bad, and I couldn't make out a fucking word of what they were saying. Sir."

Merkin emptied his lungs through pursed lips. "Thank you, Ray. As I promised, I'll hold off on any action until there's evidence of clear and present danger. But I want those two low-yield devices at the ready for my launch command."

"Yes, sir." Lawrence snapped off a salute and left the room.

Yung-shik, Merkin's valet, bowed low to Colonel Lawrence on the other side of the door. And then he activated his cell phone and sent a coded text message.

CHAPTER 34

DEMILITARIZED ZONE
May 1, 9:24 a.m.

Patrick winced as he strapped the rifle onto his lacerated back and began climbing the winding staircase on the eastern side of the Kumgang Dam. Suddenly, an intense whirr like an electric charge whizzed by his head and spanged off the steel cowling surrounding the staircase. He flattened himself against the side of the stairway closest to the dam where, theoretically at least, the angle would be too severe for the shooter to have a clear shot. He was pinned down, but he had to act soon to prevent the man from blowing up the dam and unleashing a tide of death.

Having no idea that the man was getting ready to deploy a backpack nuke, Patrick approached the problem in terms he was intimately familiar with from his JSOC days. He had worked with satchel charges before and knew that even the smaller ones required time to set up properly. If the man on the dam was using something bigger, the M183, say, which contained twenty pounds of C-4, even more time would be needed. Taking a chance that his adversary had gone back to arming his explosive device, Patrick took a deep breath and sprinted up the next go-round in the staircase. No shots. Following the same strategy, he paused momentarily at each landing and then sprinted up to the next. Soon he was halfway up, then two-thirds, then finally at the top. Shielded by the cowling of the staircase, he poked his head out. His foe was huddled fifty yards away in the middle of the ten-foot-wide top of the dam but facing in the opposite direction. Patrick raised the M24 and took aim. He had always hated having to shoot a man in the back, but a sniper takes out the enemy when and how he can.

But the man had already seen Patrick climbing up the stairs, and, realizing that he needed for his stalker to emerge from behind the protective cowling, he presented an easy target of himself while furtively chambering a round into his bolt-action 30.06 rifle. Not the full-metal jackets of his earlier shots, though. An FMJ will pass through five men lined up in a row and remain intact. The problem is, the shot has to be accurate to center-mass or the head to avoid leaving an enemy wounded but still alive enough to shoot back. No, to rid himself for good of this nuisance he needed more assurance than that: A fragmentation boat-tail round, essentially several bullets in one.

He slammed back the bolt on the 30.06 and pivoted around in a flash, aiming the barrel directly at Patrick's chest. Patrick was caught completely by surprise, and the two shots he managed to get off were wildly off the mark. He instinctively balled himself up into a crouch to present less of a target, but there is very little hiding place from an 11-gram chunk of lead traveling at 3,000 feet per second. He felt a crushing pain in his chest, and the wind was punched completely out of his lungs as the bullet found its mark and his rifle clattered down the side of the dam. The Kevlar vest he wore absorbed and dispersed much of the direct lethal force of the round but sent boat-tail fragments exploding outward and upward, one of which caught him in the left side of his neck. Carotid territory.

Luckily for Patrick, the bolt action of the shooter's high-powered rifle had jammed, preventing a follow-up shot, and he was able to back off the dam onto the staircase, protected again, for the moment at least, by the metal cowling.

The shooter, on the other hand, was flummoxed. He had seen with his own eyes his victim take a direct hit to the chest. How he had survived, much less retreated onto the staircase, was beyond miraculous. Not even the most advanced bullet-proof vest he knew of could withstand the immense force of a point-blank 30.06. What he didn't know was that Patrick had liberally coated his vest with Jack Fitzroy's STF--- Shear Thickening Fluid--- which instantly hardened into an all but impenetrable barrier upon impact. However, one of the boat-tail frags had scored the left side of Patrick's neck. The shooter impatiently checked his watch. The seconds were rapidly ticking down on his deadline. But first he needed to make sure that his stalker was out of the picture.

Once behind the cowling, Patrick's eyes began losing focus, and his pulse raced wildly. The bullet he had taken to the chest had caused hydrostatic shock, whereby the pressure waves of the slug had traveled to his brain, causing a moderately severe concussion. His hands were soaked by the blood that poured out of his neck, and he lay down to conserve his dwindling energy.

Lying prone on the staircase landing, he was quietly amazed at how calm he felt as he awaited the inevitable. Time stopped. His grip on life was loosening. All his dreams, aspirations for enlightenment, his love for Yumi— all of them losing color and shape and draining into the burgeoning pool of blood he lay in. A strange delight just this side of delirium drifted over him like an unseen mist, a samadhi of peace that surpassed understanding.

His mind wandered unmoored to his next incarnation, the one after this wasted one. *Hopefully, next time I'll get it right. Maybe I'll even have Yumi in my life again. Maybe we can reach enlightenment together and...*

His field of vision began to narrow and curl around the edges like a photograph being consumed in a flame.

But wait—who is that? It must be the Angel of Death himself. Are you here to take me?

The shooter stepped carefully around the cowling with his rifle raised. Patrick looked up at his Angel of Death and smiled. The shooter was momentarily perplexed by the expression on Patrick's face, but he collected himself and took aim at Patrick's head.

Patrick had once read in the Tibetan Book of the Dead that at the exact moment of death, there is a release into a light-filled realm from which one begins the next phase of the soul's journey. The light is an effulgent yellow, the book had said. Patrick indeed saw a light--- but felt a twinge of anxiety. The light he was seeing was red, not yellow. And it was not an enveloping light, either. It was focused, a scarlet pinprick piercing his darkening field of vision. And now the light seemed to travel in slow motion, becoming brighter and brighter and taking on an almost physical dimension as it grew in intensity.

He had heard no sound nor seen a flash coming from the rifle in the hands of the Angel of Death. Even so, the light increased in fullness and brightness. But how could this be, he wondered, as he saw the Angel looking down the stairway and shouting something he couldn't make out. The Angel's mouth was moving in a weird slow motion, his face filled with bewildered fear. *Could it be? Yes! The Angel of Death was screaming!* And the red pinprick of light Patrick had seen came from a laser sight that had grown into something voluminous and scarlet that issued from the Angel's chest. And then the Angel fell.

Patrick had no strength left to process any more of what was happening. The hydrostatic shock he had suffered had shut down his normal brain functions out of self-preservation. And then he lost consciousness and tumbled down the stairs.

He came to with his ghost-mind wobbling, not sure what was fact and what was phantasm. He saw the faces of Yumi, Tyler, his father, his mother—everyone who had ever mattered to him—swirling around his blinkered field of vision. Into this netherworld intruded a thoroughly corporeal voice.

"Ain't gravity a bitch?" the voice said. A hand, firm yet gentle, rested on his shoulder as if in reassurance. Patrick summoned the strength to look up. His eyes tried to focus. *Who might this be? Ah yes, I remember now.*

"General Merkin, Featherstone's hour just ended and the real-time satellite images show O's artillery tubes being readied."

"Stand by for launch orders, Ray."

"You're not going to wait for him to attack first, are you, General?"

Merkin looked at Colonel Lawrence with his eyes widening. "Why, Ray, you're sounding like a hawk all of a sudden," he said in a tone of mock-surprise. Then he turned serious again. "I haven't gone dove. But I looked into the eyes of that guy on the bridge. O's a tough old bastard, but he's a man of his word, that much I'm sure of. I know what I said before, but sometimes you just have to go with your gut. And pray to God you're right."

"General O, I have urgent information!" General O's adjutant stood breathless at the lip of O's command tent. O came out. "What is it?"

"General, our agent working for the Americans just called in. They are preparing their nuclear attack! May I humbly suggest that we take immediate preemptive action?"

General O bolted from his tent and pushed past the adjutant. The adjutant tailed him like a loyal dog waiting for his master to issue a command. O spoke angrily as he rode to the Bridge of No Return.

"Prepare a full artillery attack. Await my order."

"But General, what if the Americans are preparing to launch their nuclear weapons this very moment?"

"You will wait for my order," O barked and pushed the aide aside. He was at the bridge a moment later. He called over to the American side.

"Tell Merkin to come here immediately," he shouted to the sentries on the other side of the bridge. He didn't have long to wait. From around a curve in the road, a jeep appeared carrying the American general.

"Why are you preparing a nuclear attack on my position?" O shouted from his side of the bridge.

"Why are you preparing an artillery attack on mine?" Merkin countered angrily.

O's adjutant ran up to him with a frightened look on his face. "General," he said in a low voice, "our agent says that they are preparing a *second* nuclear weapon for immediate deployment."

Colonel Lawrence's jeep screeched to a halt at the American end of the bridge. Lawrence ran to Merkin and took him aside. "The satellite images show that they've now got their entire artillery capability ready to launch any second, General. Shall we proceed with preemptive action?"

O and Merkin looked at their respective aides and then back over the bridge at each other. Each was slowly raising his hand to order an attack. But then they stopped with their arms suspended in midair.

In fact, all motion of any kind ceased in the immediate vicinity of the Bridge of No Return. Even the rain that had inundated the area stopped.

The only sound was birdsong drifting over the DMZ, the largest unintended wildlife sanctuary in the world. And the reason for the silence was the unlikely entourage approaching the bridge from the North Korean side: three white men, only two of whom were alive. Of the two still alive, an elderly one carried the dead man in his arms, and a younger man limped forward, his bloody neck bound with one of his shirt sleeves.

Generals O and Merkin watched them approach with looks of absolute incomprehension on their faces. The dead man in the arms of the old man was young, perhaps in his mid twenties. He had ash-blond hair, a fair complexion—and a hole in his chest. He was wearing a blood-soaked U.S. Army uniform. No one moved or said a word. It was as if they were holding still for a portrait painter. Finally, the old man spoke.

"I've come to bring my son home," he called out in a southern American accent, and began to walk across the bridge with the body of the young man cradled in his arms. Sentries on either side moved to block his way, but were waved away by their generals. When the old man reached the south side of the bridge, he gently placed the body of the young man on the ground, stood up, and saluted General Merkin.

"Corporal John Robert Drosnik reporting for duty, sir."

Merkin, for once, was speechless. He had heard about the defectors from the 1960s, and vaguely remembered that this Drosnik had been there longer than any of the others, almost fifty years. And now he had come back. Merkin spoke to Colonel Lawrence in a low voice, telling him to take Corporal Drosnik and the body of his son to his headquarters.

Patrick limped across the bridge where he was assisted by a burly MP. The two generals regarded each other silently from opposite ends of the bridge. Even the birds in the trees ceased their singing. Then, at some unspoken signal both of them recognized, they walked to the line painted on its exact center. They held each other's eyes, then ever so slowly their right arms lifted in unison. They shook hands. Then they walked back to their respective sides of the Bridge of No Return and gave orders for their forces to stand down.

Patrick was taken to the base hospital at Camp Bonifas where he learned that he had lost quite a bit less blood than had initially been thought, a little over half a pint from a bleeder of a neck vein. His carotid artery was unscathed. To be on the safe side, he was told, they were admitting him for overnight observation. As soon as the charge nurse left his room, however, he got dressed and tiptoed out the rear entrance of the hospital. There he saw something glorious beyond all measure. In a corner of the loading dock area was a pristine flame-blue Harley Electra-Glide Evo, circa 1985. It was parked in a reserved spot with the name "Merkin" stenciled on the wall above it.

It started on the first kick, and Patrick was on his way. Once on the north side of the DMZ, he opened up the throttle and streaked up the Unification Highway toward Pyongyang.

On the ride up on the nearly deserted highway, Patrick let his mind wander back to his first encounter with John Robert Drosnik at the Basement Bar. That he had re-defected to America on the day circumstances forced him to kill his own son was tragically ironic, and a heaviness gripped Patrick's heart.

Apparently, during the years of Drosnik's drunken absence from his son's life, Andrew had fallen completely under the sway of North Korean propaganda, to the point of regarding Kim Jong-il as his spiritual father. Noting his unshakeable loyalty, the regime had recruited him as a deep-cover spy, a cunning move given his blond hair and blue eyes. The weekend earlier Drosnik discovered his son's diary and read of his "final mission in Kaesong," as he called it in the diary. He knew he had to stop Andrew at any cost and saw only one solution.

Patrick switched back to the present. The official start of the Glorious Triumvirate Celebration was mere hours away. He hunched down lower in his seat and open up the Harley to full throttle.

CHAPTER 35

THE GLORIOUS TRIUMVIRATE CELEBRATION
PYONGYANG
May 1, 11:40 a.m.

Few spectacles of coordinated human activity can equal that of the DPRK's Mass Games, a dizzying non-stop demonstration of physical prowess and military might designed to inspire the masses and overawe the visitor. With gymnastics, pounding martial music, and a human backdrop display as the main features, the Games are normally housed in the 150,000-seat May Day Stadium. This year, however, the Games had been moved to the million-square-foot Kim Il-sung Square on the west side of the Taedong River in order to accommodate the huge number of foreign tourists and journalists who would be in attendance.

The Glorious Triumvirate Celebration would begin with three solemn minutes of silence followed by a military brass-band dirge symbolizing the people's ongoing grief over the loss of the Great Leader over twenty years earlier and the more recent demise of the Dear Leader. Then it would move on to a grand military parade and culminate with the piece de resistance: the first-ever performance of the Mass Games right in the middle of Kim Il-sung Square.

Comrade Moon stood alone in a room overlooking Kim Il-sung Square, watching and brooding and swearing under his breath. Gone from his heart was the unshakeable confidence that had buoyed his spirits until only a short while ago. For things had changed.

Everything is under control, he lied to himself. *All of the backup plans are now in place. Steady, steady...*

He forced himself to concentrate on the 50,000 members of the Mass Games backdrop display that was assembled behind the Grand People's Study House holding their binders of colored placards that, when flipped to a certain page, become tiny pieces of the massive tableaux that depict Kim Il-sung, Kim Jong-il, or Kim Jong-un in one hagiographic pose of victory after another. They practiced individually and in small work cadres going back and forth from the colored placards to the interlocking *hangul* letters spelling out bellicose slogans reaffirming the nation's resolute single-mindedness in annihilating every last "Yankee bastard" on the face of the earth.

Looking from side to side, Moon took in the streets of Pyongyang teeming with a multitude of over a million that included an unprecedented number of foreigners. Even foreign television teams had been allowed in to broadcast live from North Korea for the first time ever, and they busied themselves setting up their satellite dishes in the city center as close to the Mass Games performance area as they could get. They had been part of Moon's master plan. After the expected American attack on General O and his army at the DMZ, the foreign news networks would be on hand to broadcast live the assassination of Kim Jong-un by an American spy named Tyler Kang. In this way, Moon would have documentary evidence of the abysmal depths of American treachery as he proclaimed himself Supreme Leader.

Now, with the start of the festivities growing closer by the minute, Moon's sense of foreboding deepened. For one thing, the American attack on General O had not materialized. For another, Tyler Kang had gone missing. A search for him had turned up nothing. And as if all that weren't enough, Moon had learned the night before that the Bureau 39 account at Macau's Eastern Star Bank had been completely wiped out. Not a penny remained of the half billion dollars in the account. And no one knew what happened to it.

Moon began pacing back in forth in the little room he occupied overlooking Kim Il-sung Square, his anxiety and anger mounting by the minute. Gathering his composure, he realized that despite all of his setbacks, if he were able to have Kim Jong-un assassinated, he could still declare himself the new leader of the nation and satisfy the terms of his promise to the Commission. He lit a cigarette and allowed himself to relax somewhat. At least he had found a replacement to kill Kim Jong-un, now that Tyler Kang was nowhere to be found. The assassination of Kim alone should be enough to launch him to the highest reaches of power. Or at least he fervently hoped so. The Commission wouldn't have it any other way, not after all he had promised them. At this last thought, he bolted up off his chair and went back to pacing and checking his watch every few minutes.

An hour of speeding up from the DMZ later, Patrick arrived in Pyongyang to a sky sealed off under gunmetal clouds. His first stop was Mrs. Pae's *jangmadang* market where he left the motorcycle and retrieved his father's .45 caliber pistol, the extra magazines, and his passport, as well as a backup handgun. Mrs. Pae also gave him a disposable phone that operated on a South Korean cell network.

"We get these from a friend of mine," she said with a wink, North Korean for "they fell off a truck."

"Here is my number in case you get into trouble. Which you seem to have a knack for," she said with a glance at the cuts and bruises on his face, neck and hands. She wrote a phone number on a piece of paper.

"And here's one more thing," she said as she reached into her pocket and produced a good-luck amulet of the type that Miss Ok was always polishing at the Basement Bar. She pressed it into his hands.

Patrick thanked her, put the amulet and the cell phone in his pocket, and began threading his way impatiently on foot through the crowds that sauntered with maddening slowness in the direction of Kim Il-sung Square. As he quietly cursed his snail-like progress, he caught a fragment of a conversation between a five-year-old boy and his father.

"*Aboji*, is it true that the Great Leader could perform miracles?"

"Of course, son! The Great Leader raised our country up out of nothing!"

"And did he also make the birds carry him into the sky? That's what my teacher said."

"And she was right! When the Great Leader died, the birds were so sad that they came down and took him up to the heavens. But then they saw the tears of us, the people, and they brought him back to us."

"Is he here with us today?"

"The Great Leader is always with us, son."

Patrick stopped abruptly. The crowd eddied around him, but he saw and heard nothing. He had an idea.

The Great Leader is always with us...

He snapped out of his daze and continued to where he had last seen Tyler: the Foreign Outreach Institute, but when he got there, it was completely deserted. The next logical place to search for him was Kim Il-sung Square which he reached ten minutes later. Looking out over the Square, he saw that the viewing platform for Party dignitaries was directly opposite the Grand People's Study House which made the latter a likely location for a sniper hide. He made for it posthaste.

Once there, Patrick went around the back where the gymnasts had assembled. In the bustle of preparation, no one gave him so much as a second look. Except for one person. He picked the lock and ducked inside, sure he had not been spotted. Walking toe-to-heel into the darkened Study House, he stopped his breathing and listened. The only sound was a slight wind coming from one of the upper floors. A window was open on a day the Grand People's Study House and all public buildings were mandated to be closed. He began climbing the stairs.

When he got to the top, he stopped and listened again. The sound of wind was stronger now, and it was coming from a room that faced directly out onto the Square. After three quick breaths, he kicked the door open, and sprang into the room in a low crouch with one of the pistols he had gotten from Mrs. Pae panning the room. Tyler spun around from the window with a rifle in his hands. Patrick took aim at his center mass.

"Drop it!" he yelled to Tyler.

"*You* drop it, idiot!"

Patrick kept the gun leveled at Tyler who groaned in frustration through gritted teeth. "I'm not going to kill Kim Jong-un!" he shouted.

"Then why the rifle?" Patrick shouted back.

"I'm looking for the shooter, that's why! I'm sure they've got someone in my place."

Patrick hesitated. There was nothing deceptive in Tyler's demeanor.

"Go ahead, keep standing there all day for all I care," Tyler muttered dismissively and turned back to the window overlooking Kim Il-sung Square.

Patrick slowly walked over to him, his pistol still raised.

"Come to make yourself useful?" Tyler said without looking up. "Take a gander out there and tell me if you see anyone with a gun."

Patrick looked out the window at the million-strong crowd. He turned to Tyler with his mouth hanging open.

"You got a better idea?" Tyler asked wearily.

Patrick pulled up a chair and joined Tyler at the window. Now they had two sets of eyes, instantly elevating an exercise in complete and utter futility into an exercise in complete and utter improbability.

"Where'd you get the rifle," Patrick asked, nodding towards the Chinese QBU-88 Tyler was holding.

"I was supposed to use it for the assassination."

"What changed your mind?"

Tyler turned away as he spoke. "I thought about what you said about Moon. That he's a mass murderer and all. I didn't want to take the chance that you were right."

"But what about your fiancée? She was pushing pretty hard for you to go through with it."

"Oh Jesus, you had to ask." Tyler hung his head. "Did I really call her my fiancée?"

"You did."

"Well...I guess we're not engaged anymore. Anyway, enough of her. We've got a shooter to find. You take the left and I'll take the right."

They sat for a long time without a word, engrossed in scanning the immense throng. Twenty minutes later, Tyler finally broke the silence without taking his eyes off the crowd below.

"Sempai?" he said softly.

"Yeah, what?"

"I missed you, bro."

Patrick scowled and clucked his tongue. "What is this, a beer commercial all of a sudden?"

"Hardass."

"Alright, I missed you too. But no hugs."

"Not a chance. I haven't had my shots."

As they spoke, a solitary figure made his way across the Taedong River to a building with a perfect vantage high above Kim Il-sung Square and overlooking the dais on which Kim Jong-un would be reviewing the day's proceedings. The structure was high enough to give him a clear, unimpeded view of the square.

Long live the Great Leader! the man thought. *Comrade Moon, that is.* He chambered a three-inch round into a Russian-made 7.62 Dragunov sniper rifle and began to adjust the telescopic sight on the barrel rail. The man was Tyler Kang's replacement as the assassin of Kim Jong-un. Suddenly his body went rigid as his eyes casually traveled across the river. Kim Jong-un had just begun walking up the stairs to the dais a full half hour ahead of schedule. The man collected himself and did a spot windage assessment using the sea of flags floating everywhere in the Square. The gusts had died down for the time being. He pressed the telescopic lens to his eye, found Kim Jong-un's head in the reticle...and then lost him again in the crowd of dignitaries that surrounded him.

CHAPTER 36

PEOPLE'S STUDY HOUSE, PYONGYANG
May 1, 12:28 p.m.

Patrick and Tyler silently scanned opposite sides of Kim Il-sung Square, searching for any sign of a shooter. Patrick relaxed his eyes and let them wander around his side of the Square. He had long ago found it better not to focus his eyes too intently when scouting for a target. That way his peripheral vision could pick up more in the way of things that looked out of place. "Nothing is regular in nature" had been the watchword in his sniper training, but the challenge on this day was just the opposite. For the Glorious Triumvirate Celebration, nothing was permitted to be unplanned or spontaneous.

With upwards of a million people in the square, Patrick and Tyler began to share a sense of hopelessness, especially with the shadowplay of the clouds across the sun. The afternoon sky was gradually brightening, and a section of the square might be totally enshrouded one moment, only to be dappled in sunlight a moment later. Then, the last of the clouds raced over the square, leaving a boundless expanse of blue overhead, a welcome sight for those in the crowd below, but one which presented an even greater problem for Patrick and Tyler.

"Everything's too bright. I can't make out a goddam thing," Tyler muttered from behind the scope.

"Let me take a look." Patrick replied, and Tyler handed him the rifle. Patrick panned the immense crowd and then widened the ambitus of his search beyond the square itself. He slowly scanned the hilly area northwest of the city and brought the rifle sideways across a 180-degree arc. And then he stopped.

"Got it."

"Got what?" Tyler asked, excitement rising in his voice.

Patrick indicated with his head the side of Kim Il-sung Square closest to the Taedong River. Tyler's eyes followed Patrick's. They both looked across the river.

"Oh, no way. Can't be," Tyler said.

"I just saw a glint off a scope. It makes total sense. Only place with the proper angle and an open shot."

"Too far. Too high."

"I know what I saw."

Tyler grabbed the rifle out of Patrick's hands and aimed the scope across the Taedong River where Patrick had seen a glint of light, and then he saw it too. A rifle, tiny in the distance, being placed on the ledge on top of the Juche Tower, the Tower of Self-Reliance, rising 500 feet into the sky. He and Patrick had focused so intently on the Square that they had never even considered the Tower before. Nor had they heard the door to the room they were in opening slowly behind them.

"He just moved!" Tyler called out.

The assassin had changed his position on the Tower when the sun broke through the clouds. Sniper 101: Never shoot into the sun. But the man had forgotten Sniper 102: Always assume the enemy has you in his sights.

"Let me see, Tyler."

Patrick took the rifle and re-sighted in on the top of the Juche Tower. "There he is," he murmured a moment later.

"Then take the shot," Tyler said with urgency in his voice.

Patrick said nothing. His breathing had slowed to next to nothing and his finger was exerting 3 pounds of pressure on the trigger. Just an ounce more would be enough. He was waiting for the shooter on the Tower to raise his head just a fraction in order to seal the deal.

"Patrick, either you take the fucking shot or I will."

And then, not one but two shots rang out almost simultaneously. The first was from a handgun that had been aimed through the half-open door of the room where Patrick and Tyler had set up their hide. The second came from

Patrick's rifle a nanosecond later. He had been applying the final fraction of an ounce of pressure to the trigger when the surprise of hearing a gunshot directly behind him caused the rifle to jump in his hands at the exact moment the round was exiting the barrel.

Patrick turned to Tyler whose face was turning white. He had taken an in-and-out to the thigh, and blood was flowing from both entrance and exit wounds. Patrick rotated completely around and held down the trigger on full auto until the QBU-88 had spat out a hailstorm of heavy-ball rounds at the door. Whoever had been on the other side was either cut to ribbons or very lucky. He threw down the empty rifle and slithered over on his belly to Tyler.

"What day is it, Kohai?" he shouted, trying to assess Tyler's mental clarity.

"Rock and roll day, Sempai. Don't worry, I can take care of myself."

Patrick yanked a curtain down from one of the windows and tore it into strips to bind Tyler's leg wound. He then made a pillow of the rest of the curtain and lay Tyler down onto it. Tyler's breathing was calm and steady, his mind alert, and the bandage appeared to be stanching the bleeding. He was in pain, but he managed a smile.

"I've taken worse, bro. Besides, I got a note from my doctor that says I get to stay here and watch the parade. You, on the other hand, are gonna need to haul some serious ass if you're hoping to find any bad guys."

"In that case, enjoy the view. Beer's on me later."

"Roger that."

Patrick gave Tyler one of the handguns from Mrs. Pae. His next stop was the Juche Tower a quarter mile away.

CHAPTER 37

JUCHE TOWER
May 1, 12:51 p.m.

The shooter was a lucky man. The round that Patrick had sent his way would have taken off his head had Patrick not been distracted at the last moment. Still, the bullet had not gone entirely astray, and a creasing gash had opened up on the left side of his forehead, directly above his shooting eye. Facial wounds are notoriously bloody, this one exceptionally so. He pulled down a banner that was draped over the tower, tore it to pieces, and turned it into a makeshift headband which helped stem the flow.

But what concerned him more than the wound was the mystery of who had shot at him and from where. He hadn't heard anything above the din of the festivities across the river, so whoever had taken the shot must have done so from a distance. Then again, what if it was a freak stray bullet from one of the tens of thousands of soldiers across the river, all of whom would be marching with live ammo? What if some idiot private had accidentally discharged his rifle during the inspection preceding the parade? He dismissed anything more sinister as out of the realm of possibility. To be on the safe side, though, he lay his MAC-10 machine pistol on the ground next to him within easy reach. Then he picked up his rifle from where he dropped it when he was shot and set it up on the sandbag. But the fall had bent the scope. He swore loudly, tore the scope off the barrel rail and slammed it furiously to the ground.

Patrick was across the river within minutes. He got to the main entrance of the Tower and peered inside. Nothing. He tried the door, but the shooter had locked it from the inside before ascending to the observation deck. Patrick hoisted up a thirty-pound red-painted decorative rock from the walkway, leaned back, and with both hands pushing forward from his torso, sent it slamming into the glass door. No need for noise discipline now. Only a dead man wouldn't have heard the rock crashing into the glass door. He sprinted up the stairs that spiraled through the middle of the tower, and half a minute later, he reached the last section of the winding staircase and was face to face with a steel door leading out onto the observation area.

The shooter refined his aim at Kim Jong-un's head and center mass as best as he could using the iron sight on the end of the barrel. All he needed was for the Supreme Commander to hold still for just two seconds... *There!* Kim had profiled his head to listen to something one of the generals was saying. Hold that pose, you bastard! The shooter's breathing slowed to next to nothing as his finger squeezed tighter on the trigger, when suddenly the door to the observation deck flew open. He spun around, dropped the Dragunov rifle, reached for his MAC-10 that lay on the ground, and sprayed the area around the door with a curtain of lead. But the split second between dropping the rifle and picking up the machine pistol had allowed Patrick enough time to fling himself low and flat across the ground, with the hail of .45 caliber slugs whizzing harmlessly over his head. His momentum landed him right at the shooter's feet, and he wrapped his arms tightly around his legs, twisting them in a direction never intended by nature.

The shooter yelped in pain as something snapped in his right knee. He had exhausted the MAC-10's mag in a few seconds, and he began bashing Patrick over the head with its butt and barrel. Patrick shot the heel of his hand up into his jaw and followed that up with a kick to his left temple. The light momentarily faded from the man's eyes, but he came roaring back like a wounded animal and grabbed hold of Patrick's shoulders. As he leaned back in preparation for a head butt, Patrick countered with a finger to his throat directly above the supercostal notch, a *kakuremu* move he learned from Professor Park designed to crush the bundle of nerves that control the movement of the neck. An ordinary man would have been gasping for breath at the very least, but the shooter merely staggered a bit like a *soju*-besotted peasant before leaping to the ground, grabbing the Dragunov rifle, spinning back around again, and aiming at Patrick's head, all in less than a second. Endgame.

The weird calm of imminent death came over Patrick for the second time that day, and he watched what was happening as if disembodied, his mind percolating up the thought, *you have no hwallo*— 'escape route' in the game of *baduk*. The shooter's trigger finger went through 3.8 of the 3.9 pounds of pressure necessary to fire a three-inch projectile that would blow Patrick's head apart. But then he stopped and looked up. All of Pyongyang had suddenly become deathly quiet, where only a second earlier it had echoed with a million voices. His eyes went to the Square where the three minutes of silence had begun, signaling the official start of the Celebration. Patrick saw his opening, and swept his legs under the shooter's, throwing the North Korean off balance and sending his rifle flying up out of his hands.

The man reflexively reached for the rifle that continued its trajectory up and over the ledge of the Juche Tower. In an act of blind desperation that was oblivious to the unyielding laws of physics, he jumped up further and came within millimeters of catching the rifle on its descent. In doing so, he lost his footing and went careening over the ledge. At the very last second, he managed to grab hold of a metal lightning rod bolted onto the side of the tower— a flimsy length of copper that had never been designed to support the weight of someone his size. He grabbed futilely at air as the clamps holding it in place popped out of the concrete one by one.

Normally it would take fifteen seconds to fall the distance from the top of the Juche Tower to the ground. But the shooter never made it that far. At the base of the tower proudly stands a steel triptych statuary symbolizing the worker, the farmer and the intellectual. The intellectual is represented by a pen pointing straight up. The man hurtled down the side of the tower at 32 feet per second and came to a sudden stop—and end— impaled face down on the pen. His body writhed momentarily and then was still.

CHAPTER 38

PYONGYANG
May 1, 1:21 p.m.

Patrick sprinted down the stairs of the tower, his chest on fire from too many surges of adrenaline. He willed himself to maintain a steady jog across the Taedong Bridge and within a few minutes was back at the Grand People's Study House. Forcing his aching legs up the stairs, he threw open the door to the room where he had left Tyler. It was empty. He sat on the floor to catch his breath and suddenly remembered that Yumi would be coming in any time now with the Rising Tide group from Kaesong. He summoned reserves he didn't know he had, hauled himself to his feet and let gravity propel him down the stairs.

Over the course of the previous day she had spent recovering from her near-execution at Special Unit 14, Yumi had listened without comment as several members of Rising Tide revealed their plan to stage a pro-democracy demonstration at the Glorious Triumvirate Celebration. Their primary hope was that the presence of the foreign media would dissuade the authorities from too harsh a crackdown. Their secondary hope was that at least half of the million or so citizens in attendance would be inspired to join them in a show of solidarity. And their dream of dreams was that so many people would join them that they could actually bring down the regime.

They told Yumi that their plan of action was to infiltrate the Mass Games performance area and unfurl their banners before a live foreign and domestic TV audience of tens of millions. Yumi found their zeal endearing in its courage but hopelessly naive, and feared that they would all be massacred, Tienanmen

223

Square-style. But she kept her fears to herself for the time being.

In the early morning of the Glorious Triumvirate Celebration, she had ridden in a truck from Kaesong with Nahm Myung-dae, the leader of Rising Tide, as well as several other members of the dissident group. They would be meeting up with the other cells from around the country once they reached Pyongyang. Yumi had passed the time nervously thumbing through the booklet that Patrick had given her. On each page was printed a series of seemingly unrelated *hangul* characters, a geometric design, and a numbered grid on the bottom. She squinted at the characters as if in pain.

"Are you alright?" Nahm asked.

Yumi nodded. "Just a little dizzy. I'll be fine."

What are you reading?" Nahm asked casually.

"This? I'm not sure. Patrick gave it to me."

"Can I see?"

Nahm took the booklet from her and stared intently at the first page. As he turned the pages, his mouth opened wider.

"Do you know what this is?" he asked with a look of disbelief.

When Nahm told her what the symbols represented, an idea came to her as to how the Rising Tide demonstration might be made more effective, if not less lethal, and she spent the rest of the drive trying to decipher the booklet's *hangul* characters and coded numbering system.

When they reached Pyongyang, the various Rising Tide cells gathered at a small park near the Chollima statue, a mythological Pegasus-like creature, not far from Kim Il-sung Square. To an outsider, they appeared to be perhaps a large work unit that was attending the Glorious Triumvirate Celebration in a spirit of solidarity. When all were assembled, they began the ten-minute walk to Kim Il-sung Square.

1:43 p.m.

Red shards of fatigue and strain stabbed into Patrick's optic nerves as he swept the enormous crowd in Kim Il-sung Square for any sign of Yumi or Tyler. A growing sense of hopelessness came over him as he trudged up one side of the Square and down the other. Everywhere he looked, an absolute sea of humanity. How would he ever be able to find two people in...Suddenly, his eyes were drawn to a group of what looked to be a work unit walking toward the Square from a side street, most of them young, but a few older ones as well, mostly men, but a few women and...

Out of the corner of his eye, a Rising Tide group-leader on the lookout for State Security agents noticed with alarm someone staring at them. He turned slowly. Then his face relaxed. Yumi was still scribbling furiously in the booklet she carried when the group-leader tapped her on the shoulder. She jumped in surprise, and the leader turned her by the shoulders to face the man who had been staring at them. A faint smile lightened her face as Patrick walked over to embrace her.

Nahm Myung-dae gently placed his hands on their shoulders. "We need to keep moving. We'll make our way toward the foreign television cameras and unfurl our banners in front of as many of them as possible."

He signaled the rest of the Rising Tide group to get ready to move.

"Wait," Yumi said. "I have a better idea." She turned to Patrick. "If I learned anything from my studies, it was that art rearranges reality on its own terms." She held up the booklet that Patrick had given her. "What if we could use art to rearrange reality a bit today?"

She went on to tell Patrick that the booklet contained the cues used in the flipping of the placards of the human backdrop, and that she had deciphered its numbering code. The interlocking *hangul* characters of the backdrop, she continued, could now be rearranged anyway they liked— if they could somehow get inside the restricted Mass Games staging area and persuade the backdrop section leaders that the changes were legitimate. The three of them conferred on the next course of action which had Patrick and Yumi going one way, and Nahm Myung-dae and his Rising Tide cohort going in the opposite direction into the crowd of spectators. As they were setting out, a young *kotjebi* boy from among their number poked his head out of the crowd and handed several objects to Nahm. Nahm in turn passed them to Patrick and Yumi.

"You might find some use for these," he said as he gave them a pair of official Mass Games ID cards and an international press pass the flower-swallow boy had pickpocketed.

Patrick and Yumi walked to the staging area for the human backdrop. It was fenced off and accessible only by a single gate manned by an armed guard; they needed a way inside in order to put the first phase of Yumi's plan into effect. The stolen Mass Games ID cards and international press pass for Patrick had gotten them into this outer area, but no one could just walk through the gate without further authorization. As they tried to devise a way into the staging area, Patrick saw a familiar face— a beautiful young woman dressed in a white track suit who strode unchallenged past the guard at the gate.

2:11 p.m.

Hundreds of performers limbered up on the other side of the fence that Patrick and Yumi stood behind. It was the performers' last chance to perfect the brilliant display of mass effort in which each of them played a small but indispensable part. Acrobats flew high into the air, so deeply focused as to be oblivious of the hoops and balls that the gymnasts hurled all around them. Several of the gymnasts of the Hashin Middle School troupe looked around worriedly as they ran through their routines. They were scheduled to go on in less than two hours, and there had been no sign of their coach. Finally, one of the young girl's eyes lit up.

"She's here, Coach Seo-mi is here!" she shouted with delight. The dozen girls in the troupe mobbed Coach Seo-mi as she came closer. She in turn beamed at her gymnasts with pride.

"Miss!" they squealed. "We're so nervous! What if one of us falls?"

"None of you will fall, believe me! You must just concentrate on what we practiced and everything will be fine!"

"But the Supreme Commander will be watching us! We're afraid we won't be able to give him proper glory!"

"You are doing it for the whole country, girls! Everyone wants you to succeed, and I know that you will!"

The girls swarmed around her, and Seo-mi winced in pain as they hugged the kindest coach any of them had ever had.

"You're hurt, Miss," one of them said, pointing to a bandage on Seo-mi's arm.

"It's nothing. Now go and do your best!"

Their confidence restored, the girls went back to their warm-up exercises. Seo-mi's face turned serious as she took the cue-booklet for the human backdrop over to the staging area. She had made several fundamental changes to it over the past few days. The various component groups of the backdrop were going through one last dry run with the colored cards that together would create magnificent images of the Great and Dear Leader and the Supreme Commander, as well as inspirational slogans to fire the masses up into a frenzy of patriotic devotion. Patrick and Yumi stood watching from behind a first-aid tent on the other side of the fence as Seo-mi marched up to the Mass Games General Director. They were close enough that they could just make out what she was saying.

"Comrade, there are some changes in the backdrop," Seo-mi began. "I would like for it to incorporate some additional slogans so as to better praise the Supreme Commander."

The director's eyes bugged out of his head. "What? But that's impossible! We can't just make changes at the last minute without it affecting the entire tableau! And it's all synchronized with the music and the gymnastics, you yourself signed off on it!"

"You do not wish to honor our Supreme Commander?" Seo-mi replied evenly.

"Nothing could be further from the truth! But I want to honor him properly, not with something that's just thrown together at the last minute. I'm sorry, I'll need higher authorization for this. Otherwise it's completely out of the question."

Seo-mi took a cell phone out of her pocket and dialed a number. She spoke into it and passed him the phone.

"Here is your higher authorization," she said.

The director took the phone and pressed it to his ear. His eyes widened as he heard the voice on the other end identify himself and order him to do everything that Seo-mi had said.

"Ye-e-s, Comrade Moon, I am terribly sorry to have troubled you!" He handed the phone back to Seo-mi with a trembling hand and called over to the cue-leader of the backdrop to come get the new changes. Seo-mi turned away from the Games director and spoke into the phone again not five feet away from where Patrick and Yumi were listening with their backs turned.

"There is one other thing. It's about the American spy, Tyler Kang. He's dead."

Patrick's stomach lurched. *Tyler dead? But how?*

Seo-mi ended the call. The director went scuttling off with the backdrop cue-leader to make the changes in the slogans. But, rather than trumpeting the greatness of Kim Jong-un, the changes Seo-mi had made would instead herald Comrade Moon as the savior of the nation in its greatest moment of crisis, namely the imminent assassination of Kim Jong-un himself. She looked at her watch, concern tightening the corners of her mouth, and then looked across the river to the Juche Tower. The shooter was late.

As Patrick and Yumi continued to cast furtive glances at Seo-mi, Patrick happened to look over to the opposite side of the staging area fence. His head shot forward in shock, and he began running around the fence.

"Wait here!" he shouted to Yumi. Thirty seconds later he was on the far side of the staging area fence.

"Tyler? My God, it is you!" Tyler spun around and limped over to Patrick. He pulled him around the corner of a tent, out of Seo-mi's field of vision.

"It was her, Sempai," Tyler said, his breathing fast and shallow.

"I had a feeling when I saw the bandage. I must have winged her at the Study House."

"She's mine," Tyler said, not with the possessiveness of love, but in the way he and Patrick had once called dibs on targets. He turned back in Seo-mi's direction with a feral look in his eyes. Patrick released a jet of breath.

"Ease up, Kohai, that's a dish best served up cold."

"She tried to kill me," Tyler rasped, not taking his eyes off her.

"I know. But maybe we can set her up, too."

Tyler turned back to Patrick. "How?" he asked skeptically.

Patrick led him back around to the opposite side of the fenced-off staging area where Yumi was waiting. He quickly introduced them and explained the plan they had developed. As Tyler listened, his jaw gradually softened and a light came into his eyes.

"The only thing is, we can't figure out a way to get into the staging area," Yumi said.

Tyler turned to Patrick and spoke slowly as if to an idiot child.

"'Can't'? Did I just hear the word 'can't', Sempai? Were you or were you not the second best sniper in the world at one time in your life? You need a diversion, rookie."

"Damn straight, but if we do anything too obvious, they'll be on us like a coffin lid."

"You've forgotten what we used to do in training when we needed to relieve the quartermaster of his beer supply?"

Patrick's face lit up. "Wait here!" he called out and began running.

"Where are you going?" Yumi called after him.

"To the bar."

"*Now?*"

But Patrick was already on his way. Five minutes later he returned with eight bleary-eyed, red-faced foreigners from the Koryo Hotel Basement Bar to whom he had promised free booze and loose women. He huddled them together for their assignment.

"Hang on, mate, where's the booze and the women?" one of them asked before Patrick could begin.

"Believe me, if this works, you'll have the nubile maiden of your choice pouring wine down your throat," Patrick said and filled them in on their part of the upcoming drama. He had them wait and went back to Tyler and Yumi by the human backdrop staging area, where they took their assigned positions. For his part of the plan, Tyler limped over to where he had last seen Seo-mi. He searched the throng of gymnasts and members of the human backdrop, and then saw her exiting the fenced-off area. Moving toward her, he smiled and waved.

"Sorry I'm late," he called out to her breezily. Her face froze as if seeing a ghost in broad daylight. Tyler reached out his arms to embrace her, turned her away from the crowd, and brought a practiced fist sharply up into her chin. Her legs gave way, and he called over a man in the security detail to help him get her to a first-aid tent.

"Coach Seo-mi has been overcome with exhaustion!" he shouted. "She's been working much too hard." As he and the security man half-carried her back into the fenced-off area, Yumi flashed her stolen Mass Games ID card to the armed guard at the gate who had been distracted by the commotion with Seo-mi, and took her own booklet with its revised cues over to the director of the Mass Games.

"Coach Seo-mi has made some additional changes to the backdrop," she said authoritatively, holding the book of cues that she and Patrick had revised.

"And who are you? I've never even seen you before," the director said.

"I am Coach Seo-mi's assistant." She flashed the stolen ID before his eyes. "We must hurry, there's not much time before we're to begin," she said with an edge of irritation in her voice.

The director just stood there with a look of disbelief on his face. "She wants to make more changes?"

"You know her, never satisfied. Probably why she fainted."

"But I just gave the cue-leader the last changes she made!"

"Take your positions," Patrick said sotto voce. "Prepare for action."

The men divided into two groups and proceeded to fight among themselves, beginning with a bit of shoving but growing into wrestling on the ground. The fight spilled over to the fence of the staging area where Yumi, as anticipated, was having little luck getting the Mass Games director to make even one more change to the human backdrop. One of the two groups pretended to retreat in the face of the drunken attack, and lurched into Yumi and the director just as Patrick had planned. Tyler took the hand-off of the booklet from Yumi and approached the cue-leader.

"New orders from Comrade Moon," Tyler said and handed over the booklet.

By this point, the cue-leader had gotten so many changes that he just shrugged and trudged resignedly over to his sub-leaders.

"New orders from Comrade Moon," he repeated to his underlings in a bureaucracy-deadened voice.

All afternoon the assembled masses had shouted themselves hoarse as the grand military parade made its way through Kim Il Sung Square. Now they were ready for the sheer spectacle of the Mass Games which would begin at 3 p.m. sharp. The General Director of the Games raised his hands up over his head as a signal for the backdrop to begin its sequence of placard-flipping.

"All Honor and Glory to the Great People of this Nation!" the first slogan read as a taekwondo demonstration began in the middle of the Square. It was a quote from the Great Leader, Kim Il-sung, that everyone in the massive audience recognized. A deafening cheer went up among the million people in the Square. The director heaved a sigh of relief that the last-minute changes to the backdrop hadn't been too disruptive.

"I Am Always with You!" read the second Kim Il-sung quote, again to fervent cheering from the crowd. Patrick watched as the slogan materialized and thought of the father and his young son he had seen earlier. *The Great Leader is always with us, my son.*

"Let Us All Dedicate Ourselves to Lifting up the Masses!" followed to the greatest cheering yet.

But when the backdrop's next slogan was flipped into place, instead of wild cheering, there was only mortified silence. The Mass Games director began madly waving his arms over his head in a futile attempt at ordering the human pixels to lay down their placards.

"My Son Betrayed You," it read. Before the Games director could make any progress, he was intercepted by the men from the Basement Bar, and he found himself tangled in a scrum of foreign drunks, unable to get any closer.

"Comrade Moon = Traitor!" the next slogan read.

"The People Must Rise Up Against False Leaders Who Rule In My Name!"

The placards were turning hard and fast. The next slogan read simply, "Tyrants!"

Nahm Myung-dae, who had positioned his people into strategic positions among the crowd began a low, rhythmic chant that his Rising Tide followers picked up.

"Ty-rants, ty-rants, ty-rants..." they chanted as the word appeared before a million people in the square and countless others tuned in to their televisions in North Korea and abroad. The original word had been "heroes" but a readjustment of the interlocking *hangul* characters had completely altered the meaning.

The masses in Kim Il-sung Square had initially stood dumbstruck through the unthinkable displays. But then, a voice here, a voice there began tentatively to chant along with the Rising Tide members until an entire section of the audience was shouting out the new slogans as they appeared one after the other in the backdrop. Before long at least half of the throng of over a million had joined in.

A final slogan appeared in the backdrop: "Rising Tide!"

Giant swaths of the audience clapped their hands in rhythm as they chanted in one voice, "Rising Tide! Rising Tide! Rising Tide!" For years there had been rumors of this dissident group, and now the day had come for them to make themselves known. And ushered in by a miracle performed by Kim Il-sung himself, no less! *The Great Leader is always with us, indeed*, thought Patrick.

As the crowd stamped its feet and shouted in exultation, Patrick ran over to Tyler and Yumi, and told them over the din of the chanting what he needed to do next. Tyler offered to come with him, but Patrick waved him off. This was personal.

Fueled by the heady exultation that filled Kim Il-sung Square, his physical and mental exhaustion forgotten for the time being at least, Patrick's steps were light as he jogged out of the Square toward a nearby section of town.

CHAPTER 39

PYONGYANG
May 1, 3:42 p.m.

Three blocks southeast of Kim Il-sung Square, Patrick slowed to a trot as he neared the Puhung subway station. On the train down to Kaesong, Choy had revealed a most interesting feature of its construction. Patrick took the stairs down two at a time but came to an abrupt stop at the sight of a ticket taker in his booth. Practically everyone in Pyongyang was already in Kim Il-sung Square, however, and the man sat dozing with his head on his chest. Patrick carefully tiptoed past him.

At the far end of the platform he saw a mural depicting Kim Il-sung in his fedora and a wind-billowed overcoat dispensing subway-building wisdom to a group of civil engineers. Choy had told him that a section of the mural concealed a labyrinth of tunnels. Hiding in plain sight. Brilliant, Patrick thought. No one would ever dare get too close to an image of the Great Leader. He walked up to it and ran his hands over its glossy surface but felt only seamless plaster under the paint. Suddenly, his concentration was jolted by the sound of cleated heels echoing sharply off the concrete platform. The formerly napping ticket-taker was wide awake and heading his way.

Patrick appraised the diminutive man's height from twenty feet away. A leaping kick to the head would dispatch him with ease. But as the ticket-taker closed the distance between them, he suddenly broke into a trot, passed Patrick, jumped straight up and tapped the top border of the mural. Instantly, a panel to the right of the Great Leader's outstretched hand loosened. The ticket-taker jogged back to his booth, and Patrick's eyes narrowed in bafflement. "How the hell did he know?" he marveled aloud.

Pulling the panel back, he lifted himself up and squeezed through a narrow opening. Once inside, he again heard trotting footfalls. The ticket-taker began moving the panel back in place and tossed in a flashlight. Patrick caught it and murmured his thanks. A voice came back as the panel closed: "Rising Tide."

Patrick trained the flashlight beam down a narrow, pitch-black passageway that immediately ate up almost all of the flashlight's illumination. Choy had told him of a splay of tunnels that ran like catacombs beneath the capital, with the one terminating at Puhung Station leading directly to Bureau 39, the mother lode of criminality in North Korea. Descending further, he came to a round, hub-like chamber that was fed by four other tunnels. Three of them were pitch-black and silent, but from the dimly-lit fourth came the murmur of faraway voices and the muted whirr of machinery of some sort. As he moved toward the sound, the flashlight flickered out. He gave his eyes a few seconds to adjust and set off down the fourth tunnel.

Twenty feet later, the walls curved to the right. Directly around the corner was the source of the voices and the whirring sound. Patrick reached into his jacket for his father's ancient Colt pistol, realizing as he did so that he had violated the first rule of combat: always know how much ammunition is in your magazine. He swore under his breath. He had an extra mag for the .45 in his pocket, and he ejected the one in the gun he was uncertain about. Holding both mags in his hand, he was about to insert the full backup when the cell phone Mrs. Pae gave him began to ring in his pocket. The ring volume was on a low setting, but his surprise was such that he frantically reached for it before it rang again, sending both mags flying out of his hand and onto the concrete floor with a double metallic plink.

He held his breath and listened. The whirring sound continued, but the conversation had come to a complete halt. Then the conversation began again, but this time in urgent whispers. He had been made.

Patrick squatted down and swept the ground with his hands for the two pistol mags as a clatter of footsteps echoed in the near distance. Finally locating and scooping up the mags, he raced back to the hub connecting the five tunnels. When he got there, he forced himself to think calmly but quickly. They would probably expect him to take the tunnel leading back to Puhung Station, so he ducked into the darkness of a different one and guided himself by touch along its inside wall. The footsteps grew louder. He frantically tried to slam the full mag into the .45 but it jammed when he racked the slide, so he ejected the mag and pocketed it and the gun, and began searching for something, anything, to use as an alternate weapon. Running his hands up and down the tunnel wall, he felt a length of pipe that ran along its higher reaches. Grasping it with both hands, he furiously began pushing and pulling until a two-foot-long section broke off. More rust than metal, but it was all he had.

Moving deeper into the tunnel, he felt his way along using the curvature of its walls to guide him. Hoping he had put enough distance between himself and whoever had been chasing him, he stopped and listened. His pulse lurched. For from around the next bend came the same whirring sound he had heard before. The tunnel had merely clover-leafed around to where he was earlier, and he was cut off on either end as his pursuers closed in on him.

Flattening himself against the wall, he gripped the length of rusty pipe tightly and braced himself. As the first pursuer came rushing headlong around the corner, Patrick swung the pipe and connected squarely with his upper lip and nose with a cracking sound that echoed down the tunnel. The man cried out in pain and his hands shot up to his face as he staggered about drunkenly, blood pouring out of his nose and mouth and onto his Korean People's Army uniform. Patrick drew his foot back and dealt a kick of his instep into the soldier's solar plexus, sending him crashing to the ground. He tried to grab the man's pistol, but before he could reach it, another soldier appeared from around the corner and stopped with a perplexed look at his comrade lying on the ground. When he looked up, Patrick tagged him in the eye and followed up with a left cross to the mouth, breaking his lips against his teeth with a sickening squishing sound. But despite the geyser of blood gushing from his mouth, the soldier charged again. Patrick shifted his weight to his right leg and torqued from his foot to his fist in a scythe-like haymaker. This time the man stayed down.

He stripped the soldier of his rifle and inched ahead toward the whirring sound which increased in volume with every step. Soon the tunnel opened onto a chamber similar to the hub he had seen earlier. Poking his head around the corner, he could see that the sound came from a conveyer belt leading out of a dumbwaiter in the wall and from which a lone soldier was frantically loading canvas bags onto a truck. And standing atop the truck supervising the placement of the bags was none other than Comrade Moon himself. Patrick carefully thumbed off the safety of his captured rifle.

For a man in late middle age, Moon's hearing was acute, and his head bolted around at the sound of the safety clicking off. He leapt behind the truck and called out to the soldier who had remained with him. Patrick shot out all of the sodium lamps hanging from the walls of the tunnel, with the only light now coming from one inside a far tunnel that curved out of range of his rifle. He ran in a crouch to a corner of the chamber and hunkered down behind a brick wall that protruded out a few feet. Moon spoke in a low voice to his loyal soldier, but Patrick was able to pick out the words, "go" and "together." He dialed the rifle to full auto. "Group therapy", as they called it in JSOC.

Moon quietly counted backwards from "three" and then shouted, "Now!" The young soldier sprang from his position and began running towards Patrick with his rifle spraying, while Moon stayed where he was, clearly hoping to home in on Patrick's location at the expense of his naive bodyguard. Patrick had no choice. He switched back to single shot, aimed at the soldier's non-shooting shoulder, and fired. The soldier went down, moaning but still alive. Moon caught sight of Patrick's muzzle flash and responded with a magazine-emptying burst, a round of which whizzed past Patrick's ear, ricocheted off the brick wall behind him, and nailed his rifle between the forestock and the barrel, rendering it completely unusable. Patrick then heard the click of a mag being changed. A long moment later, Comrade Moon spoke.

"Pointless, isn't it, Mr. Featherstone? Why are you doing this when I can make you rich beyond your dreams?"

Patrick said nothing but took heart. It appeared that Moon was unaware that his rifle was useless.

"What are you, an idealist? Some kind of storybook hero?"

Patrick still said nothing.

"How about $1 million as a starting bonus? Will that earn your partnership? You can work for me from now on, or you can stay here and die. Your choice."

As Moon dictated his terms, Patrick adjusted his position behind the brick wall so that he was farther away from him. He took his father's .45 out of his waistband and began smashing the butt on the stone floor. On the second strike, the inside grip panel broke off and out popped the spare bullet inside. He called out to Moon.

"Make it $2 million and you've got a deal."

Moon laughed. "A greedy man! We will work well together, Mr. Featherstone. Please come out with the rifle above your head."

Patrick held the pistol with its one shot in his left hand, lifted the rifle up over his head, and then hurled it like a javelin so that it sailed through the air and clattered a full fifteen feet away. Just as he had expected, Moon opened fire in the direction of the rifle. Patrick darted out in a low crouch, jumped up and over the truck, and tackled Moon, sending the rifle hurtling out of his hands. He pressed the .45 into Moon's temple.

Suddenly, the sound of footsteps echoed from one of the far tunnels and a lantern gradually began to illuminate it. Patrick's stomach fell. Moon's reinforcements? He roughly grabbed Moon up off the ground by his collar and turned him around so that he would be facing the intruder. He heard a woman's voice.

"Father!"

Patrick squinted and saw Seo-mi emerge from the shadows pushing Yumi ahead of her. As her eyes settled on Patrick, she brought a pistol up to Yumi's head.

"Do you want her to die?" Seo-mi called out tauntingly. Yumi squirmed slightly, but her face betrayed no fear. Patrick set his gun down on the ground.

"I knew you would come!" Moon exclaimed to Seo-mi.

Seo-mi smiled and pushed Yumi forward so that she stood side by side with Patrick, her gun trained on both of them. Moon picked up Patrick's .45 and aimed it at Patrick's head. Then he stopped. More footsteps began echoing through the chamber, this time coming from a different tunnel.

"Who's there?" Moon shouted.

"It's me, Comrade," a male voice shouted back.

All eyes went to the sound of the voice. The man walked into the illumination of the lantern Seo-mi had set on the ground.

"Choy?" Moon said in disbelief. "I'd given you up for dead!"

"I might as well have been, Comrade." He walked forward another step. "I have been disloyal, and I wish to criticize myself. I allowed myself to be taken in by an enemy of our fatherland. I have done all sorts of things for which I am truly sorry. Now I want to apologize from the depths of my heart to the people of this great nation."

"Choy, Choy, Choy, always such a sentimentalist! There's no need for any of that now. The important thing is that the enemy of our fatherland is about to die." Moon drew back the hammer of Patrick's gun. Choy stepped forward.

"I would like the enemy to criticize himself first, Comrade."

Moon stifled a chuckle at Choy's patriotic fervor, then turned serious. "Well?" he said to Patrick. "You heard him. Any words of remorse?"

Patrick lifted his head in silent defiance.

"Here is the evidence against the enemy, Comrade Moon," Choy said, coming another step closer with a file folder in his hand.

Moon reached for the folder, but Choy handed it instead to Seo-mi.

"Please read this," he told her.

With a look of impatience, Seo-mi set her gun down on the truck and took the folder out of Choy's hands. After she had begun reading the opening page, Choy spoke again.

"The enemy of our fatherland is one who would kill the mother of his only daughter in order to advance himself in the eyes of the Great Thief, Kim Jong-il. The enemy of our fatherland is one who would then prostitute his daughter to the same Great Thief so that he could gain control over Bureau 39. The enemy of our fatherland..."

"Stop!" Seo-mi screamed. "These are all lies!" She waved the file at Choy as if trying desperately to put out a fire.

"Those are all original documents from the Ministry of State Security,"

Choy replied calmly. "If anyone is an enemy of the people, it is this man who calls himself your father."

Seo-mi frantically turned the pages of the file. Then she turned to Moon.

"Father! Is this true?"

Moon's lip quivered. "Of course not!" he shouted.

"It *is* true," Seo-mi hissed in a tremulous whisper. "I can see it in your face!"

Taking advantage of the confusion, Patrick pulled Yumi to the far side of the truck out of Moon's sight line, but Moon jumped onto the hood and squeezed the trigger. Patrick pushed Yumi down and threw himself upon her just as the gun fired. But then another shot rang out from an unexpected quarter.

The soldier whom Moon had double-crossed into charging Patrick was sitting upright with the smoking barrel of his rifle aimed at Moon. A stricken look came over Moon's face, and as he fell to his knees, Patrick's .45 dropped out of his hands. Seo-mi pivoted and pumped four shots into the soldier, killing him instantly. Choy ran behind the brick wall where Patrick had hidden and called out to Seo-mi.

"He betrayed you! He betrayed us all!" he shouted.

"He is still my father, you bastard!" she screamed, firing at him and missing. As she knelt down to tend to her father, Patrick scooped his .45 off the ground, grabbed Yumi by the hand, and pulled her back behind the truck. Seo-mi looked up and opened fire at them both. With lightning speed, Patrick took the mag that had jammed from his pocket, popped out one of the rounds in desperate hope that the spring would release its excess of tension, and slammed the mag home just as Seo-mi appeared from behind the truck with her gun pointed at him.

A split-second later, a shot thundered through the tunnel system. Patrick flinched and turned to see if Yumi had been hit. She was trembling but appeared to be unscathed. Patrick ducked lower and swung around to face Seo-mi with his gun leveled. Her face was creased in pain and confusion. The pistol in her hand went up as her legs gave way from under her. She managed a wayward shot, then collapsed on top of her father with mortal finality.

Patrick turned to the entrance to the chamber. A figure was slowly limping from the shadows. Patrick raised his .45 into firing position.

"Looks like I still have to rake your coals out of the fire, Sempai," Tyler sighed as he came closer. Choy emerged from his hiding place and began walking over. Suddenly, Yumi screamed out.

"Patrick!"

Patrick crouched low to the ground and turned in her direction, only to see Moon gripping his dead daughter's gun with trembling hands and aiming point-blank at Yumi. Without a thought, Patrick pumped the entire magazine of his father's .45 into Moon's center mass. Moon grimaced and tried to lift the gun, but its weight was too much for him. As he fell back against the truck, it dropped from his hand. And slowly, ever so slowly, his eyes lost their focus and finally looked out onto a literal vanishing point.

CHAPTER 40

PYONGYANG
The same day

"'Every time I think I'm out, they pull me back in'," Choy said in an exhausted monotone as he, Patrick, Yumi, and Tyler exited the tunnel and dragged themselves up the subway stairs one halting step at a time.

"Never mind the Godfather quotes, how did you find me? And why did you come back?" Patrick asked hoarsely.

"The cell phone you got from Mrs. Pae. I tried calling you a while ago, but I guess you had your hands full. Anyway, the phone has a built-in GPS. You're lucky it worked all the way down there. I told you I'm no hero, but I felt guilty just leaving you on your own. After all, you had no *hwallo*." Choy smiled.

"Really? By my count, I had three of them," Patrick said, looking at Choy, Tyler and Yumi in turn. "And how about you two?" he said to Tyler and Yumi. "How did you know where I was?"

Tyler answered. "When Seo-mi came to after I clocked her, she got hold of Yumi when I wasn't looking and forced her to go with her. I didn't realize she was carrying a gun. I guess she knew her old man would be down in the sewers with the rest of the rats. I followed them to the tunnels from a distance."

"Listen to that," Choy marveled, nodding in the direction of Kim Il-sung Square where hundreds of thousands of voices were still rhythmically chanting "Rising Tide!" over and over. As the four of them emerged into the daylight, an atmosphere of jubilation filled the streets, the likes of which barely a single one of the participants had ever genuinely felt before. For their entire lives they had acted a part in order to avoid punishment for insufficient socialist zeal, and now the ability to express themselves freely was almost too wonderful to bear. In the back of everyone's mind, however, the exultation was leavened with dark foreboding: surely the regime wouldn't allow this to go on for much longer. But as the minutes turned into hours, not a single figure of repressive authority had come forth to squelch anything or anyone.

The four of them walked with fatigue-weighted steps along the waterfront as revelers spilled out from Kim Il-sung Square.Mrs. Pae, never one to miss a sales opportunity, had moved her entire *jangmadang* to the southern part of the Square and was at cheery wit's end trying to keep up with the volume of business. When the four of them happened by, she called them over excitedly, sat them down, and immediately had her servers bring over a steaming pot of *yukgaejang*, a hot spicy stew. In a flash, they were noisily slurping from their bowls.

When they finally pushed their bowls away, Patrick turned to Yumi, Tyler and Choy. "Not exactly how anyone thought this would turn out." He sighed in blissful contentment.

Choy groaned from an overfull belly, let out his belt buckle a notch, and relaxed back in his chair. Yumi said nothing, but her slumping head jerked back as she fought a postprandial nap.

Choy looked over at her and with great effort hoisted himself up. "Well, I should be going."

Patrick's face fell. "But why? The party's just started." Choy gently pulled him aside. Yumi slumped further in her chair.

"You already have someone to celebrate it with. I believe the English expression is 'third wheel'?"

"How will we keep in touch? Don't just disappear on me again."

Choy took out a piece of paper from his pocket, wrote on it, and handed it to Patrick.

"Here's an email address and password. We can write emails to each other, but instead of actually sending them, save them in the 'draft' section. We'll be the only ones who'll be able to see them."

"Very clever," Patrick said as he looked down at the piece of paper. Then he looked up. "How can I ever repay you?" he asked softly.

"Repay me? Are you crazy? Take a look around you!"

"You saved my life, what? About five times?"

"And now it's time to live it, my friend." Then he took Patrick by the shoulders and pulled him into a tight embrace neither was in a hurry to end.

"Goodbye for now, Patrick."

"Goodbye for now, Inspector."

Choy pulled away. "I think that after today I'd like you to call me by my given name: Jung-hee."

"'Jung-hee'," Patrick repeated. "'Righteous' and 'fun-loving'. It fits you to a T."

"And 'Patrick' fits you to a P. You helped drive the snakes out of this country."

They embraced again, and then Choy turned quickly around. As he walked away, his shoulders shook. Patrick watched him sadly until he turned a corner and was out of sight.

Tyler spoke next. "I have to go, too, bro."

"What!?" Patrick said, turning around to face him.

"My parents always wished that this country would someday go back to being normal, and it looks like it finally has a fighting chance. I'm going to stay and help things along as best as I can. I feel like I owe it to my parents. Korean filial piety and all that."

"Don't go yet!" Patrick implored, but he could see that Tyler had made up his mind.

"It's not as if I'll never see you again, Sempai," Tyler said. "Who knows what adventures lie ahead." His tone was jocular, but it hid a heavy heart. He looked over at Yumi who now had her head down on the table.

"She's a special one, Sempai. Take good care of her."

"I'm really sorry about how it turned out with Seo-mi, Tyler," Patrick said, casting his eyes down.

"Shit, I'm not. I just wish I saw through her earlier. But...all's fair in love and war, especially when they're one and the same."

An awkward moment ensued. Finally, Patrick took his old buddy in his arms. "You're a special one, too, Kohai. We *will* meet again soon, and it better be a hell of a lot sooner than the last time."

Tyler bit his lower lip. "What is this, a beer commercial all of a sudden?" he croaked, and then buried his head into Patrick's chest. Neither wanted to let go. Finally, Tyler clapped Patrick on the back. "We'll raise some hell, you foreign bastard!" He turned and walked away.

Patrick blinked the tears away.

"I hope you stay in touch with them," Yumi said. Patrick turned to face her.

"Oh, I will," he said, brushing at his eyes. "How are you feeling?"

Yumi shrugged. "Okay."

"Up for a walk?"

"Sure."

Mrs. Pae laughed at Patrick's attempt to pay for the meal, and he and Yumi threaded their way through the crowd until they got to the back area of the Grand People's Study House.

"Let's sit here," Yumi said. The sun was on the opposite side of the building, as was the crowd, and the steps were cold.

"I...I don't know what to say," Patrick said after an awkward silence. Yumi sat with her eyes downcast. Patrick soldiered on. "For the past couple of months I've thought about this moment and all that I would say to you if it ever happened. But now I find that I have no words."

Yumi exhaled softly. "Neither do I," she said. "It's as if I've just awakened from a nightmare. Which I guess I have."

Patrick nodded. A jagged energy filled the space between them.

"Anyway," Yumi sighed, "I've been able to think a bit since I got out of Senghori and that other place...what was it?"

"Unit 14."

"Yes. Special Unit 14." She paused. "What I've been thinking had to do with when I saw you again. What I'd say."

"It's been the same with me," Patrick said. "It took all of this to happen for me to realize how selfish I was toward you."

He looked at Yumi intently, a knot forming deep in his stomach. Yumi returned his gaze with what he could see she wanted to look like toughness. But when her eyebrows lifted and knitted together and her lower lip began to tremble, Patrick knew there was nothing at all tough in her at that moment.

"I'm so, so sorry," she murmured and held onto him, sobs spasming in her chest.

"Sh-sh-sh, it's alright," he whispered in her ear, holding her as tightly as he could, trying to forestall what his intuition told him was next. "It's all over. The nightmare is over."

He drew his head back so that he could look into her eyes. A profound sigh shuddered out of her lips. An icy hand gripped his heart.

"Oh, Patrick. My sweet, sweet Patrick. It's not what I've been through that makes me sad. It's what I have to do now."

That same heart now shriveled and sank to the bottom of a burning sea.

"When I was at Senghori," she began, her voice trembling, "I went through every pain that can be imagined. But harder than that pain was the torture of never seeing you again and knowing that my father would be killed. He *was* killed, wasn't he?"

Patrick nodded, tears again filling eyes.

Yumi's head went down.

"I knew it. As soon as they told me why I had been kidnapped, I knew they would never let him live, no matter what." She took a deep breath, held it for three seconds, and then expelled it slowly. She no longer trembled.

"I'm so grateful to you for coming back for me—twice. You could have been killed but you came anyway." She tried to smile. "For once you weren't thinking of yourself!" she joked weakly. She looked away and then back again. "Patrick, there was a time when I couldn't imagine a life without you…"

She took still another deep breath, held and released it. "… but when I was at Senghori, seeing what they went through all their lives, I realized that I *can* be alone. Before, I wanted to marry you because I didn't think I had the strength to be alone. But that feeling died at Senghori. Now I know I can be alone my whole life and nothing can touch me. Do you remember what you told me about *samadhi*, that deep meditation? That feeling of *I need nothing*?

When you said that, it hurt so much, because I thought you were telling me that you didn't need me. But now I think I know what you meant."

Patrick felt the muscles in his neck slacken. He lay his head on her shoulder. "It's been just the opposite for me," he said in a weak voice. "It wasn't until all this happened that I realized how much I love you."

Yumi shook her head slowly from side to side. "No. You wanted someone to hold onto. An anchor. It was need, not love. For me, too."

Patrick buried his head deeper into her shoulder. "Don't... go," he pleaded and looked up at her face. Yumi's eyes wavered. But then, ever so gently, she lifted his head from her shoulder and kissed him on the forehead.

"I'm sorry, Patrick. I'm so, so sorry." She took one last deep breath, expelled it quickly, stood up, and walked down the steps.

As he watched her fade from view, a keening wail rose up from within the deepest part of his heart, a wail that evaporated into the exultant jubilation of the nearby crowd. He desperately wished he had his father's gun back with its single all-ending bullet. He began to run.

CHAPTER 41

KAMAKURA
One week later

Yasuhara Roshi sipped from his cup of tea.

"And so this Inspector Choy deposited money into your bank account without your knowledge? I didn't know that was possible."

Patrick nodded. "Quite a lot of it, too. He's a computer genius and he somehow got into my account online. He emailed me that he had made an electronic transfer that nobody else knows about. It seems he was looting Comrade Moon all along. He said that the money he gave me is a gift from the people of North Korea. But I'd like to use it to help them in some way."

"As you should. From what you've told me, this Comrade Moon was the one who was looting it."

Patrick nodded. A tense silence ensued. Patrick could see that the Roshi had something else to say but was reluctant to bring it up. So Patrick brought it up himself.

"Yumi is still in North Korea."

Yasuhara Roshi just nodded and held Patrick's eye, willing him to explain further.

"The situation over there is up and down," Patrick began. "There's talk of civil war if the regime doesn't meet Rising Tide's demands. But at least Kim Jong-un hasn't been seen. I'm betting that his former aides saw an opportunity and took it before he could execute any more of them. Plus, the Politburo closed the prison camps, which is a good start. There are a lot of orphans from the camps, and I hear Yumi is working with a group that looks after them."

"Do you think there will be civil war?"

"Nobody knows for sure. But one thing I do know is that the people won't go back to the old way of just doing whatever the government says."

The Roshi paused and looked down. "And you and Yumi?" he asked with his eyes still cast downward.

Patrick's mouth tightened and a sigh escaped his lips. "I don't think she's ever forgiven me for wanting to become a monk instead of getting married."

Yasuhara Roshi reached across the low table that separated them and refilled their teacups. "And you? You no longer wish to be a monk?"

Patrick thought for a long moment. "If it doesn't work out between Yumi and me, then I'll become a monk."

The Roshi said gently, "I think someday it will be good between you two again."

Patrick nodded solemnly, sadness in his eyes. "I hope so."

Yasuhara Roshi eyes widened as he took in the look of resignation on Patrick's face. Then he frowned. A minute later he broke the silence.

"It's not like you to be so passive. It worries me."

KAESONG, NORTH KOREA
Four days later

A hastily scrawled sign had been posted on an old farmhouse a few miles outside of Kaesong. "Children's Refuge House" the sign read. The children who sat listlessly on the porch of the farmhouse seemed barely capable of putting one foot in front of the other. Most of them had the raccoon eyes of pellagra, and all of them were dangerously underweight. Several adults moved through the crowds of children spooning a thick, pleasant-tasting vitamin syrup into their mouths and gently helping them back to their mats where they resumed their vacant stare into the middle distance. None of them would be ready for solid food for at least a week.

The adults themselves looked barely better than the children they ministered to, but just the joy of seeing most of them showing signs of recovery from day to day animated their steps. Some of the children, however, were so far gone that all they could do was sit with them as they took their final breaths. These were the "kings and queens" of the Kim dynasty, innocents who had done nothing except be born to parents who had gotten on the wrong side of the regime. As the last of the children were tucked into their beds for their midday nap, the adults sat on the porch of the farmhouse chatting softly. Suddenly, they all stopped when they saw a lone soldier with a bundle under his arm approaching from down the road. But unlike before, when they would have tripped over themselves in a show of deference, this time they stood sullenly with their arms folded while one of them went into the farmhouse and reappeared a moment later with a shotgun. He cranked in a round, raised it, and called out. "Stay where you are!"

The soldier, whose eyes had been on the ground as he walked looked up sharply. He began walking toward the farmhouse again, and the man with the shotgun brought back one of the hammers.

"Stop!" a voice rang out. It was a woman's voice, and she was shouting to the man with the gun, not the soldier.

An hour later Patrick had changed out of the North Korean army uniform he had ridden in from Pyongyang. He had found the ancient Bugang motorcycle and uniform where he had left them in a field just outside Pyongyang. The motorcycle had finally breathed its last two miles up the road, and he had walked the rest of the way. He sat on the steps of the porch, while the former prisoners who had started this makeshift orphanage chatted lazily around a table, enjoying each other's company and the crystal-clear spring weather. The children were still napping inside while their frail and wasted bodies tried to recover from years of malnutrition. Looking over at Patrick sitting by himself on the porch, Yumi rose, went to the kitchen, and brought him a cup of tea. Patrick took it from her without looking in her eyes. Yumi returned to her group of former prisoners.

That evening Patrick had not moved an inch from his spot on the porch. One by one, the other adults had turned in for the night. A full moon was beginning to rise from behind a nearby mountain, its light incrementally crosshatching the ground through the pine trees. Behind him the door opened and footsteps approached.

"Why did you come here?" Yumi stood with her arms folded in front of her.

Patrick didn't look up. "What else could I do?"

Yumi said nothing. She sat down on the other end of the porch with her arms still folded and looked up at the moon rising above the mountain.

"How long will you stay?"

Patrick was silent for a moment. Then he turned to face her.

"Forever."

Yumi shook her head emphatically. "No. That life is over."

Patrick pressed on. "Do you know what Yasuhara Roshi said? He said we'd never be complete without each other."

He waited for a response. Yumi said nothing. It was as if she hadn't heard him.

"Are you going to stay here?" he asked finally.

"Yes," Yumi said without a moment's hesitation.

"And how will you survive? There's barely enough to eat here."

"I don't need much after Senghori."

"What about these kids?"

"What about them?"

"They'll grow up fast. What will happen to them then?"

"The future has a way of taking care of itself."

"'The future is the present before you know it, and then the present turns into the past. Unless you prepare for the future.' Choy taught me that."

"Nice words. But there's only so much you can do to prepare for the future."

"Maybe I can help."

Yumi snorted. "Since when do you like children?"

"I wasn't thinking of adopting them."

A chuckle escaped Yumi's lips before she was able to stop it. Patrick saw an opening.

"I have money," he said.

"We need a lot more than you'll ever have."

"I have a lot more than you think."

She looked out over the pine forest that was gradually becoming bathed in moonlight. "We need to set up a network for the children of the prison camps. There are tens of thousands of these kids."

"My parents ran an orphanage. Maybe it runs in the genes."

"To you? Don't make me laugh. How would you ever reach your precious enlightenment in the midst of a hundred screaming kids?"

"'This very place is the Lotus Land'. 'Everything can be enlightenment'. Yasuhara Roshi taught me that."

"You're big on quoting other people today."

"I could fund it, you could manage it," Patrick said, ignoring her comment.

Yumi said nothing for a long moment. But then she slowly shook her head from side to side, rose up, and began walking to the porch door.

"Wait. I want you to have this," Patrick called out as he reached into his pocket.

She stopped and turned around. "What is it?"

Patrick stood up, walked over to her, and pressed Mrs. Pae's good luck amulet into her hand. A faint static charge from the cool dry evening zizzed from skin to skin.

Yumi smiled faintly and rubbed the amulet between her thumb and forefinger. "Thank you. It's probably wasted on me, though. I've never believed in good luck charms."

"That one seems to work even if you don't believe in it."

Yumi chuckled softly and continued to smooth the amulet with her thumb. Then she looked him in the eye for the first time. "I guess I need all the luck I can get. I'll keep it forever."

Patrick lowered his head and smiled tenderly up at her. "I needed to hear that." He took a long breath and looked out over the moonlit meadow fronting of the orphanage.

"I'll be leaving in the morning," he said. "Is there any tea left? I'd like to stay up awhile longer."

Wordlessly, Yumi turned and entered the kitchen just off the porch. She returned a moment later with two cups, not the dainty Japanese type, but sturdy mugs used by North Korean mountain folk. She held out one of the mugs to Patrick. He took it from her. Their fingers briefly touched.

"So how did you come by all this newfound wealth?" she said, warming her hands on the cup.

"It's a long story."

She looked up at the moon that had finally crested the mountaintop, and took a sip of her tea. "It's not all that late."

THE END

ACKNOWLEDGMENTS

I would like to thank, first of all, my literary agent, Susan Gleason for her expertise in identifying areas where the dramatic thrust of the story could be enhanced and the characters brought into sharper focus.

Many friends and colleagues were of immeasurable help in reading through the manuscript and offering critical insights and corrections, and to them I extend my deepest thanks. Among these were Michael Breen, Monica Chung, Thomas Grollman, David Hagberg, Dale Hall, Deborah Hayden, Gary Hughey, Richard Lessa, Bradley K. Martin, Barbara Phillips, Naomi Shepherd, Todd Shimoda, Robert Vieira, and John Wehrheim.

Lastly, I would like to thank my wife, Virginia, for her love, patience and support as I struggled to bring the manuscript to its final form.

The poem quoted by Inspector Choy is *Invocation* by Kim So-wol (1902-1934).

R I N G S   O F   F I R E

"In war, truth is the casualty".

-Aeschylus

PROLOGUE
Kaesong, North Korea
May 1, 2017
The day of the Glorious Triumvirate Celebration

Comrade Ahn Mun-yin couldn't get enough of the echoing silence of the cave system he explored for his job several days a week far from the crowds and noise of the "surface world", as he called it. And the crowds and noise would be worse than ever today, the day of the Glorious Triumvirate Celebration, a national festival marking the radiant brilliance of the dynasty of Kim Il-sung, Kim Jong-il and Kim Jong-un. His wife was content to spend a few hours relaxing topside on this beautiful spring day, quietly reading to their child as she waited for her husband to emerge from the depths. An hour after his expected exit time, though, she began to worry, as did the man himself when he suddenly heard the sound of rushing water and realized the danger he was in. He hurriedly made for the cave entrance a quarter mile above, with the rumble of the flood pulse growing in intensity like an oncoming freight train. It took him a full hour to reach the surface, the entire cave shaking the whole time as if by an earthquake. He was only fifteen yards from the cave entrance when an enormous torrent of white water suddenly broke forth from the ceiling spewing tons of falling rock and debris that almost completely blocked the cave entrance. He could just barely see daylight, but there was no way he could get out any time soon without help, so he checked for a signal on his cellphone. He was picking up one bar, but it flickered in and out of receptivity.

He repeatedly tried calling his wife on his phone, but there was no answer, so he yelled at the top of his lungs toward the cave entrance over and over but again heard nothing. Sensing that something had happened to her husband, the wife had hurried back in the direction of Kaesong forty minutes earlier to try to get help. Her husband got as close to the cave entrance as possible and made a call to Pyongyang. Then he turned on his headlamp and began digging. The next morning when he emerged from the cave, he ran all the way home, but his house was deserted.

C H A P T E R 1

TOKYO
Three years later
July 10, 2020

I'm dead! Adrenaline ignited the shooter's viscera, and his grip stiffened against the trigger. He relaxed slightly when he looked up into the rafters of the Olympic Stadium and saw it was only a *tombi*, a type of hawk, carrying a mid-sized carp from the lake in nearby Akasaka Palace in her beak. The tiny squeaks of her hungry chicks in their raftered nest pinged off the canopy as their mother landed and began shredding the fish with razor-like claws. The man swore silently. Although he had breached the highest levels of security and made his way to his hide undetected in the middle of the night, he had just come close to a panic-pull of the trigger. Swearing again, he took several deep breaths, feeling his pulse gradually decrease.

It was just after 3 a.m., exactly two weeks before the Games of the XXXII Olympiad were set to begin, that the squat, powerful-looking figure clothed entirely in black began his ascent of the south wall of the stadium. The raucous frenzy of nightlife in the area had evaporated after the last subway pulled out at midnight. Now the only sounds were the occasional shout of a drunk in the distance. Or the roar of a passing taxi. Or the stifled grunts of the solitary figure as he shimmied himself up the pylons, pausing every once in a while to re-chalk his hands and look down on the main concourse. He had timed his ascent to the clockwork punctuality of the eight security guards who were posted below. None of them ever looked up. They had been told that the 5G AI security system was fully operational even this far out from the start of the Games, and that it was well-nigh impossible for anyone to fool sensors that could distinguish between those taxis in the distance, or that cat skulking in the shadows, or that human attempting to scale the south wall. But the solitary figure in black who was indeed scaling the south wall had trained in a place called Keumsung Military College where from morning till night he hit things, broke things, had things broken on his head, had driven nails through boards with his forehead, rolled around in broken glass, pulled trucks filled with soldiers, and hit tiny bull's-eyes 100 yards away. So breaching a stadium with state-of-the-art security? Child's play, although even he had to admit that architect Kengo Kuma's design, with its tiered gardens protruding twenty feet out on the way up, challenged his climbing skills like few structures had at Keumsung Military College. But now he was settled in his perch high up in the stadium and waiting for his targets to appear. His trigger finger was on hot standby, as he beheld the stadium that surrounded him, lit only by starlight.

Situated in what had been designated as the "Heritage Zone", the area where the 1964 Tokyo Olympics were held, Kengo Kuma's 68,000-seat stadium recalled Frank Lloyd Wright's philosophy of creating structures in harmony with their environment. Kuma expressed a desire to go beyond the era of concrete, and restore the link that Tokyo lost with nature during the reconstruction of the city after the Great Kanto Earthquake of 1923. His stated goal with his design was what he figuratively called "defeated architecture", by which he meant a stadium that would transcend its design. But if the man in the rafters had his way, "defeated architecture" would come to mean something quite a bit more literal in the weeks ahead.

Having breached all manner of security on his way up the south wall, the man had found a recessed gap between the nosebleed seats at the top of the stadium and the rafters of the oculus that opened up onto the sky. The gap would be used for TV cameras during the Games, but for now it would serve very nicely as his sniper's hide. He crawled inside and waited, enjoying the hum of quiet as the faint stars in the black sky began to fade into the spreading shades of purple and pink of astronomical dawn. An hour later he watched through his rifle scope as a hundred or so men in blue jumpsuits and peaked caps marched in smart files to the middle of the field. He noticed that his finger had unconsciously tightened around the trigger. He relaxed it. *Not yet*, he thought. *Not yet.*

Up until a week earlier, security for the Olympics had been the responsibility of a joint venture made up of fourteen private companies, but Prime Minister Adegawa had decided that the measures that the joint venture had in place were inadequate for ensuring maximum safety, and thus, he had replaced it with the Japan Intelligence Agency (JIA) which reported directly to him. The JIA men on the field fanned out around the field and began, along with much of the country at the same time, what is known as *rajio taiso* or "radio calisthenics". The man in the sniper's hide shook his head and smiled in amusement. It was exactly how they did it back home, right down to the little piano ditty that played over the loudspeaker system. He peered intently through his rifle scope looking for a specific person, a foreigner with Mediterranean features who had grown up in Japan. The shooter had made the man's acquaintance in North Korea three years earlier. Finally he found him. *He's dead!* he thought. Adrenaline again coursed through his viscera. But then he relaxed his finger on the trigger. *Not yet. Not yet...*

The foreigner with Mediterranean features had skipped the morning's calisthenics, since he had gotten up at 3:30 a.m. to do his mixed martial arts kata back home in Kamakura, about forty miles away. He had been a star long distance runner at Kamakura High School, and his eyes still had the inner intensity that came from churning out mile after mile around the seaside town with nothing in his head except the classical music he loved, especially that of Bach. "Loner music", his father had called it, and he meant it as a compliment. As his eyes took in the stadium, the foreigner thought four weeks ahead to the day of the Closing Ceremony when the marathoners would be sprinting into the stadium after their 26-mile traversal of Tokyo in stifling heat and humidity. He wondered if he might have had a shot at the Olympics had circumstances been different, but he cut himself off in mid-thought. "Coulda woulda shoulda. Total waste of time, especially at my age."

He had eaten a quick breakfast and ridden his motorcycle up on the all-but-deserted Shuto Expressway, arriving at the stadium ready to begin his first full day with the men who would be serving under him, a foreigner. How Japan had changed in the years since his youth, he marveled, before remembering the many more things about Japan that would never change in a thousand years. He had been hired as Chief Security Consultant for the 2020 Olympics, but many of the old hands in the JIA, Japan's CIA, resented taking orders from a foreigner, a xenophobia that had also raised its ugly head when the stadium's first architect, the Iraqi Zaha Hadid, a woman no less, was summarily fired in order to bring in Kengo Kuma.

The foreigner had been hired by the new director of the JIA because of allegations of corruption and possible treason within his own agency. Its former director was suspected of being in league with the Chongryon, a Tokyo-based organization with close ties to North Korea, a suspicion that was only strengthened when he bought that group's headquarters on prime Tokyo real estate for a shockingly low price. The new director, Kazuo Hayashida, had been brought in to restore the agency's reputation, and to that end he had retained the services of a total outsider, the foreigner on the field, making him instantly unpopular with people in the agency who had been cozy with the ex-director. The foreigner had jumped at the opportunity, since he was, frankly, bored. His newfound domestic tranquility was deeply satisfying on one level, but on a level that he kept to himself, he missed his old life: a hunter of men. He had no idea that at that moment, he was the hunted one...

The sniper set the barrel of his rifle on the small bag of chalk which had given his hands traction on his climb up the south wall. He used the barrel to smooth the chalk powder down into a groove and peered through the sight. His eyes focused on the field below, where the men in blue jumpsuits were now standing in neat rows. He held out his hand in front of him. Steady and firm. His grip tightened around the rifle again, but only to the degree that he might hold one of the baby hawks in the rafters without injuring it. He peered through the optical sight and waited for precisely the right moment, cursing the heat that was causing sweat to pour into his eyes.

The men on the field were cursing it as well. The late summer humid swelter of Tokyo, known locally as *mushiatsui*, or "steam heat", rivals that of the jungles of Borneo to those unaccustomed to it. Adding to the discomfort is the cacophonous booty call of cicadas whose 120-decibel chirp makes them the loudest insects on earth. As the temperature rises, the earlier the cicadas begin their search for a mate. Even now, at 7 a.m., with the temperature rising above 82 degrees and the humidity already topping 90%, the brain-penetrating whine of the cicadas blared out of the hundreds of oak, cypress, willow, ash, and maple trees surrounding Kengo Kuma's stadium.

Down on the field Seiji Naya, one of several Assistant Chiefs of Security with the Japan Intelligence Agency (JIA) felt himself getting hotter by the minute, and not because of the oppressive heat and humidity. As he read through the day's security update, he swore silently and began storming toward the low riser from which the daily briefings were announced.

The foreigner with Mediterranean features stood at the bottom of the riser penciling notes onto a page and preparing to deliver the briefing. As the cacophony of the cicadas became more and more irritating, he considered that in a few short weeks they would just be dried out exoskeletons littering the ground, and the larches, oaks, and maples would be brown in another cycle of birth and death. An old haiku came to his mind: "Nothing in the cry of cicadas suggests they are about to die."

The shooter in the rafters followed the action on field through his scope as Naya got closer to the foreigner. Deputy Assistant Watari saw that Naya was once again in one of his rages, no doubt with his usual complaint of having to take orders from a *gaijin*, a foreigner. Watari, of a more cosmopolitan world view, moved to intervene, but Naya pushed him roughly aside and situated himself face to face with the foreigner. As soon as he looked up from his clipboard and saw that once again he would be confronted by Naya, the foreigner set his jaw and raised his chin aggressively.

"This is unacceptable, Mr. Featherstone!" Naya began, a vein bulging in his forehead. "We're talking about the security of 70,000 athletes and spectators at any given time! How can you possibly argue that snipers should be the main tool to counter security threats? The threat can come from anywhere, even outside this stadium! Our Japanese companies have developed a state-of-the-art 5G facial recognition system that can tell identical twins apart. Besides, we in the JIA have been charged with providing security without interfering with the Games. Snipers will only frighten people! Your directive is frankly naïve. It's completely beyond me how you managed to persuade Director Hayashida to adopt it!"

He spoke in fluent but heavily-accented English, knowing full well that Patrick Featherstone, who had been born in Kamakura 41 years earlier, was stone-fluent in Japanese. Patrick intentionally used less than honorific verb forms in his Japanese-language response to Naya.

"No one is saying that snipers should be our *only* tool, Naya-san, only one of our most reliable ones. The 5G AI facial recognition will be fully operational, but as you say, the threat could come from anywhere, and if you don't realize the necessity of having properly positioned snipers as backup for technology that can be hacked, then maybe you shouldn't be involved in guarding those 70,000 people."

As Patrick said this, his mind went back to Pyongyang a few years earlier when he and a hastily assembled team had helped to engineer the Rising Tide revolution which brought down the regime of Kim Jong-un, during which Patrick called upon his own sniper skills to take out a hostile shooter a half mile across the Taedong River from Kim Il Sung Square.

The shooter up in the rafters stifled a laugh as he watched Naya through his scope exploding in anger at the foreigner they both hated so much but for different reasons. Patrick Featherstone.

"Shouldn't be involved?" Naya shouted. "How dare you talk to me that way! You're not even Japanese, how could you possibly understand the way things are done in this country? It's completely beyond me why Director Hayashida insisted on having you play even a small role in security, let alone be the main advisor!"

Patrick smiled as Naya raged, which made Naya even angrier, but the little despot had been a thorn in Patrick's side for weeks, and Patrick enjoyed being his superior in the chain of command. Naya was about to continue his tirade when an authoritative voice from behind made them both turn. It was Kazuo

Hayashida, the new director of the Japan Intelligence Agency.

"Gentlemen, it's time we begin the day's planned drills. The Opening Ceremony begins in exactly two weeks. Mr. Featherstone, you may begin your presentation." Now it was Hayashida's turn to feel Naya's wrath.

"Mr. Director, having a foreign Chief Security Consultant would never have happened under your predecessor who understood the Japanese way!" Naya turned and glared at Patrick as he stalked away. Hayashida sighed in exasperation. Naya was a lifer and couldn't be fired.

As this was going on, a young woman in a navy blue suit came up to Hayashida's side. The contrast between the suit and her light-colored hair was striking. Her facial features were somehow both particular and archetypal. Hayashida said something to her in English. She smiled sympathetically and nodded in response.

Patrick allowed himself a parting smirk at Naya, then glanced briefly at the young woman as he ascended the riser and turned to face the men in blue jumpsuits. The shooter up in his hide squinted through his scope in deep concentration on the scene unfolding on the field below. It was almost time…

"First of all," Patrick Featherstone began, "I want to thank all of you for being part of the most highly trained Olympic security force ever assembled. I'd now like to begin with a review of the potential hostile actors we could be facing. And starting today, two weeks out from the Opening Ceremony, we are on heightened alert." He proceeded to go through a checklist of the groups and individuals he considered the main threats. Deputy Assistant Security Chief Watari, who also despised Seiji Naya, had taken his place by Patrick's side in a show of international solidarity.

High up in the canopy of the stadium the shooter keyed a text into the single-use phone he had brought. Patrick felt his phone vibrate but decided to leave it till later. The start of the briefing was already late as it was. He began to run through the usual suspects of terror groups and detailing each of their strengths and weaknesses when JIA Director Kazuo Hayashida was called out of the stadium. As soon as Naya saw him exit, he walked quickly back to the riser where Patrick was making his presentation. He had not finished with this *gaijin*.

Patrick was turning a page on his clipboard when two shots rang out in quick succession, their combined sound waves caroming around the oval structure and out the huge oculus above the track. Naya and Watari lay flat on their backs, gaping holes where their hearts had been. Everyone in the security detail froze in shock. And then chaos broke out, doubling down on Sun Tzu's adage, "Kill one, terrify a thousand."

High up in the rafters of the stadium, the mother *tombi* was alone again with her hatchlings.

CHAPTER 2

Later that day

The incongruity of meal, presentation and setting was intentionally designed to throw the diners off their bearings and remind them who held the power in this room on the third floor of Toyama Storage, a business in the dockland section of Yokohama. And what a room it was. The real purpose of Toyama Storage was revealed when a black-suited middle-aged man ceremoniously raised a red velvet curtain and unveiled a coffin which the man's two sons wheeled into the middle of the viewing room. For this was a corpse hotel, one of Japan's most recent and bizarrely ingenious methods of reconciling its mounting elderly death rate with the scarcity of crematoria in a country eternally beset by the NIMBY mentality.

The host of the day's festivities was a man known to all simply as Mr. Lee. He had been a close confidante and successor of the occupant of the coffin, Comrade Moon, one of the most notorious criminals North Korea ever produced and the patron martyr of the people assembled in the viewing room. The expression on his face in the photo atop the coffin was a repellent-to-the-point-of-fascinating mix of charm and wickedness that went far in explaining how he had risen close to the pinnacle of power in the DPRK...

A shy but friendly boy as a child, on his eleventh birthday Comrade Moon witnessed his mother being obliterated by an American bomb during the Korean War. Not a trace of her remained. From that day forward, a new person was born, one who would never allow himself to trust another human being, one who would sell his soul for power, if he had one to sell. But it had been obliterated along with his mother by the American bomb.

Attending the prestigious Mangyongdae Revolutionary School in Pyongyang, he was two years younger than the Dear Leader Kim Jong-il, a priggish know-it-all who enjoyed lording it over other students and even faculty and administrators, or as much as someone of Kim's runty stature was able to lord it over anyone. Moon, however, knowing a meal ticket when he saw one, cultivated a friendship with the son of Great Leader Kim Il-sung. Unlike Kim Jong-il, Moon was tall and athletic which caused no end of jealousy for Kim *fils*, who in later years would describe his appearance as that of a "rat turd". Moon persisted, however, since he could tell even at that age that Jong-il, through his incessant toadying up to his father, was destined for the highest reaches of the regime. And so, in order to curry favor with Jong-il, Moon immersed himself in *kimilsungsa*, or Kim Il-sung Thought, and came to Kim the younger with request after request for elucidation on some arcane point in the many volumes that had allegedly flowed from the Great Leader's pen.

Years later, Moon's encyclopedic mastery of Kim Il-sung Thought led to an audience with the Great Leader himself that Kim Jong-il arranged. But the meeting backfired on Kim Jong-il, as the father saw in Moon the role of regent for his son, a role that Jong-il deeply resented, especially since Moon was younger than he. Thus, after the Great Leader died, Kim Jong-il purged Moon from his lofty position, cognizant of his potential as an adversary. Eventually Moon wheedled his way back into Jong-il's good graces by pledging his undying fealty and guaranteeing it with his life— and that of his family. Kim Jong-il, never one to take the high-sounding words of underlings at face value, demanded literal proof. At one of Kim's legendary drinking parties not long thereafter, Comrade Moon signaled for everyone's attention and once again pledged his loyalty in effusive terms. At the end of his bathos-sodden speech, he drew a pistol from his jacket and shot his wife in the head. A shocked silence fell over the other members of the party, who then hurried away. Kim embraced Moon, pledged his own loyalty in return, and the two of them proceeded to drink their way through three days of mourning for Moon's wife. A dozen concubines from Kim's personal stable were brought in to help comfort the grief-stricken widower, and at the end of the three days, Kim awarded Moon the post of Deputy Director of the People's Office of Services.

Moon's next rung in the ladder of power was to marry Kim's sister. She died of acute alcoholism within a year, but he was now part of The Family. Overnight, he was admitted into the Dear Leader's inner circle and made head of State Security, the secret police.

He took to dressing flamboyantly, flaunting his access to the Dear Leader with the extravagances that such proximity entailed. His closeness to Kim also enabled him to act with impunity toward underlings, with more than a few of them meeting untimely deaths by his own hand. Thus, in his hand-crafted shoes of the finest Italian leather he stood splendidly astride a sinful nexus of elegance and criminality.

Moon's next act was to create Bureau 39, a massively tentacled conglomerate of wickedness shrouded in mystery and bringing in billions a year for the senior Pyongyang leadership through drug smuggling, slave labor in the North Korean gulag system, and the counterfeiting of American $100 bills, known as Super Ks. But now Comrade Moon lay in a coffin at Toyama Storage, slain three years earlier during the overthrow of the Kim Jong-un regime by a Japan-born foreigner who went by the name of Patrick Featherstone.

Comrade Moon's successor, Mr. Lee, offered no one any information about himself, not even a first name or background, although some said he was of North Korean ancestry but had been raised in the Chinese city of Dandong, right across the Yalu River from North Korea. He spoke the languages of both countries with native fluency, along with English and Japanese. Mr. Lee's coyness about all aspects of his identity stemmed not from any sense of modesty or shame, but rather from the tangled web that was his personal history. In fact "Mr. Lee" was a pseudonym that he and Comrade Moon had decided upon in order to conceal his double identity, one of them legitimate, the other viciously corrupt.

After the red velvet curtain was raised and the corpse hotel's manager's two sons had wheeled Comrade Moon's coffin into the middle of the viewing room, the main door of the room was then opened for a dozen young men who waited outside. All twelve were impeccably groomed and dressed to the nines in ultra-lightweight woolen suits by Armani and Brioni. They were members of the *Bonghwajo*, or Torch Club, children of the DPRK power structure who had been unceremoniously booted out of their luxurious homes in what was known as the "Pyonghattan" section of the North Korean capital after the Rising Tide revolution that toppled the Kim regime. The revolution had taken place three years earlier on the day of the Glorious Triumvirate Celebration, a festival marking the radiant brilliance of the dynasty of Kim Il-sung, Kim Jong-il and Kim Jong-un. After the fall of that dynasty, which their *nomenklatura* parents had helped prop up for so many years, these pampered one-percenters were down to their last few billion North Korean *won* and searching for a way to regain their former lifestyle. Mr. Lee offered salvation in the form of the insurgency he created in the DPRK known as Chosun Restoration, with *Chosun* being the former name of Korea before Japan colonized it in 1910. Its stated goal was the restoration to power of Kim Jong-un. The twelve youths assembled today were the insurgency's best and brightest.

In accordance with an initiation rite derived from that of the Mafia, Mr. Lee's twelve young apostles of Mammon would be served sake from ceremonial flat *sakazuki* cups of solid gold which they would first hold up in offering to Comrade Moon's coffin. After drinking the sake, they each would present a finger to Mr. Lee who would prick it with a pin and squeeze so that their blood dripped onto a wad of cotton they each held in their other hand. Mr. Lee would then take a taper, light it from a candle surrounding Comrade Moon's coffin, and set the cotton on fire in their hands. They had been instructed to hold it for three seconds before dropping it into a bowl of water that had been placed on the table for the purpose.

"We remember Comrade Moon today and include him in our ritual and feast." As he said the name, Lee's eyes went to the coffin in the middle of the room. "And we ask him in spirit to give his blessing to Chosun Restoration, our army of liberation." Mr. Lee then nodded to the twelve young North Korean men who proceeded to hold the cotton balls in their hands as he pricked their fingers, dripped the blood onto the cotton, and set the balls on fire. After all of them had dropped the cotton into the bowl of water, Mr. Lee led the closing of the ritual, the final words of which were repeated by the inductees: "We dedicate ourselves to Chosun Restoration, and we bind our fates to that of our fellow members."

Mr. Lee then raised his wineglass to the coffin and the young men followed suit. "We salute Comrade Moon. *Mansae!* [ten thousand years]", they toasted three times in unison. As the ceremony drew to an end, the unearthly aroma of flesh and fat roasting in butter, punctuated with after-notes of vaporized Armagnac, drifted enticingly into the room from the floor below. To Mr. Lee it seemed only fitting that a meeting to discuss violence and mayhem should be held in this place of death and have ortolan as the featured item of the menu.

After the final toast ended the initiation ceremony, a long table was set in front of Comrade Moon's coffin and the appetizers were brought in. One of the young men likened the lobster bisque and spider crab in sweet-savory foam to inhaling sea spray. Then it was time for the main, highly illegal course. No larger than a baby's fist and weighing less than an ounce, the delicate ortolan songbird is a French delicacy of yore. The birds are encouraged to gorge themselves, and when they are two to three times their normal size, (that is to say, the size of a typical American, Mr. Lee jokingly told his new acolytes) they are drowned in Armagnac brandy, plucked and roasted.

As the roasting birds, speckled with an autumn-leaf-fall of truffle shavings, were being carried into the room, their aroma becoming more and more maddeningly tantalizing, everyone murmured in fevered expectation as their individual cocottes were set in front of them. They all then placed oversized linen dinner napkins over their heads as French tradition dictated, hiding their faces from God at the impending sin of eating such a rare and delicate creature.

After the meal, largely silent except for the crunching of bird bones and primal grunts of gustatory passion, Mr. Lee addressed the group.

"Gentlemen. The twelve of you have been chosen carefully from the most elite members of the Bonghwajo Torch Club as Chosun Restoration's advance guard. I have purposely limited your numbers to avoid arousing suspicion until our reinforcements arrive for the latter part of our mission. But you make up for your small numbers by the fact that you are all highly adept at martial arts, gunmanship, and the use of high explosives. We meet today in common cause. As you are all well aware, the interests of Bureau 39 were admirably advanced for many years by Comrade Moon. Now our dear Comrade is no longer with us, and the DPRK is in the midst of great turmoil, following the Rising Tide revolution of three years ago. We are now at a crossroads."

Mr. Lee was a master orator, and paused to let the tension build before continuing in a lower pitched voice.

"When Rising Tide deposed our Brilliant Commander Kim Jong-un on the very day of the Glorious Triumvirate Celebration, it also robbed you of your rightful claim to aristocracy, and greatly diminished Bureau 39's traditional sources of income. However, Rising Tide and its puppet leader Nahm Myung-dae have made the lives of the people far worse, with widespread hunger and the breakdown of order.

"Now, with the upcoming Olympic Games, we have an unprecedented opportunity to take revenge, and for you to regain your former status. Gentlemen, we seek nothing less than the return of our Brilliant Commander to the seat of power in the DPRK, with the twelve of you as military regents paving the way for his return. The one hundred or so reinforcements who will arrive later will be our second wave. Let me begin with the details of the first wave for which you will be responsible. My overall plan has five phases, each of which represents one of our enemy's centers of gravity, which we will systematically destroy. In so doing we will bring the enemies of our nation to their knees. Would you now please gather around this map of Tokyo. Mr. Pung, who was Comrade Moon's right-hand man, will help me explain."

A thickset middle-aged Korean man with gunshot residue on his fingers stood. He explained that each of them had a particular mission of destruction meant to sow chaos and terror during the upcoming Olympic Games in order to demonstrate to the world that Chosun Restoration would avenge the overthrow of Kim Jong-un three years earlier, and would now stop at nothing to restore the Brilliant Commander to power. Pung had begun Phase One of the plan that very morning with the double assassination at the Olympic Stadium.

After Pung had finished, Mr. Lee rose from the table and departed. He promised to come back from time to time to check on their progress.

Look for ***Rings of Fire*** by Gregory Shepherd, wherever books are sold.